RA

CW01521791

a tale of truth and illusion
by
Bernard W Roberts

dedicated
to
the people of Merseyside

Published by
NINA GIOTTI

Odyssey Works
Corporation Road
Birkenhead CH41 1HY
tel: 0151 647 2123
fax: 0151 666 1472
email: PPP_Ltd@rhino-pg.freeserve.co.uk

a trading name of Rhino PG Ltd

RATS was first published in 2000 by NINA GIOTTI, at
Odyssey Works, Corporation Road, Birkenhead, WIRRAL CH41 1HY
tel: 0151 647 2123/0151 666 1369
fax: 0151 666 1472
email PPP_Ltd@rhino-pg.freeserve.co.uk

ISBN 0–9538911–0–0

Typeset by Wilmaset Ltd, Birkenhead, Wirral
Printed by The Book Factory, London N7 7AH

Preface

In the nineteenth century the spokes of the Liverpool half-wheel were filled with short streets of damp and lice-infested houses. The rent was paid weekly. Failure to pay meant certain eviction into an uncaring society where survival and self-interest prevailed.

It was rare for the dock-workers living in the houses to earn a full week's wage, and often their children went ragged and shoeless.

In the twentieth century the welfare system provided a cushion, and the rehousing schemes, conceived in the 1950s and 60s, became a reality. Tower blocks, like the mythological Phoenix, rose from a landscape ravaged by poverty and German incendiary bombs. But many of the back-street houses stood firm.

In the 1980s the local council debated with explosive experts a feasibility study for blowing-up seven of the ten tenement blocks on the Tower Hill Estate in Kirkby. The other three could, it was reasoned, be reduced to ashes by conventional force to avoid damage to adjoining property. These buildings had been built only seven years earlier, and the council still had another 54 years of repayments of the original one million pound loan needed to build the estate. It was anticipated that a similar amount would be needed for the demolition of the nine hundred out-of-town housing units – some of which had never been occupied

Merseyside was a veritable jungle of expensive mistakes: a landscape blighted by sanctified confusion at every level of local administration.

From the inner-city slums to absolute vandalism, Liverpool was a string of tangible decay and deterioration, held together by the Social Security Office.

Of course, Liverpool had its pleasant corners – but they had to be sought-out. Any true Scouser can name them: Sefton Park, Otterspool and ... well, you need to ask a Scouser.

Against this cyclorama throbbed a city, once of great stature; a city with inhabitants rich in character, eccentricity and imagination – but a city of people with not much real hope for the future.

The Pierhead was where Liverpool seemed to begin and end. The place where cross-Mersey ferries converged. A focal point for the homeless. A place where ancient mariners sat and watched the waves, and rolled their wafer-thin cigarettes.

There, under the overhang on the southern side of the riverside restaurant, the pensioners, straight-faced and taut of limb, sat on long benches. Now a community of daytime people – but once, not so long ago in their minds, the wooers and wooed of pre-war Liverpool. The warriors and mothers of the war-torn forties. The strugglers of the fifties and sixties. The grandparents of an increasingly drug-dependent society.

In a crowd each of them sat alone. An occasional comment or smile at a blurred memory.

On another, separate slatted-bench a family of Pakistani day-trippers sipped tea from paper cups and picked at sandwiches in paperbags. The two women of the group, hidden inside brightly coloured saris, were strangely at odds with an otherwise grey environment. The men and children wore conventional dress, and blended with the afternoon and pigeons.

A vagrant, trousers tucked into holed socks, searched for an empty bench. An old man, bespectacled and stooped with a black trilby hat and grey raincoat, shuffled by, sockless in his open-toed sandals.

At the end of the Pierhead the gulls perched on the purpose and sturdily built Speaker's platform. Rarely used, it was an ideal resting place for the birds. Occasionally an orator on a wooden box attracted a small audience, but most of those with a message to convey were barrow-boys on the city's shopping streets. It was, however, the pubs and working men's clubs where the Liverpool man made his point. A place where he exposed ambition, vexation and frailty. And intimate thoughts were shared only with friends but forever secret from spouse and family. A sympathetic ear was available – face to face. Back to back that sympathy could be short-lived.

The departing ferry's siren scattered the gulls from the Speaker's platform and screeching, they circled and dispersed over the maritime museum – once the dock where Liverpool's original fishing fleet unloaded its catch, a time when seagulls, no doubt, enjoyed a richer lifestyle.

This is the story of just two volatile years in the life of that city. A period when central government turned its back.

Rats
1980

It was the awakening of another day and the clouds and sea-mist parted slowly like heavy curtains opening on a wide proscenium stage.

During the cold night the star-studded black sky, like diamonds on velvet, had moved imperceptibly until the twinkling lights disappeared over the invisible horizon. The pre-dawn darkness seemed impenetrable, until a loom of soft orange light illuminated the thin clouds streaking away, seemingly fearful of the encroaching dawn and as though first-light and night-cloud were somehow incompatible. Nevertheless, the gossamer cloud-drift, like the earlier stars, surrendered to the manifestation that backlit the mother-of-pearl horizon with turquoise fire.

In marked contrast to the muted but multi-coloured sky, the sharp silhouettes lining the banks of the awakening river stood tall and jagged like the turrets of a medieval garrison town. The ebony-black waters swirled in the turmoil of the ebbing spring tide. On a high, but narrow, mud bank against a crumbling brick-built shoreline a sodden, but determined, brown rat left its trail of imprints deep in the soft sludge. Old rotten timbers, once the foundations of a nineteenth century jetty, clung to the old bricks like seaweed covered serpents. Behind one decayed stanchion a brick had become loose. Through this hole the wet rat disappeared.

Behind the small hole in the embankment an ancient tunnel, big enough to accommodate a crouching man, continued for nearly a mile inland, culminating in a long forgotten and buried chamber that had once been the starting place for very long sea-journeys by those poor, nineteenth century inebriates snatched from the dark, sewerage streets of Liverpool. The tunnel had been built by a consortium of Tall Ship owners to fill a labour shortage caused by burgeoning demand for vessels to carry the growing trade across the Atlantic Ocean. It was from those damp, gas-lit back streets that the wretched drunks were plucked and bundled down two flights of narrow stone steps. And in small boats waiting at the end of the long dark tunnel the lost souls were moved to a half-masted ship anchored off the jetty – but straining to sail on the rising tide.

By the time Horace, as the big brown rat was known to his extended family and friends, reached the former dungeon, the grey city was stirring under a bland white sky. The streets above where Horace lived had seen many changes since the days the tall sailing ships tied-up alongside the Strand. In the middle of the nineteenth century, and with a marginally more equitable judicial system of law and order replacing rule by wealth and association, the deep cellar had been sealed. The streets above had been recobbled several times and eventually tarred over but neither that nor the laying of sewage pipes, nor the later underground railway system and under-river road tunnels had exposed the small room and its access to the sea. However, previous generations of rats had opened up a vast underground network of narrow tunnels that fed into every man-made system, and allowed the rat population unfettered access into every building in the city. Although it was not usually necessary for rats to cross a street in search of food, those rats of the commercial district were somewhat different in that at weekends when offices were closed and their waste-paper bins empty, the streets with their wealth of discarded and partly eaten take-away food offered rich pickings.

Times had changed since the plethora of small unregulated shops with their loose and open storage facilities lined the streets. In those days the rat population lived out their lives within the confines of a single shop. With regulation and the transition from unsealed to sealed food storage, life became more difficult – but not impossible. The search area for sustenance had to be extended to cover a row of shops. There were, of course, the dockside warehouses but they were diminishing, and that territory was controlled by aggressive wharf rodents who through birth inherited their district. By incisors and claw strange rats were intimidated and discouraged from sharing the food supplies at the disposal of the obese wharfinger rat-packs. There was more food than they could possibly eat, and the gigantic store-rooms were piled high to the roof with millwheel-size cobs of cheese, white flour like Egyptian pyramids and lakes of syrupy, dark brown molasses – their particular favourite. And when the supplies were reduced, new stocks arrived. The coats of the wharf-rats shone like silk but there was a downside to their over-gormandizing lifestyle: rootless, the teeth of a rat continue to grow and it is only the constant chewing on a hard surface that keeps them at a manageable size. The abundant supply of rich, soft food allowed the incisors of the wharf-rats to grow unchecked until they reached such a length that feeding became impossible. It was a short and sweet life.

Horace and his wife had arrived in Liverpool by accident: word had got around the Manchester rat population – where Horace was born – that a fleet of ships had arrived on the Ship Canal with cargoes of grapes. apples and pears. It was dusk when Horace and Betty, his young wife, scampered up the bow-rope. After a feast of fruit they fell asleep in a dark corner beside the warming funnel and it was only the sound of a ship's horn that awakened the pair. The sunlight was hitting the black ring around the funnel's exit, and they could hear men moving about the swaying deck. The ship was moving through the water close to a shore line.

"How will we get off the ship in daylight?" Betty whispered.

"I think we're moving," Horace replied, peering around the bend of the fat, red funnel.

"Moving! Oh no! What about Mother?"

3

"Shh!" Horace admonished. "There's land on both sides. We're on a river."

For an hour they crouched in the narrow crevice between a lifeboat and the hot funnel while unseen buckets of cold water were emptied over the wooden deck, and stiff bristles of searching brush-heads scraped the floor inches from their feet.

"I'm getting wet, Horace," Betty complained.

"Shh!" Horace repeated. "If we're found we'll be thrown overboard."

"Oh no!" Betty moaned to herself, and danced quietly over the soapy water that ran under the white, clinker-built lifeboat.

The sailors in their circular-striped vests and sloping black berets shouted to each other in a language that the pair didn't understand. It was obvious to Horace that they were heading for a foreign land but, not wanting to have his nerves tested by an excitable wife, kept a still tongue.

"How can we get off, Horace?" Betty whispered.

"Shut up, please," Horace whispered back, and Betty obligingly put a paw across her own mouth but stared wide eyed at Horace for an answer. Unable to tolerate the unblinking gaze of his frightened wife, he continued: "don't worry, we'll get off all right."

"But if we get off how will we get home?" she said, so close to his face that he could smell the trace of eau-de-Cologne she put behind her ears every evening.

"We can walk."

"How will we know which way to go?"

"We'll follow the river bank."

"But ... oh dear! How will we get off?"

"We can swim."

"We can't jump off a moving ship. We might get caught by the propellers," she said, surprising Horace with her imaginative thinking. He had to agree that such a venture would be fraught with danger. With an outstretched forepaw he leant on the funnel, but with a shout quickly withdrew his burnt hand.

"Blast!" he shouted.

"Quiet! Somebody will hear," Betty said, scooping up two paw-fulls of soapy water and embracing Horace's burnt paw. "Is that better?" she asked affectionately, gently leading his sore paw into a pool of cold water on the deck.

"Whatever you do don't touch that thing. It's red hot," he said protectively, pointing with his head towards the funnel. With his aching paw resting in the shallow film of deck water the pair sat down facing each other. Although he fought to disguise his fear, Horace's expression mirrored Betty's pained countenance. It was in that brief moment of contemplation and calm that the blunt end of a heavy wooden brush-head crashed to the deck, narrowly missing the worried couple. Above their heads the sky was blotted out by a round, red face behind a thick, curling moustache and beneath an equally black beret. Wide eyed, and with a toothless grin, the seaman lifted the long broom handle above his head until its wide bristly head was touching the blue sky.

"Quick! This way . . ." Horace shouted, and Betty followed her husband through a small hole in the lifeboat's metal support. Across the water-logged deck they slithered and slid, spun and rolled.

"Mort!" the pursuing sailor shouted, and soon he was joined in the chase by two other brush-wielding deck-hands. Around the wide funnel, Horace and Betty ran breathlessly.

"I can't go any further," Betty panted, but Horace pushed her ahead.

"When we get around the funnel again you get back where we started and I'll lead them away. Then climb in the lifeboat. I'll be back later."

"On my own?"

"Go on, now," he insisted, with such aggression that she did as she was told and slid back into the crevice where they had spent the night. With the adrenalin in full flood, Horace made for the open deck, and the three wheezing seamen shouted and swore as they collided with each other. From a square opening in the deck Horace could see metal steps leading down to a lower open deck and unhesitatingly descended two steps at a time. The fat man and his two thinner colleagues tried simultaneously to get down the hatch. The overwhelming drive of each man to catch the prey caused a blockage at the entrance to the stair-well. Before they could descend, Horace was well concealed inside the thick ropes curled neatly around a stanchion at the bow of the ship. Through a narrow slit between coiled rope he looked out from his dark hiding place and watched the trio – lookalikes in all things but weight – leaning over the guardrails. The otherwise grey waters of the ship canal foamed white beneath the bowsprit. The fat man threw his head back and moved a finger across his own throat. "Fini," he said with a smug smile. The three men climbed heavily back up the short, steep staircase, and resumed their deck-scrubbing duties.

The gentle roll of the ship and the constant underlying vibrations from the ship's engine conspired with the darkness of his hiding place to calm Horace's racing heart. His priority was to return to the upper deck and protect his wife, but his eyes began to close and his head was nodding. To avoid falling asleep he pressed his face against the oily rope and looked out across the empty deck. From the height of the sun above his head he reasoned it was early afternoon. Perhaps they will be going for lunch soon and the way will be clear, he thought but before he could develop the concept a pair of long black trousers appeared on the metal staircase. The legs were followed by a white teeshirt with black hoops – and then the narrow face with a pencil thin moustache and black beret of one of the earlier vigilantes. Another pair of black-clad legs followed the head and three times the exercise was completed. The three sailors leant their backs against the guardrail and each drew, from behind his own ear, half a cigarette. With cupped hands around a match, each man lit his own cigarette and inhaled deeply before blowing out a cloud of smoke. Horace watched intently through the chink in the circle of rope. It was the static nature of the smoke and the way it hung in the air that alerted him to the changed nature of his environment. The wind, caused by the movement of the ship, was no longer passing over the deck and the vibrating undercurrent had changed: it was now more urgent and strained. And then, seemingly of its own free will, the heavy, rusted chain began clattering and snaking over the deck until, tamed by the hole in the bow deck, it slid towards the water below. The ship had stopped, but the open sea lay ahead and the land was but a vague strip in the distance. For the first time that morning Horace felt lost, defeated by circumstances beyond his control. He watched the fat seaman unfasten a section of the guardrail. A fourth man dressed all in black with a peak cap and carrying two large well-filled plastic carrier bags descended the stairs. He placed the bags by the coiled rope and went across to the guard-rail where the three men stood smoking. It was impossible to hear what the men talked about as their conversation was drowned-out by the noise of a fast motorboat. The four men stood along the remaining rail watching the approaching small boat. Horace ran silently across the deck, jumped up the staircase, slid over the upper deck and leapt up onto the lifeboat.

"Betty, Betty. Are you there?," he whispered.

"Is that you, Horace?"

"Quick. Follow me," he instructed.

At the stairwell, Horace held out a paw to keep Betty back. Lying flat, he peered under the deck. The men below were still looking out to sea.

On tip-toe, Horace and Betty descended the steps. Obediently, and with total faith, she followed in her husband's paw-prints. Horace ushered Betty behind the coiled rope while he removed five apples from each bag, placing them inside the bundle of rope. With a nod of the head he indicated the bag. "Climb in," he mouthed.

"Oh no!" Betty cried quietly.

"Climb in and get buried," he seethed through clenched teeth, and Betty did as she was told. "And don't breathe."

Before Horace climbed in the second bag he re-arranged the apples over his wife so that she was completely hidden.

Horace had made a calculated guess: the man in black looked like a ship's pilot who had possibly steered the ship safely to open waters. The approaching boat was coming in to take him back to shore.

It was an accurate assessment, and suddenly the two frightened rodents were swinging freely inside their hideaways as the man in the peak cap transported the captain's gift of fruit to the smaller boat. Careful not to bruise the apples, he placed the two bags under the side seat, and settled down with his cap over his eyes.

Betty lay at the bottom of the bag hardly daring to breathe. Her body had trembled so violently that she was sure she would be discovered and thrown into the sea, and her eyes were closed so tightly she didn't notice the light was no longer passing through the thin white plastic – but she was conscious of something pressing against the outside of the bag. Horace had climbed out of his own hiding place and was tapping on the bag where Betty had achieved maximum concealment surrounded by red apples and black grapes.

With his head inside her bag, he said: "Out!"

Betty emerged from the fruits and, beneath the side bench-seating, followed her husband to the stern of the boat where three white lifebelts were stowed tightly under the seat. The boat pitched and tossed but Betty didn't mind: she was wrapped safely in her husband's arms and unless the boat began to sink nobody would discover their new hiding place.

Exhausted by their brush with death, and in the comfort of each other's arms inside the pile of lifebelts, they were soon rocked to sleep by the boat's movements. It was dark when Horace put his nose out between the top lifebelt and the under-side of the seat.

"It's dark and everybody's gone," Horace said, in a low voice.

"Where've they gone?" Betty asked.

"How do I know," he replied irritably. "What does it matter?"

"Have they fallen over the side?"

"Don't be daft, doe. The boat's tied up against the harbour wall. Come on. We can't stay here all night. We've got to find some-where safe to spend the night."

Betty followed Horace onto the narrow, creaking jetty by

stepping on the old car-tyres nailed to the side of the timbered pier. She followed him up the damp stone steps cut into the mossy harbour wall.

"Where are we?" she asked, relieved to be on level and solid ground once again.

"Just wait there. I'll go ask a policeman," Horace replied, with sarcasm built out of frustration.

"I thought you were knowledgeable," Betty said timidly. "Are we in England?"

"Of course we're in England."

"Those sailors didn't speak English – and I can see lights across the sea."

"It's not a sea. It's the river we sailed along."

"Those lights seem a long way off!"

"It's the mouth of the river. This is where it widens out and goes to the sea."

"It's been a long day," Betty sighed

"It was very nearly a short day. If those scoundrels had got hold of us they would have shown no consideration for life. We'd be floating in there," Horace said, pointing to the blackness below.

"Don't say things like that, Horace." Betty said with a shiver. "It makes me feel quite weak."

The night was dark and the dots of light too distant to provide illumination.

"Come on, no time for sitting down dreaming," Horace ordered. "We'll follow the coastline."

And so it was that the pair, due to Horace's misfortune, found their new home. They had been walking for only ten minutes when he stepped into space, but landed softly in the black mud.

"Horace. Horace," Betty cried in despair.

"Don't panic. I'm all right. I'm coming back up. Just keep away from the edge."

It was as he climbed up the remains of the burnt-black timbers attached to the sea-wall that he discovered the hole in the ancient brickwork.

"Where are you?" Betty shouted from her prostrate position, head over the embankment. "Where've you gone?"

"I think I've found somewhere we can spend the night," he said, reappearing from the hole. "Climb down this plank, but be careful. It's rotten."

With utterances of fear for her safety, Betty edged slowly down the wooden structure that had, a hundred years before, secured a jetty to the wall. She followed Horace's instructions and climbed into the partly concealed hole. "We couldn't spend the night here, Horace. It's too damp!"

"It's a tunnel. Follow me."

"It's too dark," Betty whispered. "And wet."

Rattus norvegicus, as the rodent population prefers to be known, are generally nocturnal by nature. And because of their preference to move about in the dark their eyes have adapted accordingly. It was not difficult for Horace and Betty to follow the winding tunnel: narrow gauge lines had been laid beneath the brick-lined arching roof, and in the nineteenth century those stupefied prisoners of the 'Press Gangs' had, in small wagons, been transported towards the sea. The pair hurried to their unknown destination.

"What if the tide rises?" Betty called, struggling to keep up with her determined husband.

"All the reason to go faster," Horace shouted back over his shoulder.

"What if we come to a dead-end, Horace?"

"Don't be pessimistic, Betty."

"Let's go back," she whined.

Horace responded to his wife's inate defeatism by increasing his pace and Betty, as was her wont, moaned and groaned, but followed his lead. Although Horace's level of optimism was more than enough to counter-balance his wife's lack of confidence her words repeated themselves in his thoughts: '... what if the tide rises? What if the end of the tunnel is a blank wall? What..?'

Out of the corner of his eye he noticed water trickling down the black brickwork, and other demeaning imagery entered his head.

"My feet are getting soaked," Betty cried.

"Get up on the rail line. It's above the water-level."

Like tight-rope walkers, with their noses to the rusted metal rail, Horace and Betty pushed forward.

"Keep your tail still. It's hitting me in the face," Betty called.

"And how do I keep my balance? Keep your distance."

"I'm afraid I might lose you."

"In a tunnel? I couldn't lose you if I wanted to!"

At last the railway line ended, and the tunnel opened out into a large room divided by a ragged grey blanket hanging from the ceiling.

"This is nice – and a blanket," Betty said.

"It's dry – and look, a table and chairs."

"Who the jasus is dat?"

In shock, Horace and Betty jumped back apace. Through the thin blanket a spectral light floated-apparently unaided. Slowly the curtain moved, and a white-haired rat with a candlestick in hand revealed itself.

"I'm sorry. Is this your home?" Horace said.

"Tsis!"

Horace apologised for the intrusion and explained their plight. The middle-aged rat and his equally white-haired wife listened intently to the trials and tribulations the younger couple had experienced that day. At length the older rat introduced himself. "You were lucky to escape. Listen . . . I'm Paddy and this is Glad. Glad the mad!. What's your names?" Horace and Betty in turn introduced themselves. "Your luck is changing," Paddy continued. "The place next door is empty. The couple who lived there moved out only two days ago. They've moved down to the underground. Wanted a bit of excitement."

"What is this place called, Paddy?" Horace asked.

"Called? Jase, we don't have any fancy names down here. We're working-class. This is number one, next door is number two."

"I meant . . .the name of the town?"

"You don't know?" Paddy asked with a smile. He looked towards his wife and winked.

"They wouldn't ask if they knew," Glad interjected. From her few words Horace detected a Midland accent and an ally.

"It's Liverpool! I came here like you – on a boat. Met Glad and settled down. Best thing she ever did."

"More like best thing you ever did," Glad said, putting her elbow in Paddy's ribs.

"How long will it take us to walk home tomorrow?" Betty asked.

"To Manchester? Impossible! Too much traffic."

"Couldn't we follow the drains?" Horace asked, putting a comforting arm around Betty.

"They're in too much of a mess. Some haven't been seen to since they were built in the last century. I hear things were easier then than today. You wouldn't believe that, would you! Do you know they've still got bomb-site up there – and it's thirty-five years since the war ended!"

"Why is that?"

"The local politicians are all pulling in different directions. No unity. One thing in their favour: there's plenty of rubbish about."

"Don't go on, Paddy," Glad chastened. "Horace and Betty need some rest. Come on ducks, we'll show you next door."

Paddy and his candlestick led the way along a narrow corridor, and Glad followed with a blanket and a second candlestick.

Paddy pointed to the stone steps off the passageway. "At the top of the stairs is a hole in the wall. It leads into the underground cable ducts in one direction and the main sewer in the other. The hole in the ceiling goes straight into a pub cellar. Couldn't be better. I'll show you around tomorrow."

"Don't you go getting Horace into bad habits now, Paddy," Glad said, handing the blanket to Betty and the candlestick to Horace. "He goes up to the pub nearly every night. Goodnight!"

No sooner had Horace and Betty crawled under the blanket

12

than they were dreaming they were back on the ship being chased by knife-wielding pirates. But exhaustion soon overcame their anxiety and they fell into a deeper sleep.

TWO

Betty had spent her first day in their new apartment scrubbing walls and floor and dusting and polishing the few pieces of furniture the previous occupants had left behind. Horace had been out and about exploring the inter-connecting burrows. Industrious and focused by nature, it didn't take him long to scavenge an old settee. Despite the horse-hair spilling out from both of the round, black plastic-covered arms it was an acquisition of which he was justly proud. When he dragged it through the door, Betty showed her appreciation by throwing both arms around Horace's neck and giving him a loud kiss on the cheek.

"Get away, doe. I've got work to do," he shouted, deflecting attention from himself towards the comfortable chair. No sooner had he pushed the double arm-chair at an angle to the corner of the room than Betty was polishing it and plumping-up the seat cushions. By the end of that afternoon Horace had found enough bits and pieces to provide all the creature-comforts for their inner-city dwelling-place. In a day, and by their joint efforts, the couple created a place in which to live and, in the fashion of their near-neighbour's home, had, by the use of a hanging blanket, made two rooms out of one. It must be said that Horace had expressed surprise at how many discarded items he came upon – especially as Paddy had hinted at high human unemployment and mismanagement by the elected council.

By pre-arrangement Betty called on Glad with whom she was going to spend the evening learning about available facilities. And Horace, with Paddy as his guide, was going to explore the streets and alleyways of his new neighbourhood. Paddy was enthusiastic at the opportunity to show off his geographical and sociological knowledge of his adopted city; and Horace was eager to absorb the strange atmosphere that Paddy had described as peculiarly insular and surviving on self-praise. "Don't criticise Liverpool to a scouse rat or you'll be in trouble," Paddy warned.

"What's a scouse?" Horace asked.

"A member of the local community. You'll be able to recognise them by their accent. All the 'hairs' are 'hers'. They like you to be truthful in all things except the state of their city. And by the way, don't say you're from Manchester They've got a thing about Manchester. They say it's down to football but I think that's an excuse. Liverpool used to be a wealthy city – not that the ordinary bloke saw much of it. One day I'll show you some of the grand buildings down town but they're surrounded by mouth-watering squalor. Come on. Let's see the sights."

Horace followed Paddy up the stone steps and through the hole in the wall. Without hesitation and, for his age, quick on his feet, Paddy led Horace along narrow, winding pipes.

"Where are we going, Paddy?"

"This'll bring us out near the Pierhead," Paddy said without stopping.

"What if we get separated?" Horace asked.

"No bother. In the early days before I got the knack of the pipeways I used to head for the river and make my way back down the tunnel."

"How would I know where to find the river?"

"It's always down hill to the sea. Whatever you do, don't try to cross the Strand. Too wide and dangerous – a bit of a racetrack. Keep to the pipes. We could have used the tunnel but you get wet feet. It's only for emergencies."

Horace followed Paddy into an old dry-dock beside the river. The early evening sky was darkening but a long, thin strip of pink light broke through the mackerel-sky and stretched over the estuary before disappearing below a skyline across the water, described by Paddy as Wallasey. There was a strange quiet in the air. It was that time of day when the buildings came into their own: the shoppers and retailers had gone home; the revellers had still to arrive and the traffic was scarce. It was 'tea-time'.

The river was swollen but smooth and a tanker was making use of the high tide to journey up the Mersey to the oil terminals at Eastham. Paddy was a font of knowledge but Horace thought he would never be able to remember all those strange place names. With an early lamp at bow and stern, the small ship glided low in the water, its bow slicing and churning the polluted river. A plume of white smoke trailed horizontally from its stern-positioned green funnel. Beyond the ship the evening cloud was fragmenting, and a large red sun lay low behind the shipyard cranes lining the Wirral banks in stark black silhouette.

"Well? What'd yer think?" Paddy asked.

"It's very interesting."

"Come on; we've got a lot to see," Paddy said.

In the shadow of a dusty high wall the two new friends followed the dock road north, and by a rodent underpass outside the Princes Dock headed east and inland. The new moon was up when they re-emerged on Scotland Road.

"Used to be a pub on every corner here, Horace," Paddy said, as though he had spent his whole life on Merseyside. "They catered for the thousands of dock workers who once inhabited the back streets around about here. Looks like most of those houses have been flattened. Plays havoc with the drains when they do that."

"I know. Where are all the dock workers now?" Horace asked.

"Gone. Jobs gone. Self-respect's gone. Most have moved out of town or into those high-rise buildings. Word of warning, Horace. Never go near the drains under those multi-stories. You wouldn't stand a chance. You wouldn't believe how they live. Side by side, above and below, all packed on top of each other – and the smell: fish and chips and cabbage. In the old days they had their own roof and backyard. The women used to chalk the doorstep and stand on the street talking. Never see anyone these days. They even board up the shop windows now – what corner shops there are."

From the grassy knoll where the pair stood on Everton Heights the view of the city centre below was panoramic. The neon lights dressed the streets like a giant brown Christmas tree stripped naked of its pine-needles.

It was only a short walk from the concrete surrounded hill to the festering back streets of Anfield and Everton and their rows of cheek-by-jowl black and brown-bricked houses. Refuse, sodden and decaying, spilled out of a dark alleyway blocking the entrance and adjacent footpath. On the edge of a small wasteland, broken walls exposed backyards where damp, grey clothing hung limp from string stretched between nails. In a dimly-lit upper room, uncurtained and brown ceilinged, a thin, old woman in a loose vest struggled to pull a tight black jumper over her head. Her arms were inside the long sleeves but her head would not pass through the neck opening. Bending at the waist, her arms writhed above her head – but the shrunken jumper remained anchored around her armpits. Her shadow danced on the yellow wall. From behind, a youth, lank haired and also lean of stature, wrapped his bare, fleshless arms around the woman and through the flimsy vest took her empty breasts in his hands. On the wall their black shadows combined, at first, like a frantic crab struggling to escape the lincrusta walls, but when the woman's bony head burst out of the jumper and her arms waved in the air it was a giant, black praying mantis that slid down the wall and out of sight. On the yard wall below the window a cat howled.

"What do you make of that, Paddy?" Horace asked.

"Human stupidity. Live in squalor and behave the same way. They're conditioned by their environment. Don't suppose it's their fault. Circumstances of birth."

"Some go on to better things!"

"A few. For most of the inner-city back street dwellers there's no escape. They're tarred with the same brush that tarred their mas and pas. And so it goes on: no drive, no imagination, no nothing. And to make matters worse their brains are in their underpants. Come on, let's head back. It could be catching!"

Hugging the shadow where the wall and paving-stone converge they turned a corner and stopped. Two youths, each with a shoulder to the fluted cast-iron lamp-post, leaned in conversation. The pool of soft light from the street lamp was narrow and barely reached to the toecaps of the robust boots they wore. A young woman, similarly pre-occupied – but with her own thoughts – approached from the opposite direction. The baby pushchair she wheeled rattled but, although she had difficulty steering a straight course, she managed to cross the street before reaching the lamp-post. A second, and slightly older child, clutched at her three-quarter length black leather-jacket, struggling to keep up with its mother's hurried steps.

The shadowy streets of Anfield were no place to be on Saturday evening – and most certainly not after the Liverpool Football Club had been beaten on its own Anfield-based ground.

Paddy knew from sorry experience that in those parts a street could be empty one minute and teeming with a pack of wild children the next. At the junction of Kirkdale and Scotland roads they joined the main sewage pipeline where they were assured of safety and security. Paddy led Horace to Whitechapel where there had been serious underground pipe decay and in consequence had become a major terminus for the city rat population. At Whitechapel they descended to the underground railway line that led directly to Bold Street, Horace's new address.

Bold Street, before the onset of government-inspired deflationary policies and the switch in trade from West to East, had been a rare jewel in a crown of thorns. Surrounded, on one side by a British Rail valley of wasteland, and on the other side by grotesque empty buildings that would not be tolerated in Calcutta, it once offered quality furniture, expensive shoes and – but before the Animal Liberators arrived with their red-painted sheep-skins – beaver, fox and mink furs. The liberators need not have bothered, for, at the end of the seventies, even those with money feared for the future and kept their hands clasped inside their pockets. And the 'less-than-a-pound' products from China were quickly filling the shops and the people's wants.

As the merchants of the inedible moved out, small food retailers, cafes and bars moved in to create an environment the rodents occupying the dangerous superstructures in the square mile to the south east had never dreamed possible. No longer would they need to risk life and limb walking down to Church Street after the market traders had gone home. Suddenly food was on their doorstep. And so the rat population of Fleet Street and Duke Street and all those other decaying streets as far as the inappropriately named Park Lane multiplied. And the City Council did everything within its power to encourage it.

"For us rats, Horace, I think you'll find the quality of life here is much better than you'll find in Manchester," Paddy said, as they followed the drain down the kerb-side of Bold Street.

"I think Betty wants to be going home, Paddy. She was worrying about her mother this morning. They usually meet up on a Saturday."

"They're all the same. Does! Don't want to leave their mothers. It's the protection thing. I had it with Glad. When I met her she was crying her eyes out. She'd arrived on a lorry-load of pottery. She was bruised all over. It was out of pity I took her in. I didn't want to get tied down – but that was a long time ago. Look at us now. Two peas in a pod. We're both white and full of aches and pains. Betty will get use. Listen, Horace, it's better to live a long life here than a short one trying to do the impossible. You'll soon both get into a routine."

"If things are so good for the rodents but bad for the citizens because of the confusion, what if they get a really dynamic council?" Horace questioned.

"We'll have to watch and pray that doesn't happen. Come on, this way. Nearly home."

"Why have the people got a council that does nothing to improve things?"

"It's like a business, Horace. Once a city gets into difficulty and starts losing money it's almost impossible to stop the bleeding. Bank charges get heavy on borrowings – and you wonder if those council people managing the budgets are really the kind of people who would be running a successful multi-national private company."

19

"How do they get the jobs, Paddy?"

"Say anything they think the voters want to hear, but haven't got a clue about what to do when they get elected."

"What about central government? It seems to be filled with educated people," Horace said.

"Not doing much for Liverpool with their policies of switching trade to Europe. This is the gateway to America – not Amsterdam. We don't count up here. What worries me though, Horace, is if the dock warehouses get any quieter we'll have the wharf-rats moving in here and you know what they're like. And that government woman's out to get the unions. She'll go too far if she's not controlled. You've got to keep women in their place!"

As they emerged into the open street for the short journey across the footpath, young lovers in doorways huddled and cuddled. The excitement was too high for the caressers and caressed to notice two tired rats – even if one was white.

"The young folk seem happy enough," Horace said, as they climbed down the steps.

"Young people the world over are happy on Saturday nights. It's the other six days when they have no money that they are unhappy."

THREE

The following morning Horace and Betty had a lie-in as was their practice every Sunday. The fact that they were living in a strange place disturbed neither their routine nor metabolism. They were creatures of habit and comfortable in the dark. However, although their new home was two stories below the ground, the daylight, through a series of fissures and natural prisms in the earth, scattered pencil-thin sunbeams throughout the rodent complex – for a complex, Horace was about to learn, is what it was. No less than twenty-two apartments lined the corridor, constructed in the early seventies as overspill accommodation for those rats attracted by the socio-economic decline on Merseyside. The complex had been a major undertaking carried out by a mixed social group, including a team of Irish immigrant rats, working under Paddy's supervision. As the owner, by long-term occupation, of a brick-lined room with direct access to the mud banks and salt water of the Mersey he saw an opportunity and seized it enthusiastically. All he asked in return was free access for life to the communal food stores without the usual obligation of having to contribute to the stockpile. It was a deal welcomed by the younger rats: modern apartments with naturally refracted light and constant fresh water leaking from the city's main water supply pipes. The accommodation would also provide direct access into a long row of ground level retail shops including a choice of restaurants and a pub. Weighing this against the requirement to provide food for an ageing couple with not too many years left to live seemed a bargain and contracts were exchanged.

"Do you know there are twenty young families living in this

street, Horace," Betty said, her nose peeping over the edge of the blanket.

"Street? What street?" Horace asked, his eyes still firmly closed.

"This is the beginning of a long street. It has a store-room and a communal hall. It's all very exciting. There are all kinds of things going on. Jugglers and acrobats come and put a show on each month – and they have talks by elder rats."

"Twenty other families?" Horace asked rhetorically and with his eyes still closed. "Who told you?"

"Glad."

"How many kids?"

"I don't know. Why?"

"Why! We'll never have any peace," he said, opening his eyes wide. "You know how some of those young rats breed."

"What are you talking about?" Betty asked, sitting up in bed but keeping the blanket just up to her nose.

"Paddy was telling me there's a lot of Irish influence here and they like large families."

"I don't see what that's got to do with it. Anyway, we'll have to think about starting a family soon." Betty concluded and, turning her back to Horace, lay down and went to sleep.

"Top of the mornin' ter youse! Are you up and decent?" Paddy called from outside the archway leading off the corridor. Egalitarian by both philosophy and instinct the rodent population had no need of doors – a rat would never dream of entering another rat's property uninvited. Offenders of this doctrine were considered to be mentally ill and banished from society. The punishment of being sent to an isolated and barren habitat meant certain death. In ratland the rules were clear and unequivocal and sub-cultures, on pain of similar retribution, were dissuaded from creating naive pressure groups that could, by their innate malleability, undermine the solid foundations on which their law abiding society had been constructed.

"Come in, Paddy," Horace shouted through the hanging

blanket that curtained-off the bedroom. "I won't be a minute. Have a sit down on our new sofa."

"Very nice too," Paddy called back, settling into the corner of the armchair. "I could sleep on this."

"Good morning, Paddy," Horace said, entering the room and brushing his head as he walked.

"Morning. Sleep well?"

"Excellent. I think I must have been worn out by the traumas."

"Aye, it catches up on you," Paddy said knowledgeably. "Sleep is a fine medicine. I've come to show you around the village – well it's not really a village, more of a hamlet. That said, upstairs we've got an excellent selection of city shops at our disposal. And, furthermore, to us they never close." Paddy slapped his knee and laughed out loud. "I'm sorry, Horace. Is Betty asleep?" he whispered.

"It'll take her a week to get over that boat-trip." Horace said, putting his hairbrush on a small shelf over the sink.

Horace followed Paddy out into the corridor. It was a five minute walk before they passed the entrance to the next apartment, but from then the other accommodation units were close together and built on two sides of the tunnel. Intermittent slivers of light radiated from the ceiling like the silken threads of a water spider.

"This is the primary store," Paddy said, pointing through a double-width archway. "You have to bring in more than what you and Betty need 'cause some of its for Glad and me. I don't charge any rent. Fair enough?"

"That sound's fair enough to me, Paddy."

"And in that store-room we keep bedding, and that room opposite is for candles. We use a lot of those in winter. And these are shower rooms. One for bucks and the other for does."

"I've never seen such a well equipped complex. Did you do it all, Paddy?"

"You ain't seen nuttin yet. It's all down to teamwork with encouraging leadership. There has to be some reward for all the participants."

"Wait till I show Betty all this. It might get her thoughts off going back to Manchester."

On their long journey along the semi-dark corridor they did not encounter any other rat. It was so quiet that Horace assumed everybody must still be sleeping. At regular intervals arterial passages sloped gradually up to the ceiling where small holes had been cut to provide direct access into the cellars of retail outlets above. As they continued along the main corridor the ground sloped sharply downhill until they had descended the equivalent of four stories below the accommodation level. Horace asked Paddy several times where they were heading, but he just smiled.

At the bottom of the shaft a heavy, metal-studded door barred the way. Slowly Paddy pulled the door open and, with the gesture of a quarter bow, his left paw across his stomach and a swing of his other paw, exclaimed: "After you, sir!"

Cautiously, Horace stepped inside but couldn't believe his eyes. The area was of such massive proportions that he could barely distinguish the rich carvings covering all four walls. Giant stone pillars lined two sides of the huge room but like the walls themselves the pillars, from the mosaic floor to the high architraval ceiling, were engraved to the finest detail. Rodents rode on the backs of naked humans carrying the spoils of victorious battles; swam in mountainous seas and hung in heroic postures from cliff faces. No part of the surrounding walls nor offset pillars were left unembellished. From every part of the pastel blue vaulted ceiling golden rays of sunlight fell like rain over the sculptured architecture. And, as if the monumental construction was, in itself, not sufficient in breath-taking design, proportion and grandeur to awe-inspire the most indifferent onlooker, in the middle of the capacious and multi-coloured floor a flat-topped Mayan pyramid had been built, carved with the same careful attention to detail. Tapering down to a wide base by incremental steps on all four sides, it at first appeared to Horace insurmountable. Closer inspection revealed a steep narrow staircase of one hundred small stone steps. At the top of the steps, and immediately below the flat summit, a square black hole contrasted starkly with the artistic carvings that covered the stonework. Ornate designs, hieroglyphic writings and pastoral scenes filled every inch of the enormous monument.

"This is our Isenergic temple, Horace," Paddy said in a low voice. "It is there to remind us that in strength we are all equal. That the muscle of youth is no more powerful than the wisdom of age."

"Who built all of this?" Horace asked, breathless at the scale and beauty of the monastic-like complex.

"The Merseyside rats. Everything you see gnawed out of solid rock by their own incisors!" Paddy said, adding with pride: "With the help of the Irish immigrants, of course."

"How long did it take to build?" Horace asked.

"It began with the decline of the docks and the parallel growth of cronyism and ineptitude in the local authority. Those factors conspired to create unemployment, lethargy and self-interest. The population became less but the number of buildings remained the same. Ideal circumstances you might say for the rodent population. Indeed as the people moved away in search of work the rats moved in. It was a recipe for disaster but, in accordance with our inate conditioning and natural energies, the rat elders organised communal work and good came out of bad."

"I've never seen anything so beautiful!" Horace exclaimed, running his paw over the carved door. "Were they rewarded for their efforts?"

"Yes, of course. There were too many rats and not enough food to feed them. The council had built multi-storey housing complexes for the humans but then started rehousing those same inhabitants in out-of-town estates. It was like having hundreds of hotels without kitchens and dining-rooms. Word got about in places like Southport and Widnes that free accommodation was abundant in Liverpool. For years it had been the natural order of things that food and accommodation went together ... like a hand and a glove – but suddenly the order was unnatural.

Something had to be done. It was a programme of tertiary concepts. All sexual active bucks and does had their day divided into three parts. Eight hours working on the communal halls, eight hours foraging in allocated sectors and eight hours sleeping. Apparently it worked very well. The level of fitness reached new heights, bodies were toned and teeth were honed. All the rats eligible for work put their eight hours in. They had to. No work, no search sector. It was work or starve. That was the reward – but a remarkable thing happened. As the work progressed the workers began to see what they were achieving and a sense of pride emerged. The work in itself became the reward and many rats were working ten and twelve hours a day. There was no additional incentive – only a beauty they themselves were creating. Like members of a finely tuned orchestra they became intoxicated by the contribution each rat made to an exciting work of art.

"That's a very poetic way of putting it. You Irish have a way with words," Horace said, following Paddy along a paved pathway that cut a swathe across the mosaic floor, laid in the images of rats at work and play. "Where we going now?"

"There's more," Paddy said, pointing to a second door.

On the wall opposite the point of entry to the hall a similar arch-door of dark polished wood and brass studs stood ajar. With two paws Paddy slowly pushed open the door. He stopped, ushering Horace to enter the second gigantic chamber.

Of similar massive proportions to the first room it was constructed to a completely different design. Without the central pyramid there was nothing to diminish the perception of space in the four storey high rectangular room the size of a football pitch. Inlaid at one metre intervals into the four roughly hewn rock walls small pieces of quartz glowed and pulsated from a self-conducting electrical charge – but rather than project light into the room, the orange light was absorbed into the rock creating a thousand minute luminescent caves. Any light that escaped the caves into the room was absorbed by the peat-black ceiling. Yet the whole upper atmosphere was filled with fitful and vibrant fireflies that seemed impervious to the strange omnivorous canopy. As the living ceiling sucked at the delicate orbs of light, they floated upwards towards the hungry roof, but with sudden determination and surprising agility the flickering flames swooped down towards the mirrored floor that held in captivity their dancing reflections. And so the fireflies were suspended in permanent limbo and, like flickering candles in a cathedral, they provided both light and shadow.

"This is our son et lumiere, our theatre of reflection. This is where we come to watch the struggles between good and evil. We are reminded here that we should not allow ourselves to be overwhelmed by black thoughts but should fight against them," Paddy said.

"I'm lost for words, Paddy."

"Impressed? Everybody is."

"I don't see many rats about?"

"Most of the rats who helped build these temples have moved on to where the food is. The few that remain are out foraging. It's Sunday and the shops are closed. This is when we revictual. It is also the day when the fisher-rats bring home the day's catch."

"Where have they gone to?"

"Who?"

"Those rats you say have moved on?"

"Warrington, Chester. Some managed to get the trains to London but I hear accommodation's scarce down there."

"I suppose Betty and I could try getting a train back to Manchester."

"Two of you? One at a time perhaps, but not two together. There isn't the cargo to hide in these days."

"What about the coal wagons?"

"Coal? They've started to run that down. Although, come to think of it, they're bringing it in to the docks from Poland and moving it inland to the power stations. Don't worry yourself now. I'll take you through the resource area and then we can go down town to meet me cousin, Douglas," Paddy said, striding over the mirrors.

"Is it all right to walk on the glass, Paddy?"

"It's an inch thick – and anyhow it's self-healing. All glass has a floating molecular structure that eventually moves over itself. We've just speeded up the process. Doesn't work with vertical glass but this surface is dead flat. Spirit-levelled to perfection."

Despite the reassurance, it was on tip-toes that Horace followed his intelligent friend over the mirrored floor. Their reflected images, however, did not conform to recognized mirror images but rather had a life of their own. Detached, and as though standing in a shallow basement, the reflections smiled and waved. Paddy waved back but Horace was so disorientated – as though confronted by an over-gregarious stranger – he avoided eye contact with his own reflection.

Unlike the previous two heavy wooden and brass doors, the third door, built into the rock face on the far side of the semi-dark hall, was a continuation of the rough stone wall. It could be distinguished only by the absence of the inner-glowing quartz lights that covered the rest of the walls. There was no door handle nor seams in the stone surface but, conversely, the reflected door was fitted with a round metal wheel that Paddy's reflection rotated, and its shoulder pushed against the door. Quietly it opened, and Paddy waved to his counterpart in gratitude. With a smile he turned to Horace – but said nothing. He was interested only in seeing the expression on his companion's face.

In contrast to the previous and surreal edifices, the third chamber was nothing more than a huge cave with a massive black lake. A narrow strip of white sand surrounded the still water, separating it from the steep granite rocks that created an impenetrable barrier and reached to the cave roof where stalactites radiated green light. At the water's edge a dozen rats sat with total concentration on their bamboo rods and upright, bobbing fish-floats.

"They're on supply duty," Paddy whispered.

As they walked around the lake, silver spider-crabs emerged from the sand and either re-buried themselves or scurried into the opaque pool.

At a narrow cleft in the rock face, Paddy began to climb the almost vertical cliff; reluctantly Horace followed.

"Not too fast, Paddy. I've never been rock climbing before."

"It's no different to climbing on a building-site," Paddy shouted over his shoulder. "This is a short cut. We call it 'the chimney'."

Scrambling over the summit, the pair crawled under the cave roof until they reached the junction where the strata converged. At that point, Paddy and Horace climbed through a loft door leading directly into a straw-lined tunnel. It was in total darkness and Horace was unsettled by the sound of panic that was manifest without there being any coherent noise to define the concept. Horace sensed fear – not in himself but in the air.

"What's that sound, Paddy?"

"It's the mice. They don't like us passing through their territory."

As his eyes grew accustomed to the darkness, Horace could see the tiny unmade beds lining the wall. But there was no sign of the mice themselves and Horace commented on their disappearing act.

"They're under their beds," Paddy said, with a paw cupping the side of his mouth. "They always do that."

"Could we not have gone the other way?"

"Aye, but this way takes us almost to Seel Street where my cousin resides. He lives alone in the vestry of an old church. He doesn't like company. As a matter of fact he's very anti-rat. In other words he's a real nark, but I call and see him on the first Sunday of every month and – as we moved into May last week – another Sunday has suddenly come upon me."

The tunnel led directly into a drain on Slater Street – a street of decaying small shops that had seen better days when, before the war, it had thrived on a once-prosperous community in an atmosphere peculiar to Liverpool. The nineteenth century terraced houses had then an inner-city elegance with railed-off cellar windows, alcoved doorways above a flight of stone steps and sturdy boot-scrapers. As a major British port the demand for warehousing had grown and the dockside store-houses spread up the hill until they had moved in and around those once desirable town houses. With its own delightful little church the community had been well-served by the up-market shopping offered by the Bold Street traders.

Net curtains twitched nervously for the short period the two opposing aspects of city life co-existed. The residents were the first to move, but followed closely by the employees of those warehouses that had, unexpectedly, fallen victims to a changed economy. Shell-shocked, in more ways than one, the rot had set-in and the once elegant quarter of town was reduced to a shanty town. An eyesore for those humans who remained – or parked their cars on the dark back streets while they did their Saturday shopping. But an excellent source of accommodation for the rat population – although, as Paddy had earlier explained to his new-found friend from Manchester, it was fool's gold: with the reduction in the human population there was a correlating fall in the food supply. The windows were the first to go, and then the slates fell off the roof-tops, and the pigeons flew in and nested in upper rooms. Wood-rot, damp and festering brickwork combined to create a square mile of decaying and empty slums.

Paddy was first to climb out of the drain-grid outside the corner bank. The midday sky was light grey, and a disparate group of men wearing ill-fitting suits stood inflexibly with their backs silhouetted like a lost generation frozen in time. The apparent inaction of the men was an illusion: their movements were slow but deliberate. Each of the twenty men, all of assorted ages, walked alone but as a group spread unevenly across the otherwise empty roadway and both footpaths. Following Paddy out of the grid with his nose sniffing at the air, Horace commented on the smell.

"Worse than the sewer!" Paddy said, putting a paw over his own nose.

"What is it?" Horace asked.

"That lot."

Rounded at shoulder and with his eyes to the ground, each

man shuffled forward – yet no man moved faster than his neighbour. The pace of the shuffling crowd was slow but constant, a manifestation of the palpable, but invisible, cloud of noxious gas that trailed in their wake.

"Who are they, Paddy?"

"Homeless! Humans who have no home. They're off to the soup kitchen for Sunday lunch. Don't get too close. Might catch fleas!"

"I've never seen so many. They don't seem very friendly to each other."

"They depend on charity, you know. There's no system to care for weak humans. No safeguards for the homeless."

At a distance the two rats walked behind the depressed group, following them along the Fleet Street alleyway backing onto Seel Street. At intervals each man stopped, leaning his back against the long, continuous brick wall. The two rats stepped into the recess of a back-door and watched. Some of the men inhaled on small, flat cigarettes. Many coughed and spat. Metal on metal signalled the opening of a door.

It was only a very short walk from those remaining couturiers of Bold Street to the shanty town where six, comparatively young, Sisters of the Order of Missionaries of Charity, an order founded by Mother Theresa, were based. From India and other distant places, the attractive, dark skinned women had travelled to Liverpool to dispense care and soup to the helpless inhabitants of the once-noble city. The tables had turned.

From late afternoon, and up to ten o'clock in the evening, the homeless female members of Liverpool society either made their own way, or were helped by the Sisters, to the Seel Street Shelter, a terraced house set amid the squalor described previously. It was only a five minute walk from the epicentre of the city's main concentration of fashion retailers that separated the abject poverty and indescribable odours from the perfumed spenders of Church Street. But even so, the two halves of the city rarely met.

Unobserved, the two rats mingled with the homeless men in

the concealed vegetable garden behind the high, back-street wall. Only faith and constant care could have provided the fertility that the soil exuded. For the high surrounding walls limited the hours of sunshine. With little money, but considerable determination, the Sisters of Charity had converted a wasteland into an oasis; a damp hovel into a dry and hospitable refuge for those humans who had fallen below the minimum required standards. Trade unions would not allow their council members to care for such degradation – not even for wages! Those poor homo sapiens, as Paddy referred to them, were beyond redemption. Compassion was their only salvation. Paddy was familiar with the lay-out of the garden and house, for his relative lived diametrically opposite the Sister's front door. He led Horace along the inner wall of the garden.

In the warm sun an old man hoed the weeds around the firm vegetables while a second, younger man, beat the dust out of the threadbare carpet hanging over a washing-line. A third man, of middle-age, was bent over an upturned straight-backed chair screwing a sugar-twist leg back to the base of its seat.

The garden, Paddy explained in a hushed voice, had originally been part of the church-owned house next door. As a gift, St Peter's had presented it to the Sisters. Equipped with its own kitchen, toilets and a room with trellised tables and chairs it provided the perfect setting for the dispensing of bread and soup – and occasionally cake supplied by Cousins, a local and sympathetic retailer.

The garden door leading into the back of the house was open and Paddy gestured for Horace to follow him into the scullery. ''A short cut. The front door's usually open,'' Paddy said, his mouth so close to Horace's ear that Horace felt his warm breath. ''Stop,'' Paddy instructed, with his outstetched arm preventing his friend's entrance into the sitting room. ''Back, back, back,'' he repeated with quiet urgency.

Quietly the two rats retreated towards the garden door, but their exit was blocked by a young, dark-skinned women dressed in a flowing white robe. She was approaching the house and carried in her right hand a brown bottle. "Now don't you ever, not ever, ever bring alcohol into these premises again. There'll be no more soup for you, Archie Clark, if you do. You mark my words now." She spoke to nobody in particular, but at the rear of the line an old man, his white hair yellow and falling over his jacket collar, stood bowed, his thin upper body, supported by an ancient suit, flexing as though his stomach muscles were in spasm. On each downward movement a limp hand moved up to touch lightly his wrinkled forehead.

"In here," Paddy said, taking Horace's paw and leading him to the linen-filled wicker-basket by the stone sink. Barely had they climbed in and pulled the soiled towel over their heads than the Sister strode into the small room. Through the side of the whicker strands they watched as she emptied the bottle's contents into the white sink. Still talking to herself, she returned to the garden.

Alcoholic, deranged or simply desperate, the women, young and old, arrived at number 55 Seel Street at all hours of the day and night. At night they were never turned away. The more capable of these women were asked, in return, to assist with the cleaning. In the middle of the living room two of those volunteers, on their knees and side-by-side, moved slowly backwards scrubbing the worn, brown linoleum covered floor with small handbrushes. They shared one pail of soapy water. The older woman, broad faced and fat, smiled occasionally to herself, revealing the gap where her front teeth had been. To an imaginary observer she moved her eyes towards her more industrious companion and, with a fixed smile, shook her head.

It was the sight of these two women working at ground level that had stopped Paddy in his tracks.

The second woman seemed younger, but similarly ovoidal and dishevelled. Their work rates were in profound contrast: the younger woman attacked the floor with the stiff brush and with each stroke made a guttural noise. When she lifted her head to resoak the brush, her long mousy hair, that had hung to the floor, parted around a small, round and owl-like face. With a newly watered brush the thin-armed younger woman, with renewed vigour, scoured the floor. By comparison, the bloated and pink-faced older woman's hard brush skimmed the surface, and she continued to communicate with the imaginary third person – rolling her eyes and laughing silently as she continued to nod in her companion's direction. At regular, but brief, intervals the fat woman's features became serious, and throwing her head back she mouthed, for several seconds, silent communications to the ceiling. In tandem the two women moved slowly backwards, and the young woman grunted and groaned.

Both Paddy and Horace were concerned the situation was getting serious. Not only had they to cross the sitting-room floor, where those abundant chairs that normally offered good cover were now stacked high in a corner of the otherwise bare room, they had to then navigate a long dark corridor to reach the front door and the street. Paddy could sense, by the stillness of the air, that the front door was shut. And the soup-kitchen was underway and the door leading into the back-entry closed. Paddy admitted that their dilemma was of his own making.

"We'll have to climb out and try the back-garden," Paddy said, but before they could move a door-bell rang.

"Get me a Sister. Get me a Sister," an agitated and high pitched female voice shouted through the front door letter-box. "Get me a Sister," the voice continued, accompanied by the bark of a dog. The two rats looked at each other.

Without rising from her knees and in a surprisingly loud voice the fat cleaner shouted: "It's Annie."

From the rear garden a second and darker skinned Sister wearing a similar white robe entered the scullery. She threw a soiled hand-towel into the basket. The young, black and rounded woman crossed the sitting room, but before continuing down the corridor stopped, put a finger in a bowl of water resting on a ledge beneath a cross, and with the wet finger touched her forehead.

The two rats, hearing the unlocking of the front door, again looked at each other. "I think we should make a dash for it. Are you ready, Horace?" Paddy asked. Horace nodded – but before they could climb out of the linen-basket a brown mongrel dog, with a white patch over one eye, charged in through the door, ran down the corridor, slid over the wet floor of the sitting-room and jumped into the scullery where it stood barking at the basket.

"Is that your dog, Annie?" the Sister asked, in a soft Caribbean accent.

The tall, heavily built woman with bleached hair stood on the doorstep, shook her head and said: "I need new flip-flops."

"Just a minute, Annie. Wait there while I get the dog out."

Paddy and Horace had worked their way to the bottom of the dirty linen, but the dog continued to press its nose against the wicker, and bark fiercely.

"Get out!" the Sister, from a distance, shouted at the dog. But the dog salivated and began pawing at the basket. "Hughie," she called into the back garden, and the man with the screwdriver entered the room. "That dog's just broken in the house and it's after the food on the towel I've just thrown in there. Get it out, Hughie. Give it a biscuit. It must be starving."

"Yes, Miss," Hughie, the odd-job man and reformed alcoholic, replied and with the aid of the repaired chair, ushered the dog out of the house.

In the confusion, and contrary to house-rules that non-helpers, whether homeless or not, were not allowed inside the house between mid-morning and late afternoon, Big Annie, as she was known to the homeless community, repositioned herself in the doorway between sitting-room and scullery.

"Annie, you is not allowed in the house at this time of the day and you know it," the black woman said, softly.

"I need new flip-flops. I can't walk in these. Look at the sole. It's falling off," the irate woman said, lifting up her right swollen and varicose-veined leg.

"I'll get Sister Josenn. Just a minute."

The smile had gone off the face of the fat woman on the floor. She made light circular movements with the hand brush, but kept her eyes fixed firmly on big Annie.

"Don't look at me, you lazy cow," Annie said to the kneeling woman. "I'll kick yer soddin' bucket over."

35

The cleaning woman said nothing, but continued to stare at the big blonde woman.

"Annie!"

"Sister Josenn," Annie said, her voice and posture suddenly submissive in the presence of the senior Sister

"Size forty-three isn't it?"

"No sister. Size nine."

The two women walked into the sitting-room.

"That was Sister Josenn, the boss," Paddy whispered. "She was born in Southern India and trained under Mother Theresa in Calcutta! For a human, she's a good person. She's sympathetic to the insane. Treats them as though they are normal, she does. Heard her say once that she'd worked in Rome and London as well as Calcutta but she'd never seen vandalism such as she's seen here in Liverpool. Can you believe that, Horace?"

"I seem to be spending all my time hiding these days, Paddy."

"You know what she said? She said: 'violence is everywhere but vandalism in Liverpool is endemic'."

"What does that mean?" Horace asked.

"I think it means it's like an illness. There's a lot of sickness about."

"Do you come here often, Paddy?"

"Call in occasionally for fresh vegetables. I don't rob the poor or anything like that. Don't get me wrong. Just the odd carrot."

"Shouldn't we be concentrating on getting out of here?" Horace suggested tactfully.

Paddy already had one paw over the side of the dirty-linen basket when Sister Josenn re-entered the room. His hurried movements went unnoticed for the Sister's attention was fixed on the old sobbing woman she accompanied to the white, stone sink. "Wipe your eyes with the flannel," the Sister said, turning on the tap and allowing the water to run over the cloth in her hand. "You'll feel better." Pushing a small stool beside the sink, the Sister lowered the crying old woman into a sitting position. "Do you want to tell me what happened, Freda?"

The black overcoat the old woman wore was two sizes too big, making her appear more diminutive than she actually was; and the black, high collar of the coat heightened the white of her small, waxen head. Her red-ringed eyes pleaded with the Sister, white robed and perhaps young enough to be the old woman's grand-daughter.

"I don't know what to do, Sister," the old woman sobbed, bending forward to pull up her thick brown stockings that had fallen wrinkled above her ankles.

"Go on, Freda. Start at the beginning," the attractive, dusky-skinned woman said, her large brown eyes responding sympathetically to the woman's eye-contact.

"You know I moved in ter me council flat on Friday," the woman said, pausing for breath. "In the Ugly Sisters."

"Yes, I know you moved in Friday We helped you. Don't you remember?"

"I do! I do! I was grateful to you for helping me. As sure as God is my judge, I was grateful to you. And to the Social for the table and chair and the bed. The next day I cleaned it as best as I could. Couldn't do much about the damp and the roaches an' all that. And I could just about cope with the stairs – you know what the lift was full of, don't you, Sister?" The Sister nodded knowingly and Freda continued: "There was only me on the landing and the Social said I'd be all right 'till they found me somewhere else. It was terrible, Sister," she said, putting her head in her hands. "I thought they were going to kill me."

"Who, Freda?"

"There must 'ave been ten of 'em. I was listening to the wireless this morning when there was a knock at the door. 'Who's there?' I says through the door. 'The rent collector', somebody shouts back, but I could tell it was the voice of a child. 'Go away or I'll call the police', I said, but they kept banging on the door. I got a blanket off the bed and sat in the chair with it wrapped around me. But the banging got worse. I kept shouting for them to go away but they..."

"They what? What did they do, Freda?"

"Broke the door down. None of 'em could 'ave been more than

37

ten or twelve. They took everything I 'ad: me wireless, shopping bag with the bit of food you gave me and, and me purse."

"Here, put the cloth to your eyes, Freda," the sister said, running fresh water over the small square of fabric. "God will be with you and everything will be all right."

"I, I thought I was getting on my feet again, Sister. I said my prayers last night, but today I've lost everything. It's 'opeless, Sister. They set fire to my bed and ran off laughing. Everythin's cindered."

"Well you're still alive and where there is life there is hope. Have you been to the police-station, Freda?"

"No I came straight 'ere, Sister."

"Dry your face, Freda. We'll go see a policeman. Tomorrow we'll go back to the Social Security office. Tonight you can sleep here."

As their voices trailed away Horace and Paddy leapt down from their hiding place. The back garden was empty. The odd-job men and the other homeless people had returned to their own city centre hideaways. Two of the white-robed women remained but they were too busy washing cups and plates in the garden kitchen to notice the two rats run past the door and scramble under the rear gate.

"We'll have to call on my cousin another day," Paddy said, hurrying up the wide back-entry.

"Where we going?" Horace asked. Despite his younger years he was struggling to keep up with his determined friend.

"Urgent business. We're going to sort out those young hooligans who did that terrible thing to that old lady. We'll teach them a lesson."

"You and me?"

"You, me and some friends of mine who live in the area of the three Ugly Sisters."

"Three Ugly Sisters? What are they, Paddy?"

"Three monstrosities of tower block accommodation. Near Everton Brow where we were yesterday. Nobody'll live there. Not fit for pigs. I thought they were empty. Hooligans, that's what they are. We'll teach 'em a lesson," Paddy seethed, unable to control his anger at how the gang of children had robbed old Freda and vandalised her home.

"Wouldn't we be better going there by the under-ground?" Horace asked.

"Nobody about on a Sunday afternoon. The streets are deserted. They're all watching television."

"They seem to do a lot of that, Paddy – even in Manchester."

"Humans are not industrious by nature, like us. Some of them can think all right and that's the trouble. They make fancy electronic gadgets and lose their drive."

"Then there are all those cars."

"They'll forget how to walk next. And that's when we'll take over. It'll come about."

As Paddy rightly predicted, the dusty streets East of the city were empty, but to avoid any traffic on Renshaw Street they descended to the cable ducting running under Copperas Hill and skirted around the back of Lime Street Station. It was never advisable for a rat to go near the railway station in the middle of the day. The employees of British Rail in their black serge suits were often to be found lurking in dark corners. Not for the purpose of rat catching but for a catnap or smoke. In their uniforms they were difficult to spot.

The number of railway employees far exceeded the available duties and with little to do their workdays seemed unreasonably long. Nevertheless they were all rather keen to extend the number of working hours as pay for additional weekday hours increased by twenty-five percent. And for Sunday attendance the reward was doubled. Paddy knew that on a Sunday afternoon there would be many idle hands in and around the railway station. And as Paddy said, it was those idle hands that did the devil's work and chased the rats. It would have been quicker to cut across the platforms but the danger far outweighed the saving and Paddy led Horace across London Road and through the back streets to Islington. It was from here that they detoured to Shaw Street, a road still cloaked in its nineteenth century origins. At the back of that grey street of old houses and old schools lived three Irish rats. They had worked for Paddy on the construction of the apartment complex, but they chose rewards alternative to the offer of accommodation. They were, by nature, itinerant. At least they were before they came across the tatter's yard with its tons of waste fabric. So high was it piled that the lower layers of wool and cottons never saw the light of day, and more comfortable and warm accommodation would have been hard to find. It had other advantages in that a simple re-arrangement of the remnants offered redecoration for little effort and the colours were manipulated, especially in winter, to off-set depression. With wool in winter and cottons and satins in summer, the three friends, for all their rough-and-readiness, realised they had found their Utopia. Unpretentious, the environs were suited perfectly to the 'tough guys' as they liked to be known. In times of famine the materials were edible and their different dye contents offered a variety of tastes. And, as if all of those many features were not enough to satisfy any freedom-loving rat, the Rag Yard was out of doors with just an overhanging corrugated tin roof to keep the waste dry. Paddy knocked on the double doors, their rotting timbers held together by cross-members and rusted nails.

"Who's dare?" a thin voice shouted from within the yard.

"Tis yer old mate, Paddy," he replied. With a wink, he whispered to Horace: "They owe me a favour. They're a bit rough-and-ready but their hearts are in the right place."

"Paddy, be-Jase. And what brings you down to der backside of town?" the red-haired rat said, holding the two doors apart for Horace and Paddy to squeeze through.

"I thought I'd bring me new mate, Horace, to meet youse. This is Ginger, Horace."

"Pleased to meet you," Horace said, holding out a paw. The rat looked at the outstretched paw but kept his own paws by his side.

"Is 'e a posh one?" the ginger rat asked Paddy, the back of his paw to his mouth.

"No he's all right, He's one of us."

"Which part are you from?" Ginger asked, his shoulders visibly relaxing and his face breaking into a half smile.

"He's not from across the sea, Ginger. I mean he's a good lad," Paddy said, answering for Horace and patting Ginger on the shoulder. "Where's Lofty and Porky?"

"Come on. We'll wake 'em up. They're down the yard 'aving a doze."

"Are you well?" Paddy said, walking alongside the short and slightly-built red-haired rat.

"Top of the world. Couldn't be better. You and Glad keeping fit?"

"I've got something on my mind. I'll tell you when we wake Lofty and Porky."

For Horace it was easy to remember the names of the three co-habiting rats: Ginger got his name from the colour of his hair, Porky was round with a flat face and Lofty was, naturally, tall.

Lofty was alert when he emerged from underneath the cloth tents but Porky, who had been in a deep sleep, at first had difficulty focusing. Standing in the middle of the yard, Ginger, Lofty and Porky listened attentively as Paddy related the story of Freda and her tears.

"What you say then we give 'em some of their own medicine?" Paddy asked. All three agreed enthusiastically.

"Where do they live, Paddy?" Lofty asked, stretching his body to its full length.

"Ugly Sisters," Horace said.

"Now dat's a stroke of luck," Ginger said. "We sometimes talk to a group of young girls who live around there. They like our kind."

"They were brought up with rats," Porky interjected, yawning widely and showing his tonsils.

"They'll be there now. They'll know where the hooligans live," Lofty said, twisting the bristles at both sides of his mouth.

"Stop that! It irritates me," Porky said to Lofty.

"Why should it irritate you? They're my whiskers to do what I want with them."

41

FOUR

Paddy and his four allies dropped down a kerbside drain for the short journey to the three tower buildings where, until recently, nearly a thousand Liverpudlians had lived out their unemployed lives. The three fourteen-storey buildings had been built around a small and raised central area of dark grey concrete and with total disregard for the old and original terraced houses that encircled them. Such was the design and proximity that half the population of those flats and houses had lived in permanent cold, black shadow.

"Look at dat," Ginger said, leading the group out of the grid in the middle of the deserted rotund. "De Irish get everywhere."

It was an area of unrelenting concrete and brown brick relieved only by the graffiti that covered all wall space not more than two metres above ground level. "PAISLEY SHIT" had been scrawled emphatically along the side wall of an open passageway in metre high white gloss paint. The five friends walked down the passage where the same invisible hand had scrawled, in the same, but highly visible, paint: "CELTIC". The vicissitudes continued and followed the incline of the thirteen damp, grey stone steps to a subterranean level where the initials, "I.R.A." completed the mural.

On the lower level of the communal walkway a small group of pre-puberty girls hopped and skipped over white squares chalked onto the ground.

"Look it's Ginger," the tallest of the girls shouted, running over to the steps where the five rats were sitting. Her young friends followed, obviously very pleased to see their visitors.

Taking the five young girls into his confidence Ginger

explained the purpose of their mission. The girls were appalled to hear what had happened to old Freda and promised to help. Lorna, the tallest girl, knew the name of the boy who was the gang-leader.

"They are always causing trouble," she said. "They are really hateful. We saw the fire engines this morning, and we saw those boys running away laughing. The police never come down here."

"I didn't see any old lady," the girl with dark curly hair said.

"I did," a third girl shouted

"No you didn't," another girl cried.

"Yes I did – and I saw those boys just now going in that block."

Paddy stood up. "Are you sure?"

"With me own eyes," she confirmed.

"It looks boarded-up with corrugated iron," Horace said.

"They squeeze through. It's easy. Your gang should be able to get in, Ginger."

Ginger thanked the girls for their help but pledged them to secrecy. "I'll sort out some dresses for you all. On Tuesday. There's a new delivery in tomorrow."

It was a dull Sunday afternoon. The thin grey sky had thickened making the day seem later than it was.

The tower block had been emptied of its last few remaining inhabitants, and the Authorities had thrown a fence of metal and barbed-wire around the building while those inhabitants of the surrounding, and still occupied, small houses had added to the barrier with their own waste.

For Paddy and his companions the external obstacles were easily surmounted. They had no difficulty in squeezing through the slim gap between the overlapping corrugated sheeting that led directly into the main entrance of the once overcrowded multiplex housing unit. The wide, stone staircase leading off the dark, cold lobby was, like the entrance itself, littered to a depth of a metre with refuse: car-tyres, broken supermarket trolleys and torn and stained bed mattresses were piled high and filled the stair-well so comprehensively that the five able rats found it difficult to climb to the first floor. It was as though all those hundreds of former inhabitants had, before they left, collectively thrown their mattresses down the staircases and there they remained, a testament to incontinence and eating in bed. The broken but highly polished dark wood handrail attached to one of the two encasement walls added a touch of unnatural quality to an area of devastation.

At each level on the zig-zagging staircase a narrow door led onto an equally narrow, and exposed to the weather, communal passageway. The doors on the first four floors were nailed fast to the frames – but the door on the fifth floor had been removed. Putting his head into the door space, Paddy cupped his ear in his paw.

"Anything?" Ginger asked.

"A few blue-bottles, that's about it," Paddy said, stepping quietly onto the external passageway with an upright digit before his mouth.

In a line, the five vigilantes tip-toed along the passageway to the first doorless accommodation unit. The apartment was very small, built on two levels but with access only possible from the one door. It was, surprisingly, furnished with a dark brown square table and three mismatched dining chairs, complete with a similarly colour sideboard on the first level. The second level, at the rear of the living quarters, was sunken to a depth of just six internal concrete steps and contained a metal bed-frame.

"I think people are still living here," Paddy whispered.

"But the door's gone," Horace said.

"And so has the glass out of the windows," Lofty concurred, putting a paw through a window-frame.

"And there's no mattress on the bed," Porky conjoined.

"They must have left in a 'urry," Ginger said, putting his head into the room and sniffing the air. "Damp!"

"It's there to see. Look at the state of the walls," Paddy exclaimed, pointing to the black marks on the flowered wall-paper.

The adjacent apartment also contained an old table and assorted chairs of utilitarian design – but nothing more. By the entrance, the pea-green painted plaster hung from the ceiling like a sliced onion, and fungus grew freely on the red and white Regency stripe wallpaper that, like the ceiling plaster, had detached itself from its anchorage and now swayed gently in the unrestrained wind. The third, fourth and fifth apartments also contained old furnishings.

"They can't be short of cash to leave all this behind," Horace said.

"It's as though the people who lived here just vanished into thin air," Lofty suggested.

"Maybe the council threw them all over the balcony," Paddy joked.

"It's economic," Ginger announced knowingly. "It's all supplied by the Social. It saves on removal costs."

"Won't they need it wherever they've gone to live?" Horace asked.

"New address, new furniture," Lofty explained.

"Not new, Lofty. It's all second hand. The council will collect this lot, redistribute what's worth saving and burn the rest," Paddy said, stepping into a puddle of water inside the living room of the fifth apartment. "Water everywhere, and look at those window frames, full of red rust."

"They must have built these on the cheap and I bet –," Porky began, but Ginger clasped a paw over his mouth and, wide-eyed, put another paw in the air pointing to the upper floors.

"Shh! Listen," Ginger said, and the five rats stood in frozen animation.

"Can't hear anything," Porky whispered, the moment Ginger removed his paw from his mouth.

With words barely discernible and in a cracked voice Lofty said: "I can hear something." Ginger nodded, moving his first digit up and down at the ceiling above, and the group began to communicate in hurried, whispered tones:

"Voices," Paddy said.

"Not far away," Horace thought.

"They're not up there," Paddy said, emphasising the word not. "They're on the stairs."

"Shh!" Ginger instructed. And the group, with ears and noses cocked, fell silent.

The voices grew louder until it seemed they were very close and the subject of the unseen gang's conversation became clear. And then the sound diminished as the group of youths continued to climb the staircase.

"How many would you say, Ginger?" Paddy asked.

"About six or seven."

"Let's go get them," Porky proposed, thumping his inflated chest.

"Not yet. We need to surprise 'em," Ginger instructed. "Give 'em five minutes, then we'll follow."

The group of five stood on the communal walkway looking out over the desolate city scene, at each other and at the door leading to the stair-well. Nobody said a word, but with their alert eyes they communicated – with the exception of Ginger – apprehension.

"What you say, Ginger? Should we go and do our duty?" Paddy asked, deferential to Ginger's working-class savvy and aggression. Ginger nodded his head and drawing his colleagues into a tight circle said:

"Now here's the plan . . ."

In a line, with Ginger at the helm and Paddy trailing at the stern, the 'Bunch of Fives' – as Ginger had earlier baptised the group with a sprinkling of stagnant water from the floor of the gallery – crept up the rubbish-strewn staircase. At each turn of the stone steps they listened at the entrance to the communal passageways, but it was not until they reached the fourteenth landing, the last floor before the roof, that they heard voices. Ginger put his left eye around the jamb of the door leading into the external corridor. Seeing the way clear he signalled with an upright arm, and on tip-toes and in orderly fashion they moved towards the voices. The noise, it seemed, was coming from the apartment at the end of the rain and windswept corridor. At each empty apartment they passed, and to avoid being surprised by a rear-guard action, two of the advancing party made a cursory inspection while three remained in the corridor. With the exception of a few pathetic items of furniture the rooms were bare.

High-pitched and raucous, the noise grew louder. Vengeful, and following their instincts, they crouched beneath a window. Lofty raised himself slowly until he was able to peer over the ledge of the yellow painted window frame. Sliding back down the wall, his lips formed the word 'five' and then, with a shake of his head, he put his nose into his cupped paws and inhaled deeply. Ginger nodded his understanding of the mime. Horace, confused, looked at Paddy. while Porky scratched his head.

As at all the other apartments on the site, the glass in the sashes had been smashed and only jagged pieces remained at the frame edges. And all the doors had been removed.

The talking within the room had stopped. On a grey Sunday afternoon and fourteen stories high, the five friends stood on the edge of confrontation. It was only a low wall that separated the wet open passageway from the ravaged landscape way below. With a heroic shout from Ginger and racing hearts they charged into the room, but then skidded to a halt. The five youths were seated on the floor, their backs to the wall and their heads on their chests. Tubes of glue, empty tin cans and plastic bags lay between the boys' legs.

"They're asleep." Porky said, with much relief.

"Doped on glue. Vermin dey are," Ginger seethed between clenched teeth.

"I've got the evidence. Let's get them down to the police station," Paddy suggested, putting the tubes and cans in a plastic carrier bag.

With strips of white plastic, the comotosed youths were tied together, but it was with great difficulty that they were herded down the fourteen flights of mattress-covered stairs. It was only a short walk across Islington, through the cash-and-carry warehouse district and over Pembroke Place. The police station on the corner of the street was manned by an ageing constable. With an unsteady hand he recorded some notes in the Report Book, and with the other trembling hand held a black phone to his red ear.

"Send a van round to the Bullring. We've got the little buggers who tried to burn down one of the Ugly Sisters this morning. No she's not in hospital. It's one of those empty 'igh rise blocks off Islington. 'ow did I get 'em? Single 'anded that's 'ow," he said, winking at the five rats as they made their exit.

FIVE

A warm southerly wind blew along the river. The tide was on the ebb and the floating jetty at the Pierhead was low, but already creaking with the first flush of the rising tide. Seagulls, full bodied and white against a darkening sky, screeched and hovered by the safety rail where a woman stood throwing lumps of bread into the air.

Late middle-aged, her thin body was wrapped in a fur-collared, seal-black coat. The suede of her brown high-heeled shoes had been worn to a shine, and the thin heels provided no security as she leaned against the chain rail at the dockside. Stockingless, the black coat highlighted her lean white legs with their intricate blue network of raised veins. With half a loaf in her left hand she plucked at it, and like acrobats the upright birds, without touching each other, vied for prime position. With the back of her right hand she pushed back her frizzled brown hair from a sweated, narrow forehead, and blew gently.

Behind the woman, two men sat on a long, hard bench watching her feed the birds. A small, grain-carrying boat rode mid-stream at anchor, and a ferry boat manoeuvred into position alongside the jetty. The older man in a dark blue anorak pointed towards the jetty.

"See the prow of the Woodchurch. It was like that but with a higher deck," the heavily built man said, throwing back his enormous head and laughing to expose three evenly spaced top teeth. the only other four teeth in his mouth were in a line at the front of a protruding jaw. As his large chin curved up towards his nose so did his equally large nose curve down towards the chin.

49

"Well I'm glad I got me first mate's ticket. Pulls me in £200 a week," the younger and more diminutive man said.

"After tax?" the big man asked, stretching both thick and hairy arms before him in a futile effort to return his coat cuffs to his wrists.

"Naw," was the barely audible reply.

"Regular work?"

"Not bad!" the first mate replied unconvincingly.

Horace and Paddy sat in the nearby drain grid taking the fresh sea air.

"What's a first mate?" Horace asked.

"Some kind of a sailor. Used to be a lot of them around here at one time. Some of them even wore uniforms," Paddy explained.

Everything about the big human – except his tight-fitting coat – was outsized and heavy, but the gestures of his stout fingers were delicate.

"'ow many crew?" he asked his younger companion, moving his fingers in the air.

"Eight. It's all technology now – even on the coasters. Be glad to get to sea again."

"Don't blame yer. If yer want work you've got to go and get it. Jesus, I went to Australia in fifty-one and stayed fifteen years. Spent six years down a mine in Canada and three years building a rig on the North Sea. They won't 'and it ter yer on a platter! Trouble with a lot of 'em is they don't want ter work. Them on the dole brings it on 'emselves. Liverpool's 'ad it. The government never cared about it before the war so why should they bother now?" With his own special brand of contradictory philosophy the big man talked endlessly to his neighbour on the bench, and Horace felt that he was learning something new every day. The first mate watched a herring gull drift effortlessly on the wind, its legs tucked comfortably into its tail.

"There's a lot of beauty in a flying bird," he said.

"Us workin' class 'ave no time fer beauty. It's alright for them with silver spoons in their gobs. It's alright for royalty and the moneyed. They can go about looking for beauty. We workers 'aven't got time!'' the heavily-built man said, his strong guttural scouse dialect softened occasionally by Australian and Canadian inflections.

Between the two men and the woman feeding pigeons a short, bearded tramp in a multi-stained, ankle-length raincoat stopped to watch the feeding birds. In his hand he carried a large bottle of beer. In his holed, grey plimsoled shoes he was as unbalanced as the woman in her tall stiletto heels. With a toothless grin he smiled at the two men, rolling his eyes in the direction of the woman with the bread. He raised the forearm of the hand carrying the bottle, crossing it with his other forearm. The two men ignored the silent communication.

From behind, where Horace and Paddy sat watching the human and animal interaction, a youth, tall and gangling, suddenly appeared. He walked across to the man with the bottle, and with the flat of his hand to the man's shoulder pushed. The older tramp staggered back three paces, but with exaggerated body movements managed to remain standing. Recovering his composure and three paces he retaliated by pushing the youth. Before the youth could steady himself the old tramp set off along the seafront. With long strides the youth drew level with the man and, with less aggression than previously, shoved the older man. The older man again responded, as did the youth. Without speaking or stopping the man passed the bottle to the youth who put it to his lips. Like an integral part of the soiled seaport, and passing the bottle one to the other, they walked out of sight.

"Where'd you live?" the big man on the bench asked the first mate.

"Up the road in Vauxhall."

"Council?"

"Private landlord."

"Couldn't you get a council?"

"We lived in one on Page Moss. The flat was alright but it was behind the Blood Tub."

"Eagle 'n' Child?"

"That's right. You know it?"

"Used ter booze there."

"We had to move from all the hassle. The wife had a bit of a breakdown. The kids weren't safe going to school. Coming home with black eyes and broken teeth. Couldn't even go to the chippy at night unless you went in a group. The kids go around in gangs of fifty or sixty."

"I know. They want to bring back the birch."

"Believe another eighty joined the dole queue this week."

"Is that all?" the big man said with a laugh. "Been a good week."

"All from Robinson Willey's."

"The gas-fire people?"

The first mate nodded. "Said it was falling sales."

"Makes yer bleedin' sick."

"Do you know how many murders there are every month in Liverpool?"

"No idea."

"About six. Did you read about that mother on remand? Tried to poison her own daughter."

"Why?" the big man asked, a frown on his forehead and concern in the one word.

"Couldn't get it out of her."

Paddy and Horace looked at each other. Even Paddy with all his knowledge of homo sapiens had never heard of such a horrible crime. He was well aware that humans killed each other – often for no other reason than verbal disagreement. He was also aware from the rat-vine that many murders occurred inside human homes.

"Another thing they do, Horace, is kill themselves."

"Kill themselves? No I can't believe that."

Paddy was, of course, right. On Merseyside, at the beginning of the eighties, the Samaritans were handling five thousand phone calls a year from people threatening to kill themselves – or simply seeking advice before they reached that stage. Many were from the under-twenties who had never had a job since leaving school and could see no future in living.

"Are you a card man?" the big man asked the first mate.

"Since school. What about you?"

"Was! Not now. Not since I lost me job, and I'm too old now to go searchin' for work. The unions are not interested in the unemployed. They're only interested in membership fees. There's no union for the unemployed."

"Nor for the pensioners."

"It's all bloody money, money. Do you know that for every five union members in Liverpool there's one person out of work. We're relegated to the rag and bone yard of Social Security!"

"The employers don't want you. The unions don't want you and the government is talking about removing earnings-related benefit," the first mate said.

"And what can we do? We've nobody to fight for our rights."

"Gi' us some bread, missus," one of the three six-year-old boys with shaven heads asked the woman at the safety rail. She handed them the remains of the loaf of bread, and she and the birds dispersed. The spokesboy with the large hole in the front of his green jumper shared out the bread, and the small group walked towards the bus terminus. Beyond where the buses were lined up a siren sounded on the Isle of Man boat, tied-up at the Liverpool landing stage.

Next door, the Princes Dock, once the large berth for the glamorous ocean liners that ploughed the Atlantic, awaited the arrival of P & O's Irish Ferry. Princes Parade, a long cobbled roadway separating the old dock from the Mersey and its numerous waiting-rooms had, like the waiting-rooms, fallen into disrepair and weeds, tall and healthy, climbed out of every crack.

The main waiting-room itself appeared bomb damaged. All its windows were shattered, the floorboards in many areas uplifted – and the roof open to the sky. Where the floorboards remained, heavy berthing-tyres had been piled amid the pools of rain water. Electrical wires, long dead, hung limp from walls and roof supports. Down below the rotting floor joists the murky waters

53

of the Mersey were in turmoil as the incoming tide swirled around the decaying wood stumps, barely supporting the long wooden building where the wealthy once waited to board the transatlantic liners.

"Like you say, the unions don't do much for the unemployed," the first mate said, standing up and stretching his legs.

"Are you off?"

"Aye!"

"Which way you walkin'?"

"Down town. I've got to call in the ship's office on Water Street."

It was late afternoon and the Pierhead had emptied. Only the two men and the two tailing rats remained.

"Is this new?" the big man asked, pointing to the speaker's platform constructed out of bolted red girders.

"Been here a few years."

"What does that say?" the older man asked. "Can't see proper without me specs."

The first mate put his face close to the inscribed plaque countenancing the external wall. "It says: workers of Europe unite. On the 9th June 1972 the first international strike took place in Britain and Italy against Dunlop and Pirelli's multi-national capitalism."

"What does that mean?" the big man asked.

"I don't know. Don't remember reading about it at the time."

"Is that all it says?"

"No, it goes on: Spanish, British, Italian and French rubber workers met in Liverpool on August 21st 1972 to organise and defend living standards. Workers' unity has no boundaries."

"Does it say that or you makin' it up?"

"No it says that: workers' unity has no boundaries. It also says: this speaker's platform is presented by the TGWU as a tribute to the people of Liverpool and as a mark of confidence in the future of this great city."

"What a load of bull-shit. Built with workers' union fees! No mention of the unemployed is there?"

"No."

"A bag of tr_pe."

Next to the platform, and pasted to the outside of the old people's rest-home, a row of identical posters, in stark black and white, called for a general strike.

While the two men studied the robust construction by the sea the weather turned and a squall blew in. The big man and the first mate separated and went their different ways. Horace and Paddy climbed down into the drains to make their way across the city.

Saturday the 21 June 1980, the longest day of the year, brought no sunshine into the lives of the Merseysiders. It had become windswept, showery and as unpredictable as the future. Gloom pervaded both weather forecasts and news reports. Indiscriminate daylight violence had reached epidemic proportions: '... the police are on the lookout for two youths, one caucasian, the other half-caste, both with Liverpool accents, who attacked a fifty-eight year old widow returning from her local corner shop. She sustained a broken thigh, facial damage and lost three teeth. The white assailant is described as eighteen to twenty-three; five feet, two inches – with a pale complexion. He was wearing faded denim jeans and white training shoes...' The description could have fitted seventeen thousand young men living in Liverpool.

The incumbent government was being led by theory, conditioning, aspirations and lack of experience. In its infancy, the leadership was stumbling from one crisis to another and blaming its shortcomings on the former administration. Not without reason either for the previous government had appeared both leaderless and without a rudder. Its demise was sealed by the winter of industrial disputes and dubbed 'Winter of Discontent'. Industrial action paralysed the nation. Schools were shut down, industry ground to a halt, the dead could not be buried and, much to the delight of the rodent population, garbage went uncollected.

"It was a marvellous winter," Paddy reminisced about events two years earlier. "Black bin bags were piled high in all the streets for weeks on end. A nip at the plastic and you had a month's supply."

"It was like that in Manchester. The good thing about it was it was the same all over the country. We had all that available food and it didn't attract a single rat from out of town."

"It was a pity the humans got rid of that Prime Minister."

"Why?" Horace asked.

"Because he said it was only a hiccup, when it was the feast of all feasts."

"We should make it a rat public holiday," Horace proposed.

"I'd second that alright. It was a public banquet the like of which I had never before seen and I don't suppose I will see again."

"Cheer up, Paddy! The way things are going there'll be no money for refuse collecting. It could become a permanent feature of the streets."

In central government the humans discussed the Brandt Report: a document on the developed and under-developed world. The House of Commons seemed to be of the opinion that the subject could be resolved in one day. The debate in part relied on the theory that by the end of the twentieth century over 6.3 billion people would inhabit the world – a twenty-year increase of two billion humans to feed, clothe and provide with energy. Many theorists predicted that by the year 2000 the world would have used up all the oil supplies.

The main thrust of the debate was whether those matters could best be resolved by private enterprise or government control. While the private sector and governments made noises about the future, their real concerns were more immediate. Environmental issues do not contribute to profit, nor are they as attractive to the voting population as tax cuts and the National Health Service.

Against the limited debates expressing concern for the poverty of the Third World a sense of British Nationalism arose. The awakening of the spirit and self-esteem voiced by the few was self-defeated by their appearance, vocal fervour and aggression.

They tried to speak for the masses, but the general population could not relate to the 'skinheads' and their acts of violence.

Liberalism and lethargy had crept into the British psyche: the goodness in mass murderers was sought out and seemingly uncovered by knights of the realm. Competition was no longer deemed a desirable concept and sport was no longer compulsory in state schools. The British as a sporting nation, like its industry, was in decline. Technology was exported and superceded. The National Health Service had deteriorated to the stage where the sick wife of a leading Merseyside surgeon was denied access to his operating theatre by militant porters in dispute with the authorities. Workers, as individuals decent, ordinary people, were transformed by peer pressure and, in the collective situation, underwent personality changes. It was like the Englishman who goes to live in America and the very next day after arriving there is talking with an American accent. Personalities changed overnight and the individual no longer controlled his own behavioural pattern. As a member of a group he or she absorbed its philosophies. In ordinary circumstances it was latent in the sub-conscious, but immediately the right button was pressed mass hysteria became the dominant condition. For the workers, unionism was more important than Nationalism, and society was fragmenting. The employee was losing the pride in the service or industry that employed him and which he once embraced so passionately. The pride was being placed in the unions – not the work itself – that often applied policies and solutions that were misguided and misleading. The union leaderships were getting rich while unemployment was rising.

It was the Third World countries, and particularly those areas subject to natural disasters such as flood, famine and tribal warfare, that produced, on television screens, powerful arguments for financial and other aids. This didn't go unnoticed by the unemployed youth of Merseyside.

However, in the seventies the real economic growth was taking place in those Third World countries. Conversely it was the industrialised towns and cities of the developed countries that were experiencing decline.

The rain was streaming down the streets and grids, and Horace and Paddy decided to descend to the main ratway beneath the dock road. North of Huskisson Dock they took the north east bypass to the Grafton Rooms, a public ballroom, where a few dozen of Paddy's old friends lived in cavities beneath the wide entrance.

At midnight the Bold Street rat population would be celebrating mid-Summer's Day with a ball. Horace had never before been to a ball and had no idea what to expect. He certainly had no idea how to waltz and quickstep. The only thing Paddy could think of was for them to call at Liverpool's pre-eminent ballroom so that Horace could watch and learn. Paddy had only ever visited the premises in the middle of the night when the narrow back streets were silent and black. He had heard that on a Saturday night many hundreds of Liverpool's finest dancers took to the floor there, and that an excellent orchestra played from a wide and varied repertoire. Not since the days when he foraged had he visited the Grafton Rat Cellar.

After taking several wrong turns they eventually arrived at an upper drain level across the street from where the early crowds milled under the neon red and yellow lights above the entrance.

"Which way, Paddy?" Horace asked, his nose against the iron grid.

"It aint that way for sure," Paddy replied, scratching his head. "Get kicked to death. Let's go down again."

By a circuitous route and half-an-hour later they arrived at the duct connecting the main drain with the rat hamlet underneath the foyer of the ballroom. There were no doors, and they walked down a narrow corridor of ante-chambers. Every small rat-hole they passed was empty and there was no trace of anyone ever having lived there. In the very last hole at the end of the tunnel an elderly white doe popped her head out.

"Come to have your paws read?" she asked impatiently.

"No, I'm looking for me old mates from across the sea."

"That noisy Dublin crowd?"

"Sounds like them."

"Went ages ago. Couldn't put up with all the fancy music. Said they felt homesick so they moved in under the Irish Club near the cathedral."

"Well I didn't know that. Do you live alone?"

"Just me and me daughter, Ursa Minor. I'm Ursa Major," said the paw reader. "Do you want them read?"

"Naw, we're married bucks. Our future is sealed. I'll tell you why we're here . . ." Paddy explained their objective.

"I never go up there. Too noisy for me, but Ursa Minor goes up now and again to watch, and when they've all gone home she'll bring me some supper down. She's a good doe. Without her I'd be all on me own."

"You sound as though you've got a bit of Irish in you," Paddy said, catching sight of a second face peering out of the darkness behind Ursa Major.

"Haven't we all now, sir," she said, stepping into the corridor to display a ring inlaid with green glass on each leg. "Ursa Minor finds hundreds of these in the drains. I only keep the green ones. Me dad came from Belfast. Ursa Minor!" she called, but her daughter had followed her into the corridor. "Oh, you're there. This buck . . . what's your name?"

"Horace."

"Horace here wants to learn to dance. Can you take them up between the walls so they can watch. And he's married so don't get any idea."

"Mother, are you trying to embarrass me. You can't take mothers anywhere without them saying the things you don't want them to say."

"Take no notice. Children don't appreciate all the hard work we put in bringing them up. They think it happens naturally. Where did you say you lived?"

"Bold Street." Horace replied.

"Where's that?" the old doe asked.

"In the city," Paddy explained.

"You've come quite some way then. Is there nowhere you could have gone closer to home?" Ursa Major said, ushering her daughter back into the hole with instructions to brush her hair.

At a respectful distance, they followed the young doe up the criss-crossing tunnels, passing under the human ladies powder room from where there came the sound of much cackling and coarse laughter. So heinous was the noise that Horace and Paddy felt sure they were hearing the utterances of the supernatural, and closed ranks on the tail of Ursa Minor.

"I've heard they're all expert dancers who come here," Paddy shouted forward. Ursa Minor, with a puzzled look on her pretty face, turned around to look at Paddy, but continued to walk.

The young doe with the long dark and curled eye-lashes knew exactly where she was going. In total darkness they arrived at a small hole leading into the space behind the plaster-board wall. Using internal support struts as steps they were able to climb to a small platform where Ursa Minor had gnawed viewing holes in the wall. She made extra holes to accommodate her companions.

The crowded ballroom was in semi-darkness, but the rotating silver ball below the centre of the ceiling deflected the beams of the four corner spotlights around the large hall like dappled sunlight. The smoke-filled atmosphere was touchable, and women, huddled around tables, drank surreptitiously from miniature bottles of spirit, extracted from handbags, and chain-smoked cigarettes. Only their coughing interrupted the inane conversations between bowed heads. Occasionally the women pointed to a group of men standing with pints of beer and dangling cigarettes. It was then that Horace and Paddy recognised the source of the abominable cries they had heard previously.

The central floor of the hall was a black mass of intertwined bodies moving slowly to the music in a clockwise direction. Only prolonged observation revealed the motion. The more pronounced action of hands over bodies was noticeable on the periphery of the protoplasm.

When the musicians, jacketless and with rolled-up sleeves, stopped playing, the mass disintegrated. However, when the faster music began, the male and female humans reconstituted, but stood apart and jumped up and down. Others rotated their upper bodies without moving their feet. Unlike the previous dance nobody touched anyone else. Carbon monoxide and dioxide interacted with the nicotine-coated smoke. And handbags lay at women dancers' feet.

"Is this when they re-breathe?" Paddy asked Ursa Minor, who had her eye to the hole.

"Sometimes they call it a dance, but others refer to it as the twist. They all do it differently – especially the men. Don't seem to know what they are doing. At the end of the night it gets really wild. Gosh, I think it's dangerous."

"Is this what I have to learn, Paddy?" Horace asked, sitting back and feeling exhausted from watching.

"I've never seen anything like that, Horace, and that's the truth. I've seen those humans get up to some tricks – especially in the parks – but I've never seen them copulating en masse."

"They're not breeding!" Ursa Minor explained. "It's more like an excuse so that the opposite sexes can touch each other without any feeling of guilt or obligation. That's the first dance, of course. The one where they stand alone is a primitive form of self-hypnosis: they shake their brains so much that they become disorientated and lose their inhibitions."

"How do you know all of this, Ursa Minor?" Horace asked.

"It's only my interpretation – but we did live below the psychology department at the university when I was a young doe. I learned a lot."

"This is no good for Horace. It's ballroom dancing we do on Mid-Summer's Night," Paddy said, putting a paw to his aching back.

"I'll teach you. What time is your ball?" Ursa Minor asked.

"Midnight," Horace replied, rubbing the smoke out of his eyes.

"Terrible isn't it," she said with a smile.

"What?"

"The smoke! Not only does it get in your eyes, it gets on the fur and it lasts for days."

61

"We know," Paddy explained, "we go to the pub upstairs from where we live. It's nothing like that, though."

The community hall at the end of the rat corridor was no longer used but it offered a spacious area where Ursa Minor could teach Horace to dance. With his incisors over his lower lip, and without the need for fingers, Paddy whistled, from retentive musical memory, the waltzes of Strauss II and the full score from Offenbach's Gaîté Parisienne.

For an hour they danced in triple time to the array of waltzes from Paddy's lips; fox-trotting proudly and in quick time flowed to the quickstep.

As they hurried back along the rat underpass Horace felt both exhilarated and exhausted. He didn't know if he'd have enough energy left to dance, as Paddy had intimated, until dawn.

"Where've you been until now," Betty demanded, as Horace limped through the door.

Horace explained how he and Paddy had been to watch the humans dance, but how they had been disappointed by what they saw. He didn't tell Betty about his private dancing lesson, but said Paddy had told him enough to get by.

"All you have to do, Betty, is follow my feet."

"Are you sure you can lead me?"

"Positive! Anyway if I go wrong you can put me right. Your mother taught you, didn't she?"

"Well yes, but that was a long time ago. Can you fasten this ribbon behind my neck and zip me up please."

For two weeks Betty had cut and sewn the materials Glad had kindly provided for her to make a dress and an evening suit for Horace. Glad had even provided the paper patterns she had used for her and Paddy's evening wear. With slight size alterations they had proved invaluable.

"What's that on the table, Betty?"

"It's a bow-tie. You put it around your neck."

"I have to wear that?"

"Yes you do. All the bucks wear them, apparently. Glad said once you put it on you'll walk around like a peacock."

"I don't want to walk like a peacock."

"Will you please go down to the shower room and start getting ready."

"I could do with a lie down first."

"A lie down? There's no time for that. If you're tired, it's your own fault. Out all day wandering around town like a pair of playbucks."

Betty, Horace had to admit to himself, looked a picture in her pink crinoline and matching choker. And once he had climbed into his black tuxedo and bow-tie he began to think of himself as somebody more important than he actually was. Never, in all his school-buck days, did he imagine he would, one evening, be going to a ball in an evening suit with a beautiful doe on his arm. Glad had been right: Horace began to strut about like a peacock.

"Why are you walking like that? Have you got a stiff neck?" Betty asked, watching Horace's reflection in the mirror where she was applying lipstick.

"It's the collar. It sort of makes you keep your neck stiff," he replied, trying to excuse himself but feeling silly. He hadn't realised she was watching him in the mirror over the sink.

"Can we come in?" Glad called from outside the door.

"Of course. We're just about ready," Horace shouted back.

Paddy, looking distinctly uncomfortable, followed Glad into the room. Standing against the white wall in his white evening suit, Paddy would have been invisible had it not been for his red eyes and matching bow-tie. Conversely, and in deference to her middle-age, Glad wore a black crinoline, but to give more body to her thin lips she had painted a bright scarlet bow. Failing to find the beauty that is unique to every age, she had tried to turn back the clock with the exaggerated lip line and false eyelashes that fluttered, like the spiders' legs that they were, in the draught.

"Well don't we look smart. You've done a fantastic job there, Betty," Glad said, lightly touching the hooped dress. "What's your perfume?"

"Eau-de-Cologne. What's yours, Glad?"

"Lavender," she replied, putting her head close to Betty's. "Do you like it?"

"Terrific!"

"Pink suits you, Betty."

"And black really suits you, Glad. It's so sophisticated. What colour is the lipstick?"

"Cochineal. What's yours, Betty?"

"Poppy!"

"It really goes well with that dress, Betty. And doesn't Horace look handsome in that outfit."

"And so does Paddy," Betty said, running the brush through her hair. "Can you make sure there are no hairs on the back of my dress, Horace."

"Please!"

"Please! These bucks, Glad!" Betty said, a hint of excitement rising in her voice.

Betty always wore eau-de-Cologne, but for special occasions she doubled the application and it never failed to arouse Horace's procreational instincts.

"We have to follow you onto the mirrored floor," Paddy explained to Horace.

"With him being the community leader we have to make our entrance after everybody else," Glad said.

"It's the way it is, Horace. A lot of bunkum but we have to go along with it," Paddy said, thrusting his paws into the side pockets of his jacket.

"Take your paws out of your pockets. You'll spoil the shape of your jacket," Glad instructed, and Paddy complied.

"You're both on the top table next to Glad and me. The table's on the platform to the left of the room."

"Don't sit on the stage in error or they'll have you playing an instrument," Glad said, playing an imaginary trumpet. "It's the long table alongside the wall."

"They're not stupid, Glad," Paddy said, feeling his doe's explanations could be misconstrued as condescending.

Extra fireflies had been introduced into the Theatre of

64

Reflections, and suck as it did, the peat-black ceiling could not consume the luminous insects for their images, reflected in the mirrored floor, were more powerful than the abstract roof. Their golden orbs were supplemented by the thousand pieces of pulsating quartz embedded in the rock walls.

Between the round tables placed along the two side walls, citrus trees grew out of silver containers and the skins of oranges and lemons glowed like lamps. In equal measure to the illumination the fruits provided, they also perfumed the air, exhaling, in wave-upon-wave, the most refreshing scents known to rats.

The Rat Philharmonic Orchestra, in black tuxedos and evening dresses, filed onto the stage and while the twenty musicians tuned their instruments the does studied the dress of every other doe, and the bucks discussed human failings.

With a fanfare introduction the Rodent of Ceremony climbed onto the stage.

"Bucks and does! Please welcome our community leader, Paddy."

The introduction, on the instructions of the head caterer, was short. Standing in a line by the kitchen door, silent, but observant, young does in long white dresses with trays in trembling hands, awaited their signal.

The crowd parted as Paddy and Glad, to a slow paw-clap, acknowledged the crowd and made their way to the top table. As soon as they were seated all the other rats, having previously identified their name tag on the white-clothed tables, sat down. Hurriedly the waitresses served rolled oats, hemp with raw carrots, celery and wholemeal. Poppy-seeded dinner cobs were placed on side plates. The fireflies, careful not to lose their reflections, hovered over the central, and untabled, part of the mirrored floor where the dancing would later take place. Conversation and crunching of celery sticks filled the excited room, and the members of the orchestra watched the feeding frenzy and talked between themselves.

After the dessert of sliced apple and dandelions had been served and eaten the orchestra introduced itself with the opening Adagio

65

from Haydn's Clock Symphony. And the elevated tone of the evening was set.

By the time the musicians struck the first chord of the Andante, the bucks and does, on tip-toes, were circling imperiously around each other and the perimeter of the glass floor. Because of the hooped crinolines they danced at arms-length and were careful not to step into the centre of the floor above where the fireflies had congregated. The dancers' reflections, in the interest of choreography, colour and harmony, followed their partners' steps – but in an upright position. The two layers of dancers, as graceful as flocks of swans on a calm lake, glided around the gigantic room. It was a stirring display of movement, melody and colour.

At an interval the dancers returned to their tables.

"Well done," Paddy said, wiping the perspiration from his forehead. "I'm getting too old for all this."

"Me too," Glad said, trying to catch her breath. "But you two: well you'd think you'd been waltzing all your lives."

"Paddy taught my husband well," Betty said, with a thank you nod.

Glad looked at Paddy; Paddy looked at Horace, and Horace winked.

SIX

During the Summer of 1980 Horace and Betty settled well in their Bold Street environment, and both agreed they had been lucky in finding much friendship, in particular that of Paddy and Glad. Their integration into the local rat population was rapid, and they rarely talked about their home town of Manchester. And the sophisticated facilities adjacent to the warrens in which they lived were not, as Horace thought initially. unique. They were replicated throughout the undercity, but in a variety of guises that reflected the wealth that in its heyday the major port, as it had been for a hundred years, had once attracted. As a consequence, in the rat enclaves a multinational flavour evolved. For example, the 'Great George Rat Town', as it was known and located immediately below the Chinese quarter of the city, had similar massive underground chambers.

While the architecture of the above-ground Chinese community was red-bricked and bland-British the walls of the Chamber of Reflection in China Rat Town were lined with tall Madagascan palms. Colourful lanterns, intermittently round and square, were strung between the curving pinnate leaves, and the multicoloured paper shades projected elaborate oriental patterns on the centrally located pagoda. The rat population was, in some cases, seventh generation immigrant stock, but they never surrendered their identity to cross fertilisation with the indigenous population. For the most part the Chinese rats were law abiding and, like all rats, industrious. Neither had they acquired the native taste for beer and scouse. Nor a taste for the American exported hamburger concept and Italian-style pizzas that the Anglo-Saxon and black community had embraced so fervently.

67

The Chinese rats preferred the cuisine available in wholesale stores on Duke and Berry streets.

The subterranean ratways that criss-crossed the city interconnected with the man-made ducts, sewers and underground rail and road systems so effectively that, as recorded earlier, the rat population enjoyed unfettered access to every property and structure, including hospitals, universities and cathedrals. Their health and education needs were fulfilled – but they had no requirement for any human religion based on metaphysical idolatry. They had their own reflective religion based on conformity, goodwill and pain of death.

From the damaged drain inside the bombed-out shell of St Luke's Church at the top of Bold Street, an underground conduit followed Berry Street due south and on the corner of Rat China Town turned east along Upper Parliament Street, the epicentre of the Liverpool Caribbean society. Here the predominantly black rats had lived for thirty-five years in an underground enclave straddling the main sewer pipe following an east-west trajectory. As comparative newcomers to the city, the blackrats had arrived in the deep cargo holds of banana boats at a port slowly re-emerging from the ravages of a long war. During the fifties and sixties they shared marginally some of the benefits Liverpool enjoyed with the resumption of unimpeded trade with North America – but it was a relatively short-lived experience, and nothing on the scale of the high profits sustained for many generations of low wages and casual employment. Not that the workers themselves ever gained any benefits above the level of subsistence. It was the spin-off from the port of Liverpool activity: the building of ships on the west bank of the River Mersey, grand city buildings erected by ship-owners, benefactors and a nineteenth century local authority, cash-rich and competent. The commercial energy, like a magnet to filings, attracted the skilled and unskilled workforce and with them came their women and children. The human population expanded, and with it the rats came from far and wide until the supply and demand factors equalised. And so it came to pass that the energy and intuition of the rodent population was enhanced by this unprecedented influx. Their combined energies were harnessed and the subterrestrial monuments to rats' ingenuity were created. All of this happened before the black rats arrived in Liverpool. As a subculture, the black rats' history lay on distant, coral-reefed shores where warm, blue seas lapped white sandy beaches. They often bemoaned their lot, but it was merely an expression of cognitive dissonance for soon they were second and third generation immigrants with Scouse accents.

It was along the right-angled tunnel that Horace took Betty to see the sights of the city. Occasionally they surfaced for Betty to align the underground routes with the city's groundplan. It was also an opportunity for Horace to reinforce his own previous observations made in the company of Paddy. Betty was impressed by the Eastern splendour of Rat China Town, but less so with the human equivalent above ground.

"It's colourful at the time of their New Year," Horace explained, but Betty remained unimpressed. Although the couple had their own collosal community chambers under Bold Street, she said she preferred the more feminine pagoda with its array of colourful lanterns

The next time they emerged was in a narrow street of back-to-back houses off Upper Parliament Street. It was a grey, congested area the inhabitants referred to as Toxteth. A place where the adult population usually dressed in the drab colours of their surroundings although, by stark contrast, they dressed their young offspring like spring flowers.

Horace's attention was drawn to an unusual splash of colour: a string of red and white paper bunting had been secured to the iron-railing surrounding a school playground. The other end disappeared into an upper window of the adjacent beer-house. From their vantage point, between a dustbin and the old brick wall of an alleyway opposite the two uncomplementary establishments, Horace and Betty shared body heat.

Within a metre of where they stood two thin, middle-aged

women, dressed similarly in grey gaberdine raincoats and white headscarves, walked by.

"Goin' ter school carnival?" One asked the other.

"Aye, later. Promised our Elaine's boy," the second woman said.

"Yer granson?"

"Aye!"

The boredom of the wide concrete school yard behind the long row of grey iron bars was unrelieved by the carnival spirit: three, unsmiling white women stood in a circle near to where a black man sat with a black woman at an uncovered trellis table. The table was empty. Nearby a white woman, dressed in a white dust-coat, sat behind a second long table. Two green plastic milk crates stood on a table and each of the twelve compartments contained a small bottle of orange juice. Alone, but standing close to the table of orange juice, a pale teenage girl cradled a coffee-coloured baby. Partially obscured behind the two tables and standing women, four very small children, each with a different skin colour, jumped up and down on an inflated rubber bouncing-castle.

Waste paper littered the ground at the school gate where a young woman argued with a small white boy. Their faces, both clean and shiny as though just washed, were screwed-up in anger. The woman, dressed in a sleeveless frock with a low, square cut halter-neck, waved her arms above her head. The black fabric exaggerated the white of the woman's considerably exposed skin. The child, knee high and confrontational, waved his own small arms in mirrored mockery. On her veined feet, the woman wore black plastic shoes with high stiletto heels, and her attempt to kick the child was thwarted by her precarious balance. The child, little more than an infant, jumped clear of the swinging leg, and with outstretched fingers and a thumb to his nose ran past the woman to join the other children on the inflated castle. The woman did not attempt to chase the child into the school-yard, but leant against the metal upright. From a pouch pocket in her dress she removed a slim packet and, extracting the rema_ning cigarette, threw the empty packet to the ground. She put the cigarette between her rubine red lips, allowing it to rest under her upper lip and hang vertically over her small chin. While her right hand searched inside the same pocket, she ran her ringless left hand through her over-dyed black hair. By facial manipulation alone the cigarette was manoeuvred to a horizontal position. From the pocket she withdrew a single match, struck it against the metal post and, with pouted lips that covered a third of the cigarette's length, sucked the flame into the tightly-packed tobacco. With her head held back she blew perfectly formed smoke circles in the still, humid air. Flicking the match into the roadway, she walked unsteadily towards the corner-situated beer-house and disappeared into its black doorway.

The school was the educational centre of Liverpool 8, a shabby district of mixed races and deep unemployment, a place without a future. The south docks once drew its workforce from the labyrinth of two-up and two-down terraced houses, but even before the demise of the docks the workers often suffered, through the pool system, long days of unemployment. When those docks closed, the remaining inhabitants survived on Social Security handouts. The sizeable population was dispossessed and, without a Labour majority, lacked articulate representation in the House of Commons. The older residents had been conditioned to suffer in silence, but among the youth a rebellious undercurrent was developing, fuelled by the window-on-the-world that television provided. And the related advertising was the spur to the galloping frustration the young and disaffected of inner city Liverpool were feeling.

Horace and Betty followed the foul-smelling back alleyways, a grid plan as rigid and constraining to the local population as any prison wall and, without realising it, crossed the invisible border between Liverpool 8 to the equally destitute district of Liverpool 7. The two areas were close to the ever-expanding university complex, but gained no economic advantage from their proximity to massive government funding. Despite poverty comparable with Liverpool 8, the inhabitants of Liverpool 7 – where the brickwork was less worn – considered themselves marginally superior and were not averse to making such comment. As a result, animosity developed among people sitting together on the same adhesive ground at the base of the socio-economic pyramid.

From the brick alleys the pair emerged into an area where more recent council housing units had been constructed as low rise, but continuous and snaking rows of red-brick complexes. The couple rested behind a clump of congealed bricks and mortar on a small wasteland opposite a shop built integrally into one of the multi-housing units. The shop fronted the Faulkner Street flats off Myrtle Street.

Like its neighbouring district, it was a vicinity where anything that could be moved, moved, and was never seen again! As if to disprove the theory, a fractured red and white traffic cone lay on its side under the shop window, and a soleless shoe lay nearby in a similar reclining position. The word 'MOORSEY' had been heavily sprayed by an unsteady hand across the plate-glass and the over-application of black paint trailed beneath each letter, adding an artistic touch to an otherwise childish script. Strips of grass and weed grew freely out of the numerous cracks on the concrete-covered ground and, as with the graffiti-stained window, inadequate workmanship was enhanced by accident. Otherwise the area was as forbidding as a storm-lashed sea.

A small yellow van stopped at the kerbside outside the solitary food shop, and a man in a matching yellow waterproof jacket stepped out. He put a camera to his eye, but before he could return to the van a voice called:

"What yer takin' me shop fur?"

Ghostlike, on the shop doorway, a tall and heavily built young woman, white from the bandana-styled headscarf down through her dust coat to the galoshes on her long feet, stood with arms folded over a swollen bosom. "Well?" she shouted, raising her voice from the original question to a demand that needed an urgent answer.

From inside the shop two youths appeared, taking up positions

72

on both sides of the towering shop-keeper. They, too, crossed their arms and spread their legs.

"Am from planning!" the mild-mannered man stuttered, turning towards the vehicle.

"Come 'ere," the woman screamed.

Cautiously the man approached the woman, but stopped two metres away. "It's, it's only for the records. We're doin' a survey of the retailers in the area."

"What fur?"

"Nothin' really. You know what the Council's like ..," he paused, knowing not what to say further. The confident woman stared at the man, willing him to continue, "wastin' money," he concluded.

The woman agreed with the last statement. "Yer not opening any more shops are yer?" she asked, craning her head towards the man in the outsize yellow coat. "Bad enough tryin' ter make ends meet – what with the rent an' all that."

"No, of course not. Like I said, it's only for the records. Like 'istory. You know what I mean?"

"Yer not givin' me any bull – are you?"

"You've not got boarded windows like all the other shops around 'ere. It makes the area look brighter."

"Yer like the black paint on the window, do you?" she said, stepping out of the shop entrance and turning to the window. "I've told the Council about this till I'm blue in the face. They do nuttin'."

"'ave you thought about boardin'-up?"

"Why should I? It's bad for business. What you buyin' anyway?" she asked calmly, adroitly changing the subject to her own positive advantage.

"Buyin'?" the man asked, putting the camera inside a deep patch pocket.

"Come in," she demanded.

The two youths followed him into the shop's dark interior and, for security, the man put a hand inside the pocket containing the camera. The woman had preceded him and stood, arms folded again, behind the formica-topped counter. In silence the woman and two mixed-race youths stared at the man as they awaited his response. The council employee put the forefinger of his free hand inside the collar of his grey serge shirt. It had become tight around his neck. He withdrew the perspiration wet finger and lifting up the tail of the yellow coat put his hand into his trouser pocket, withdrawing a handful of silver coins.

"I'll 'ave a bar of chocolate." he stuttered.

"Please..." the woman insisted.

"Please," the man concurred.

"Only one?" she asked, taking down two large bars of milk chocolate and putting them on the scarred counter top.

"Two ... please," he said, and with a weak smile put the money on the woman's outstretched hand. While he waited for his change the two youths left the shop.

"I don't want any funny business from the Council now. Der'ear?"

"No, no. There'll be nothing like that," the man said, backing out of the dimly-lit shop.

While the man had been in the shop, heavy cumulus cloud had rolled over Liverpool reducing the amount of light reaching the ground. The unnatural early twilight was a regular feature of life on the north-west coast of England, but it had prompted Betty to suggest to Horace they return home so she could prepare the evening meal. Horace had other ideas: he had watched the two youths emerge from the shop and climb on the roof of the yellow council van.

"There's going to be trouble over there," Horace whispered to Betty.

"What are they doing?" she asked.

"Whatever it is, they're up to no good."

In the falling light, and checking the change in his hand, the man did not notice the two youths until he was putting the key in the van door.

"Come on, lads. Get off. I've got to get back to the depot," the man pleaded politely.

"We bin mindin' yer car, mate," the brown-skinned youth said, with a smile that revealed an extra wide gap between the two top front teeth.

"An we only charge ten pence – each," the whiter youth with the blotchy complexion added.

"Tek us pictures, mate," a voice called from a balcony above the shop.

On the communal balcony six youths projected their upper bodies over the low wall into space. The youth wearing the green baseball cap back to front was doing the talking.

"What's yer camera worth?" the youth asked.

Although the youths had been on the balcony when the council employee arrived he had, anxious to get the job done, failed to notice them. Before entering the shop, however, he had had the presence of mind to lock the van door. Finding the two youths sitting on top of his van, and the additional six young males on the walkway above the shop, he considered, for a split second, the consequences he may have had to face had he left the vehicle unlocked

"Not much," he shouted back, his concentration divided by the twin threats. "it's old council property."

The baseball-capped youth climbed over the balcony wall and edged along the narrow parapet immediately over the shop window. He then slid expertly down the drainpipe affixed to the wall between the window and main entrance to the block of flats. His five companions followed, and suddenly the man was surrounded. The two other youths remained on the van roof

"Tek us picture." the ring leader demanded.

With initiative developed out of fear, the man said, "Not in front of the shop. Too much background light. What about lined up on the balcony where you were before?"

"Yer! Okay! Come on gang," the youthful spokesman shouted, and as a group they disappeared into the flats.

Before the gang of six reached their original position on the upper walkway, the man had handed the chocolate bars to the two teenagers on the van, climbed in the vehicle and locked the door from the inside. The two youths remained on the vehicle. As the man attempted to start the engine one slid down onto the van's bonnet while the second youth sat with his legs hanging down the rear. At the third, unsuccessful, attempt to start the engine, the blotchy youth swung his legs up into the air and brought the heels of his boots down on the rear window. As the glass showered into the vehicle the engine burst into life and the teenagers, fearful for their safety, jumped to the ground. Before the first of the angry youths hit the ground at the base of the drainpipe, the van, much to Betty's relief, was speeding out of sight.

As they walked home along the main Hardman Street ratway, Horace imparted the knowledge gleaned from Paddy as his own. "Law and order has failed."

"There's a lot of violence on the streets," Betty said with a shiver.

"The young people are emerging into a society increasingly devoting itself to consumerism. The collective system of human employment is breaking down and there's nothing really to replace it," Horace said, paraphrasing Paddy's comments.

"So a lot of those humans have little money, but a lot of temptation," Betty suggested.

"Exactly, and the people's government is adopting strident policies that are alienating the unemployed. Paddy seems to think things will get worse," Horace said, attributing a statement to his friend. "Human strife and the ensuing lawlessness will not be contained simply by the strong arm of the police. It's the root cause that needs to be cured."

"Who said that?" Betty asked.

"Paddy." Horace replied, studying his feet.

Seven

It was a cold wind that blew down the River Mersey and greeted the dawn. All through the night, Horace and Paddy had sat at the water's edge hoping to catch fish, but their nets were empty. Paddy had heard a report that a fish had been seen actually swimming in the multi-polluted waters, and he had always preferred the tangy taste of sea fish to the bland fresh water fish of the communal lake.

Heavy eyed, the pair watched the rhythmical movements of the ponderous sea-swell, and their heads nodded involuntarily over their fishing rods. A low-lying mist covered the wide river and a fog horn, announcing the arrival of the first ferryboat of the day, brought them to their senses.

"Is it dat time already?" Paddy asked, sleepily.

"Time flies when the fish are not biting," Horace joked.

"Maybe it's just as well. Glad said she wouldn't eat anything that came out of the Mersey. Whoever saw a fish swimming in that needs to see an optician!"

"Would it be better to go around the coast a bit?" Horace asked. "Say to Southport?"

"It's a good few miles, and then you wouldn't be sure," Paddy replied.

The Mountwood ferryboat rocked slowly on the swollen grey waters and the blustery wind from the Irish Sea seemed to blow the boat at an oblique angle towards the Liverpool shoreline with its facade of Victorian grandeur. The two, tall gilded birds perched precariously atop the dramatic pinnacles of the dominant Liver building seemed to sway.

The floating landing stage was low on the water, indicating a corresponding low tide. The ferry discharged its human cargo and, like cockroaches exposed to light, they scurried into the steep tunnel rising from sea level to the flagged Pierhead.

Roped to the jetty, the black boat rose and fell with the swell, the mass of its rusted on-board chains clanging like church bells against the ice-cold guardrails. On the outerdeck by the gangway linking the boat to shore, a seaman, hidden in black wool and yellow oilskin, leaned against a bulkhead sheltering from the wind. His large oil-stained hands cupped a damp cigarette as he searched for warmth in the early-morning cold. A length of grease-covered hair hung below the grey open-weave scarf stretched over his ears and head and wrapped twice around his neck. A nomad of the river, he was watched and watcher, a journeyman of rope and chain.

At the top of the descending tunnel the Wirral-bound commuters stood passive and silent behind a gloss black wooden barrier. Less than an hour previously the weary travellers had lain in warm beds dreaming their adventures under cosy quilts. The frigid perhaps having been wrestling lustfully in perspiration-soaked sheets. And the timid fighting black bulls in Spain. In the cruel light of day-break, too soon had their individual exploits melted like spring snow, and collectively they stared at the purple-faced attendant. Many years of standing on the same spot had taught him to ignore the alarm-clock eyes that surrounded him. Peak capped and ruffled in a thick black jacket and matching trousers, his comfortable and untidy appearance combined with an indifferent stance that suggested he cared not what the commuters thought of him. His indifference was so profound, he wore it like a uniform. Seagulls screeched low around the groaning boat where shapeless figures laboured.

The complacent ticket collector moved along the barrier, and the crowd stirred in expectancy. He lifted wearily the wooden gateway and, with an outstretched gaunt hand, collected the tickets from the shuffling travellers – but in contrast to his benign appearance his brown and blood-shot eyes were alert, and vengefully he looked hard into the face of each passing passenger. Like ants, the crowd walked down the moving tunnel, crossed the floating landing stage and climbed the shaking gangway. The air was pungent with salt and diesel, but the barely-awake commuters were anxious to enter the boat's inner compartments where they sat, stiff and upright at first, on the long, hard seats. As the boat moved slowly away from the shore, the Wirral-bound ferry passengers tried to climb back into their dreams – all too conscious that another day of reality and uncertainty lay before them. For these were the lucky ones in employment. Horace and Paddy watched the boat fade away in the mist.

"Fancy a cup of tea?" Paddy asked, as they dismantled their rods.

"I wouldn't say no," Horace replied, struggling to get his three-piece rod into its carry-case.

"We'll go over to Lutyens and see Raymond. By the time we get across town the place will have been cleared out but the tea at the bottom of the urn will still be hot," Paddy explained.

"Raymond? Have I met him, Paddy?"

"Don't think so. He lives in the crypt below the Catholic cathedral-or the Wigwam as they call it. He's getting on a bit now. Older than me, would you believe? Lives beside the shelter where some of the homeless sleep. Has the run of the place most of the day when it's empty."

The south dock route they followed from the Princes jetty was less direct than the Lord Street drainage system, but at that time of the morning the central ratways were congested: as the city centre office and shop workers arrived for work, the weary rats made their way home. And the traffic was mainly one way: to the man-made Pierhead with its numerous cavities and fault-lines. The Pierhead underground system offered excellent ready-made accommodation but it was isolated with just one riverside restaurant. For the hundred of rats living in the area the food supply was totally inadequate.

In 1972, eight short years earlier, the three miles of Liverpool's south docks had closed. For many generations those same docks had been the main provider of work for the fathers and sons of Wavertree, Edge Hill, and Toxteth. The docks had also offered trouble-free food and lodgings to thousands of wharfrats, and it was down the taut hawsers of Wapping Basin, Queens Dock and Brunswick that many of the black rats arrived from Africa and the West Indies.

The Liverpool docks were constructed during the eighteenth century and eventually developed on both sides of the River Mersey. With stone shorelines, deep waters and its central geographical location on the West Coast, it was ideally placed to handle Britain's imports and exports. At its peak the Mersey docks system provided spasmodic work and low wages for more than fifty thousand Merseysiders who, in a year, would load and unload eleven million tons of raw materials and manufactured goods, as well as an equal weight of petroleum.

Along both shorelines massive warehouses were constructed to handle and store particular produce – and people. Dockyard names became synonymous with cargoes or countries. The South Docks in particular were coveted by the local rat population who regularly fought running battles along docksides and through warehouses. The imports from Africa and the West Indies that arrived regularly were commodities with special appeal to the rodent inhabitants of South Liverpool. Inexplicably, in the sixties, this trade began to fall-off. Warehouse stocks diminished, but the rat population remained constant. The battles for market-share that had been part of everyday life down the docks were but skirmishes compared with the blood-baths that ensued when the powers-that-be began transferring the irregular shipments to the North Docks of Nelson, Trafalgar and others. Those docks had, traditionally, handled the ships serving the Americas, Australia and New Zealand but, with similar reduced activity on those routes, the South Docks, in 1972, closed. Many of the rats moved inland, but without the dock warehouses to sustain them – and with no alternative skills – hardship ensued and a high percentage perished. And of those rats willing to risk violence by transferring to the North Docks only the hardy survived. In times of food shortage there is no honour – not even among rats!

From a rat's viewpoint the black, derelict buildings along the kerb-edge were touching the clouds. Windowless, pigeons flew in and out freely. For more than eight years the warehouses had remained empty and neglected. The dock gates had been locked, and Liverpool turned its back on its reason for being there in the first place. World's end had materialised and nobody wanted to visit it. It was suddenly history and, as confirmation, nobody had bothered to remove the shackles that had once restrained the black human cargo in transit from Africa to North America. In terms of British history, modern. In terms of American history, ancient. And there they were: rust-pitted, but still formidable, metal rings bolted low to black flaking brick. The straw where the lost souls once lay had, of course, long gone, but the same stone slabs covered the floor of the long, narrow passageways. Horace and Paddy chose to walk inside the road-side buildings as it was easier than trying to walk through the mud that covered Sefton Street like a thick, black carpet. Horace listened in horror as Paddy related hearsay tales about the human slaves that passed through the warehouse where they now walked. Of how they were herded into ships where many died, and how those once-free men were bought and sold by different merchants before they finally reached their new owners at the southern ports of North America.

"Did they eat them, Paddy?" Horace asked, totally unaware of the trade in human cargoes that had, in the nineteenth century, been a rich source of income for Liverpool merchants and ship owners alike.

"No. Cheap labour! A bit like the old pool system."

"The local dockers must have loaded and unloaded them," Horace said, reflectively.

Walking through the old warehouses, and in thought-provoking conversation, Paddy, still the guide, had missed Parliament Street, the lower half of the better known Upper street – of the same name – and where once five thousand dockers marched

81

four times a day in search of work. This long, sloping street to the sea was fed by major arterial roads that were themselves fed by consumptive back streets. The marching feet had gone and the dusty streets were now deserted. At the junction with Great George Street, Paddy led the way down to a subterrestrial channel that, with the advent of rail and steam in the mid-nineteenth century, had been excavated to provide a rail connection from the main Manchester to Liverpool railway line with the South Docks. It had eventually been aborted and covered and, like the South Docks themselves, forgotten. For earlier rat populations it had been their main route between Lime Street Station and the South Docks. A direct, uninterrupted passageway that had since been superseded by ducting that the 1980 rats used frequently for its route flexibility. The old covered excavations had been kept in good repair by worker rats assigned to its upkeep. With the decline of the docks, the route had become unused and suffered from subsidence. Nevertheless it still offered a good connection for Lime Street Station, where it linked with a contemporary underground system. From the station the east-bound line passed under Brownlow Hill, and from there it was only a two minute walk to Raymond's well-equipped lair.

They had travelled only fifty metres when the tunnel came to an abrupt end. Progressive by nature, the two rats began to claw the soil. Side by side (like breast-stroke swimmers) they penetrated the soft earth.

"One!" Paddy shouted, and simultaneously their forepaws pierced the earth. "Two!" he continued, and with cupped paws they scooped and swung their arms behind them. Blindly they worked, but their keen sense of smell told them they were very close to fresh air. It was Horace who saw daylight first. Marginally ahead with his breast-stroke he popped his nose through the hole, but pulled back quickly: a spade, beneath a clay-clogged boot, had narrowly missed removing half of his cherished whiskers.

"Whew! That was close, Paddy."

"What was?"

"Somebody's digging a hole. The spade just missed me head," Horace said, feeling that his whiskers were still there.

"Let me have a look," Paddy said, moving Horace aside and looking out through the hole. For a whole minute he peered out into the daylight, but there was no movement. "I think I'll crawl through and have a good look around."

"Be careful, Paddy. You could lose your head," Horace said, shuddering at the thought of how close he had been to losing his own. "Here, push this through the hole first and see what happens," he said, withdrawing a section of rod from his carry-case and unselfishly handing it to Paddy.

Paddy took the rod, pushed it through the small peep-hole and waited. Nothing happened. Keeping his hand well inside the tunnel he drew circles with the length of wood. But still nothing happened. There was no response.

"Looks like they've gone," Horace suggested.

"Be on their third teabreak of the day more like. I'll put my head through and..."

Before Paddy could continue, the sharp metal spade had plunged into the earth and ripped away the soil around their spy-hole. They jumped back into the safety of the tunnel. Daylight flooded in, and they threw their backs against the side wall to avoid detection. From where they stood they had a clear, worm's eye view of a man with a broad red face. His cheekbones were round and prominent, and his small green eyes faded into his skull. Beneath wide black braces he wore an old, pin-striped navy coloured waistcoat over a thick-knitted grey jumper. His soil-stained trousers, supported also by a heavy leather belt, were tucked into his socks. It did not appear to be his practice to attack the earth with regular strokes of his spade. Rather he removed a single clod between those long pauses when he inhaled on a cigarette. Paddy moved as close to the hole as safety would allow. He wanted to check his bearings.

It was a small section of Great George Street that was being dug up, and Paddy knew precisely where they were by the diminishing line of tall iron railings. Through the railings he could see the Anglican cathedral, medieval in all things but history. On the kerbside, beside the roped-off hole, two other workmen leaned on their own spades and smoked cigarettes. There was no conversation. The three men looked occasionally towards each other, but they exchanged no comment other than eye and forehead movement. The man with his clay-weighted clogs in the hole threw the end of his cigarette to the ground where it smouldered.

Like the word in a play that keys the actor to enter the stage, the discarded cigarette caused the dark-skinned man, leaning against the railings, to react. The connection between the two actions was as fast as the inter-action of switch and light-bulb. The ragged man in the enormous jacket was focused on the cigarette. As it left the labourer's hand he followed it into the trench, his knee-length jacket billowing like a cloak. Picking up the smouldering cigarette, he put it to his mouth. Had this been the feat of a sixteen-year-old athlete it would have been un-remarkable. But these were the perfectly co-ordinated actions of man in his middle thirties who slept on, or under, benches, depending on the weather; of a man who had not, other than internally, touched water for many years, and who survived, not on soup kitchens, but from kerbside waste-bins and razor sharp instincts. He was a solitary soul with a shapeless brown trilby pulled down over his ears.

Those parts of his naked legs visible through his shredded trousers were similarly begrimed. Striding out of the hole like a blackened miner emerging from a pit, his white, intelligent eyes revealed no provenance. He was but a shadow exposed by the red-striped and mouldy lining of his jacket sleeves that had been rolled back by several layers until they resembled arm-muffs.

Inclined, his head twitched and his body struggled in search of a more comfortable position in the oversized jacket. The shoulder seams fell to his elbows. With long, fast and slanting steps he crossed the road. The three workmen looked at one another.

"Smelt like a coke oven," the workman in the hole said, relighting a fresh cigarette.

By the time Horace and Paddy reached the Roman Catholic cathedral the clockwork city had been wound-up for the day and they had difficulty crossing Mount Pleasant. Once on scrubland north of the wigwam-shaped cathedral, they were on safe territory. Only in the failing light did humans appear, but then they were mis-shapen and, like the living dead, shuffled with plastic bags and rolled grey blankets in search of a bed.

The Lutyen's Crypt was built below and to the north end of the unusually shaped cathedral.

"It's the only part of Sir Edward Lutyen's original design for our cathedral," Paddy explained, his chest filling with pride as they walked around the glass-fluted and circular structure. "We wanted something that would shame the Proddy-dogs' church down Hope Street, but we ran out of money."

The crypt was built on two levels: ground and underground, and consisted of a series of small chambers, fan-vaulted in bare clay bricks. Dimly lit by weak light-bulbs hanging from undisguised and flexible cable attached in long loops to the ceiling, the wide staircase had all the austerity of a catacomb, Horace had commented.

"That's what it is! Two Archbishops buried down here," Paddy whispered, fearful of the powerful dead.

White fungus covered the concavities and broad discoloured patches of brickwork sympathised with the pervading dampness, but no effort had been made to rectify the generally unseen and below-ground faults.

The sealed entrance to the overnight hostel was on the west side where the grass had grown over the original builders' rubble to create a mini oasis of green hillocks, but the door was impenetrable. The implements and finger-nails of the frustrated and denied had scarred the thick brown paint, but the metal-plated door stood firm. The doorbell, however, had not escaped the destructive force of the inebriates who had arrived too late for a bed: only two short wires protruded from the small unpainted circle on the door-frame.

Horace and Paddy had entered that part of the crypt connected to the cathedral. At the bottom of the sweeping stone steps, and in a dark corner, a hole led into the solid staircase. At the end of the rat passage, Paddy dislodged a brick to reveal a second hole.

"Are you there, Raymond?" Paddy called. "Raymond?"

"Who's there?" a voice asked, from beyond the deep darkness that enveloped the short, final approach to Raymond's front door. "Who is it calling me at this time of day?"

"Paddy, be Jasus!"

"Shh! You're in church," the rat behind the torch-light exhorted. Paddy covered his eyes from the beam playing on his face. "Paddy, me old mate. How you doin'? I thought I could smell youse."

"Not bad! Not bad!" Paddy replied. "And this is me neighbour, Horace." Paddy said and, by design, diverting the light from his eyes. Horace put a paw across his own face as the thin ray of light moved towards him.

"You're just in time for a brew. Follow me," Raymond said, swinging his torch around and limping ahead of his two visitors.

Raymond lived alone in an ante-chamber that had been part of the original construction. It had been the first casualty of the cashflow crisis the church had experienced in the immediate years after the thirty-nine to forty-five war. Church and country had been gripped by austerity and money was scarce. Designs for the building were modified repeatedly until the parameters of the first plan were reduced considerably. Underground chambers, surplus to requirement, were either filled-in or simply, as is the history of the world, sealed and forgotten. A human folly is often a rat's treasure, and Raymond had acquired one of the finest apartments on Merseyside. A divorced buck, of many happy years standing, he ignored the attentions of the does who tried regularly to capture his affection – and a share of his extensive property. Having come very close to losing his beloved home at the time of his acrimonious divorce, he was careful not to become too attached to any member of the opposite sex. In any event, he had not been enamoured to find, repeatedly, his former spouse's hair in his razor. Adventurous by nature, Raymond's marriage experience had been altogether too trying and, for a hunter, the constraint of being expected to return to his own bed every night became too big a tax. Beside the usual conflicts of matrimony, Raymond had been troubled by factors at a deeper level of consciousness that he couldn't comprehend. He had lost interest. At the beginning of his marriage the sharing and sexuality were exciting concepts and the relationship seemed to him perfectly normal. He had been conditioned as a boy by his peers and adults alike that the heterosexual condition was an inflexible institution. In his youth he had never thought to question the transition from individual to partner. As a young buck, although he enjoyed close proximity with the does, he soon became bored with their company. He much preferred the free talking and dangerous exploits he shared with his buck friends.

It was this quest for adventure that drove him up the stern rope of a ship tied up alongside Sandon Half Tide Dock. For many years he sailed the world, living under the flags of no fewer than twelve different nations. In foreign ports, cloaked by the cover of dark, he would slip ashore to court the native does. And if his ship had sailed without him, as was frequently the case, he would, with the guidance of the local wharfrats, choose another vessel. Destination and cargo were the twin considerations. It was the fall through a hatch into a deep cargo hold that cut short his career at sea. Had the hold not been half-filled with grain that would have been the end of Raymond. With a broken leg he had changed ship twice to get back to his beloved Liverpool.

"Do you ever hear from the missus?" Paddy asked, settling into the leather-bound winged chair and running his paw over the smooth hide.

"Missus? What missus?" Raymond asked, a twinkle in his eye. "And don't get too comfortable there. We're going next door for a cup of tea in a minute."

"I know she's long gone, Raymond. I mean, do you ever come across her?"

"If she's got any sense she'll be living in China by now. Took all me grub, she did, Horace. Came home one morning after victualling all night and she'd gone. Me cupboard was bare."

"I've heard of that happening before," Paddy said sympathetically.

"That's when I started to question co-habitation. The more I thought about it the more ridiculous it became. She'd criticize everything I did. After much thought I said to myself, Raymond old boy, it's a bachelor life for you from now on. Never looked back since. The only sure thing about living with a doe is double trouble."

"It reduces workload, Raymond." Horace said, looking at the different beetle heads trophied around the dark wood panelled walls. He recognised the Chick Beetle, Rose Chafer and Devil's Coach-Horse. And he'd been able to identify the Stag Beetle blindfold. The bronze-green specimen with yellow spots, however, was new to him.

"What reduces workload?" Raymond, with the condescending superiority of a rat in his own home, asked.

"Marriage!" Horace absent-mindedly replied. "What species is that?" he continued, genuinely interested in the unknown beetle on the wall, but more particularly not wanting to enter into debate on a subject that he viewed differently to Raymond.

"A Green Tiger," Raymond replied with a smug smile.

"From the jungle?" Horace asked.

"Southport! Well, should we go and have a cuppa?" Raymond said, putting his paws on his own chest and patting his bosom gently.

"Could we leave these here?" Paddy asked, holding up his fishing rod case.

"What've you got there? A couple of shotguns?" Raymond asked, crouching low with a mock gun at his waist.

"We've been fishing." Horace explained.

"Fishing? Raymond said, his eyes wide and head back. "Where?"

"Don't laugh." Paddy pleaded.

"Not on the . ."

Paddy nodded. "Afraid so."

"The only thing you'll catch on the Mersey is consumption. And that's a fact. This way . . ." Raymond said, climbing an open-plan spiral staircase to an upper room.

Raymond had hand-built everything he owned. And while the living-room reflected his taste in the brooding, heavy drapes and rich mahoganies so admired by those Victorian ancestors, his bedroom, with its stainless steel and glass, confirmed a freer spirit.

Horace and Paddy followed Raymond into the Art Deco wardrobe. Its silver grey, spot-satin double doors were overlaid in frosted glass. A small hinged flap at the rear of its interior led directly into a metal ventilation shaft connecting with the hostel next door. Inside the hostel a rope ladder, one end secured to a side exit in the shaft, was piled in a heap. Raymond threw the ladder out of the vent window, and the three rats climbed down into total darkness. On the way down, Raymond instinctively reached over to the wall and clicked a switch. The three fluorescent light tubes threw a green cast over the white-washed walls. As he climbed down, Horace, from the vantage point of height, studied the room.

Most of the concrete floor space was filled by twenty-three metal framed camp-beds. The spaces between the low level beds were measured in centimetres. The stretched canvas of each bed supported a black plastic-covered mattress, and at the head lay two thin (and folded neatly by the same hand) grey blankets. The room was windowless, but a small, round fan built into an external wall circulated the disinfected air. A second room, rectangular and smaller than the first, contained another seven camp-beds and a metal trolley with steel tea-urn. Off this overspill bedroom an archway provided access to a narrow room with two showers and wash basins, assorted mops and six gallon jars of bleach.

Raymond put his paw against the side of the smooth round urn. "Still warm. He's not a bad lad that Mike."

"Who's Mike?" Horace asked, watching Raymond holding down the projecting tap to drain off the remains of well-stewed tea – the dregs too concentrated for human consumption, but ideal for the rats' reinforced taste-buds.

"Runs the place. Good looking young man he is. Came from London originally. Used to be a fork-lift truck driver. He's only twenty-nine but he and his four voluntary helpers provide accommodation for up to thirty homeless men every night."

"Is it free?" Paddy asked. "Can't remember what you told me last time I was here."

"£1.35 a night, paid usually through the Social. Never come around here on a Friday. That's when they de-louse the place. If I hadn't put the wardrobe over the vent shaft I'd have a bad chest now – or worse."

"There's a strong smell in here right now," Horace said, holding his nose.

"It's only bleach. Here you are then: a nice cuppa tea," Raymond said, handing out the cups and sitting himself down on one of the beds. Paddy pushed two beds apart and he and Horace sat facing their guide.

"It's really interesting. Reminds me of the Sisters of Charity," Horace said, watching the rope-ladder, under its own momentum, continue to swing.

"Have you been there?"

"I was just showing Horace some of the sights," Paddy interjected, not wanting Raymond to learn of his own careless behaviour.

"You're not from these parts by the sound of your accent," Raymond said, putting his cup on the floor and lying back on the bed with his paws under his head.

"He's from Manchester," Paddy said, slurping his tea from his cup.

"A Manchester man!" Raymond declared, sitting up and

swinging his legs over the side of the camp-bed to face his two visitors. "What's the rat population like these days?"

"About a million," Horace said confidently, but really not having a clue about such statistics. However, someone, somewhere must have once mentioned the one million figure and possibly he had carried the estimate in his subconscious. He had time to analyse this thought because Raymond, too, seemed to be digesting this information.

"That figures," Raymond said, at length. "Don't suppose you know Salford?"

"Not very well." Horace admitted.

"I went there once. Reminded me of Liverpool. A great place for scavenging. They don't care where they throw their rubbish. Have you been to Salford, Paddy?"

Paddy shook his head. "And I don't want to," he said.

"Why's that?" Raymond asked.

"What's the point if it's like Liverpool?" Paddy said. "We've got the real thing right here."

"How would he get there?" Horace asked.

Raymond returned to his reclining position on the bed. "Just thinking about it makes me feel tired," Raymond said, closing his eyes.

"Do you get out much these days, Raymond?" Paddy asked, lying flat on the adjacent bed and staring at the neon light.

"Not like I used to. Some nights I come in here."

"In here?" Horace exclaimed, moving to the bed on the other side to where Raymond lay. The three rats, paws under their heads and each with a leg crossed over a bent knee, lay in a line on their respective beds.

"Up there," Raymond said, opening an eye and staring at the small opening in the under-ceiling metal air vent. "Some nights I sit up there and watch the wretched humans."

"What are they like?" Horace asked.

"Probably the same crowd we saw at the Sisters of Charity," Paddy suggested.

"Most of them are," Raymond agreed. "They come here at

eight o'clock in the evening for the free soup. Some of them look quite smart for flotsam. Only a few mind! As though they've been caught in the net by accident. You know, Horace, the trouble with humans is they have strange habits. They like to do things that shorten their lives."

"Like smoking cigrettes," Paddy said.

"They stagger in here like blind men, bumping into each other. Last year I counted a total nine hundred different faces. I'd say they were all between forty-five and fifty-five."

"What happens when they get to fifty-five?" Horace asked.

"Dead! They like to mix a lot of alcohol with their blood. We've all seen those men and women sleeping under the stars – and there must be hundreds around here."

"What makes you say that, Raymond?" Paddy asked, turning over to lie on his stomach.

"I'm very observant as you know. Isn't that right?"

Paddy nodded, but with a smile winked at Horace

"How many different faces did I say I'd seen in a year sleeping here?"Raymond continued. Paddy shook his head.

"Nine hundred?" Horace ventured.

"Correct! Paddy, please pay attention. Right, so I count nine hundred different faces. Agreed?"

"Get on with it," Paddy demanded. "You're sending me to sleep."

"Nine hundred sleepers but twice as many faces at the soup kitchen. The question is where do those other nine hundred homeless sleep?"

"Salvation Army hostel," Paddy proffered.

Raymond responded curtly: "Too posh for this lot."

"I suppose your calculations mean there are at least one thousand eight hundred homeless people in the city," Horace proposed.

"I only know about the homosapien males. There are also the female homeless, but they will be considerably fewer. Their numbers will be balanced by those men who die off. Yes, I think your guess is about right."

92

"Do you think it's a genetic fault, Raymond?"

"Death, Paddy?"

"Now don't be sarcastic. You know what I mean. The way they poison their own bodies."

"Quite definitely. What other explanation could there be for filling their lungs continuously with hot smoke and drinking gallons of poisonous liquid?" Raymond said, haughtily.

"It's as though their heads and bodies don't belong," Horace thought aloud.

Paddy sat up on the edge of the his bed. "You know what I think their problem is. They are not synchronised. Those poor humans have undergone so many changes in their social behaviour that they are completely confused: they don't know if they are still hunter-gatherers like us, slaves of the feudal master, factory machines or simply a society that offers opiates on prescription and cash at the unemployment counter for doing nowt!"

"Well there aren't many factories where they can machine these days," Raymond said, also sitting up on the edge of his mattress to face Paddy. The two rats looked into each others eyes reflecting on recent rat folly that mirrored human migration. Horace remained on his back, his eyes fixed on the rope-ladder hanging from the air-shaft and swaying imperceptibly in the draught from the wall fan.

The theories of rehousing a vast population on the outskirts of Liverpool was based on the misconception that nothing had changed since those nineteenth century mill-owners built row upon row of tied-terraced cottages around the enterprising cotton mills, renting them to their employees. Times had moved on: major industry was in decline but the councillors with local taxation and central government funds at their disposal thought they had discovered the cure to that industrial decline – but they were not the shrewd entrepreneurs they thought they were. Industrial estates were constructed with large scale units – but the twentieth century counterparts of those Victorian en-trepreneurs who came to occupy the new estates were not advocates of the Laissez Faire principle. They slipped in on the lubrication of government grants; but when the money was gone they moved on.

Kirkby, one of the new small towns of sprawling council house complexes with their 'secure-from-the-sons-of-scouse' industrial estates built on the green edge of Liverpool, was the elixir that would turn unemployment into employment. Or so the local councillors thought. The concept seemed to be having some success in the South of England, but on Merseyside it was a seven day wonder: the 'for sale' and 'to let' signs rusted and peeled from derelict factory shells. The Jaguars, Mercedes, BMWs, and government grants had gone. Another anathema to debate in council chambers. There was, of course, angry recrimination, but nobody in the council was out of pocket. It wasn't a profit and loss organisation that survived by its buying and selling skills. And the rate-paying population didn't know what happened to its money, anyhow. And the stigma remained.

Discounting the housewives, sick and those who were too old, seven thousand of those participants in the concept of future prosperity were drawing, after a rigid qualification test, unemployment benefit of £18.54 a week – but payable only for three hundred and twelve days. Beyond that period, those still without work had to apply for Social Security Benefit, with a reduction of £2.19 in their weekly giro cheque. The under eighteen year olds received £12.95 a week. Job vacancies occurred occasionally, but when the advertised vacancy for a part-time gardener attracted six hundred and seventy applications, qualifications were added to the original two line card in the window of the Job Centre. When asked, by an eighteen year old youth, what his future prospects were, the man behind the desk replied, 'Bleak'. In the new town of Kirkby alone, one thousand additional unemployed were joining the dole queue each year.

Kirkby was perhaps an extreme example of the problems facing Merseyside at the beginning of the eighties. The facts and figures were mere statistics, cold and meaningless to the Londoner reading the Daily Telegraph over a full plate of eggs, bacon and toast. For many of his north-country cousins the cost of the morning paper would be an expense too far. And as for egg and bacon, well what was wrong with toast and margarine?

Down the road, in that other Merseyside new town, Skelmersdale, the unemployed were even more numerous with over twenty percent of the registered-for-work adults and youths claiming benefit.

"In the past year there has been a frightening increase in unemployment," the job centre manager reported. "Things have never been so bad in the New Town. Long term unemployment is growing and the situation for school-leavers is pathetic. We have about nine hundred youngsters looking for a job. We've even got the priest helping us find work for the kids. He's doing more than praying, but his task is hopeless. In the past year, forty percent of the unemployed have not had even one day's work!"

The poverty of Liverpool and its New Towns was not as deep and naked as Merseyside had experienced in earlier years and before subsistence allowance – but, by comparison with its southern counterparts, contemporary poverty was dire. On the streets of Liverpool the destitution was tangible with its own sour smell.

Even for an area of very high unemployment, Liverpool was dimorphic: both parents and three grown up children living in one small house and all with jobs. Next door a husband, one of the long term unemployed, with a pregnant wife and two school children to feed. Next-door-but-one a widow woman, old and bent before her time with arthritis and asthma, afraid to walk the few paces to the corner grocery shop with the permanently boarded windows. One person in six without work and the young were becoming lawless.

Raymond and Paddy had been looking deep into each others eyes and, with their powers of collective thought, had meditated on those mass population movements and the problems it had caused the rat population. Overnight whole swathes of black terraced housing and brown-bricked tower block accommodation

95

had been emptied of people. Suddenly a major food source had disappeared. The urban rat population was in crisis. The elaborate underground rat towns were not self-sufficient. Without humans and their mass production of waste there had been famine and conflict. And worse was to come, for when the bulldozers arrived they dug up not only sewer, gas and water pipes, they took with them the complex ratways that had taken hundreds of years to construct. Foodless and disorientated the back street rat population was in a state of flux. The two facing rats shivered at their shared recollections as they returned to an upper level of consciousness. Horace had fallen asleep on the black, plastic mattress and was perspiring.

"We'd better put the cups away and tidy up," Raymond said, reaching across to shake Horace. "We don't want Mike to know he had visitors."

Raymond was the last to climb the ladder, pulling it up after he had climbed inside the shaft and coiling it into a pile inside the hole. "Makes a comfortable seat when I come up here to watch the show," he said, squeezing past Horace and Paddy to lead the way back to his apartment.

Going home, Horace and Paddy took the main Brownlow underpass, one of the main rat routes into the city. The tributaries cutting across town were often congested but, on Friday lunchtimes, impossible. Paddy had never been able to reason why. The Brownlow tunnel sloped down towards the sea and soon they reached the cross-road with Renshaw Street from where it was only a short walk back to Bold Street and a much needed sleep. At the junction, Sean, the dusty controller of rat tunnels, shouted to Paddy.

"Off ter see der strippers, Paddy, I'll bet me last carrot."

Like Paddy, Sean spent his youth in Eire, the land of his birth, and like most of Liverpool's immigrant rat population he had, one day, arrived by sea. Initially the Irish rats had formed a secret society amongst themselves, but as they integrated into the Liverpool landscape their reliance on inter-cooperation and ethnic support became less. Nevertheless, bonds were formed that lasted loosely for life. This is how Paddy and Sean, living miles apart across the city, came to know each other.

"Strippers? What you talkin' about, Sean O'Reardon?" Paddy shouted back with a smile and a wave.

"Don't give me the innocent eyes now, Paddy. I've known you too long. I'll bet you and your mate here are going up to the Beer-Kellar," Sean said, walking across the tunnel.

"And what would we be wanting going up to the whatever you call it," Paddy asked, one paw on his hip.

"What you got in the bags?" Sean asked.

"Fishing rods," Horace replied.

"Fishing?" Sean started with a laugh, but was cut short by Paddy.

"What's this strip thing you're talking about?"

"Have you not heard?" Sean said, looking from one rat to the other. Paddy and Horace shook their heads. "You've got to go and have a visit. You won't believe what you see."

"Why is that now?" Paddy asked.

Sean drew close to Paddy and, inclining his head, whispered: "You won't be able to believe your eyes. Listen to this. Are you listening? The human males pay money to watch a human female take off her clothes. Can you believe dat?"

Horace's jaw dropped and he shook his head. Paddy too shook his head, but rationalised the notion: "Capitalism gone mad!"

"It's starting in a short while. You've got to see it to believe it," Sean shouted from his resumed position on the rostrum in the middle of the tunnel. "Go through up the back drain and under the ground level floorboards. The show is in the cellar and the ceilings full of holes. It's a bird's eye view. Go on. Hurry up."

With an Irish salute, they parted company.

Out of adversity someone, somewhere, will make money. In that cold climate of high unemployment thousands of young men were idle. Their drives high, but their resources low. The location of the Beer-Kellar on the apex of Brownlow Hill and Mount Pleasant and at the junction, where those heart-throbbing arterial roads of Renshaw, Ranelagh and Lime Street meet, was analogous to the centre of the spider's web.

The dark cavity in the ceiling above the vast basement auditorium was filled with rats. Lying down, each rat had one eye to a hole. Down below in the semi-darkened room, men and boys sat at long benches ranged along two sides of thirty wooden tables. Between tables and ceiling, a thick amorphous mass of tobacco smoke, purple from the stage footlights, drifted hesitantly between the stage at one end of the massive basement and the two serving counters at the opposite. Like the audience itself, the cloud was drawn between the stimuli of flesh and alcohol. Pint-sized glass-pots of beer covered the otherwise bare tables, and beer dripped down to the stone-flagged floor where ash and cigarette-ends multiplied.

The small stage, inset into the wall, was brightly lit and provided illumination for the whole basement. Secondary lighting came from three small table lamps sitting between cash registers and beer pumps. In brash contrast to the naked atmosphere, gold and silver tinsel paper at the stage edges shimmered, rotating by the heat from the halogen stage lamps. Although the day was warm, the basement was cool. A man, ignoring the packed audience, walked across the stage and switched on two self-standing spotlights. He adjusted the light stands until the two beams crossed centre stage. Walking into the middle of the projected light, he stood before the microphone and produced a piece of paper from his pocket. Reading from the sheet, he spoke into the microphone, but he was inaudible. He knocked the head of the stand. From the wings a voice shouted an instruction. Unflustered, the man lifted the stand and, walking backwards, re-positioned it where it was no longer forward of the two, stage-edge speakers. He returned to the light stands, readjusting the beams and his black bow-tie before stepping back behind the microphone.

With the sheet of crushed paper before his face, he said, "Mitzi's missed 'er train from Manchester. She's arrivin' at twenty-to-two."

In the ceiling cavity, at an excellent vantage point for viewing the stage, Paddy, lying beside Horace, nudged his ribs. "Ask her for a lift back."

"Shh!" a red rat to Paddy's right instructed.

Under a bombardment of cigarette-ends, the black-suited compere left the stage.

Irritation, like the air pollution, intensified, and the music coming out of the speakers increased in volume. More beer was dispensed, and Paddy, mindful of the red rat next to him, whispered in Horace's ear, "A ploy to sell more beer." Horace nodded, but kept his eye to the hole.

To a cheer, the man reappeared on stage. "Ladies and gentlemen" he began, but his words were lost on the shouting audience. Palms down, he waved his arms at chest level. "Quiet, you 'eathens. Ladies and gentlemen," he began, but a voice below shouted:

"The only bird I can see is you."

"Who said that?" the man called through the microphone, a hand above his eyes and leaning towards the table nearest to the stage.

"And those tarts on the bar," another voice called out of the fog.

Obscenities were shouted by the audience and, fearful of being over-run, the announcer said, "Please welcome your very own favourite lady of the strip, ... Mitzi."

The stage was empty, and the audience was filled with quiet anticipation. But the moment of respite was brief: it was the announcer who re-appeared. Ignoring the shouting and foot-stamping, he crossed the stage, placed a tape in a cassette on top of an upright piano and turned the microphone stand to face it. The tape produced a slow drum beat and the man, with a half raised arm, wiggled his fingers at the audience, and hurriedly left the stage – only for his head to reappear, side-on from the wings, mouthing '... you too'. His reappearance was unexpected and the angle from the stage to ceiling too acute for the rats to decipher the lip language. The audience, however, seemed to have interpreted his message and, in one voice, rejoined, 'and up yours, too!"

From below where the announcer's head had been a moment before, a long leg projected from the tinsel-paper covered arch. On the foot of the leg a yellow platform-soled shoe rose and fell, rose and fell.

The music increased in tempo, and the leg disappeared. To the strident rhythms of Carmen's Prelude, Mitzi, smiling and dressed in gold mandarin-collared jacket and matching short trousers, strode confidently onto the stage. Carrying an open top wicker basket she stopped and, like the music, became melancholic. The interlude was short, and soon she was tip-toeing on her high shoes. Collecting imaginary flowers, she placed them in the basket. With a hand cupped around an ear, she held her blonde head to one side and looked up and around. Both audiences, at first, were captivated by the unexpected innocence displayed by the dancer; but the basement crowd had grown weary of the theatricals. They had not gone to the Beer-Kellar for a legitimate theatre experience. They wanted to see flesh. And a real voice from the auditorium shouted: "Get 'em off."

The tape, pre-programmed by Mitzi in her Chorlton-cum-Hardy bed-sit, crackled and hissed, but undeterred she danced in a circle around the stage, unbuttoning her jacket as she went. Still moving, she put the basket on the floor, removed her jacket and, with a finger in its hanging-tab, swung it over her shoulder. Her brassiere matched the glittering fabric of the rest of her outfit. The basement audience cheered, and the rats exhaled in indignation. From the basket she removed a long feathered stole and replaced it with her jacket.

With more urgency, she stepped out of her shorts, throwing them accurately into the basket. On cue, the music reverted to the original drum-beating drone. In a glittering bikini she stood at the edge of the stage and waved the stole. A feather broke free and floated down on a tunnel of light to a table below. The table occupants fought for the memento. The rest of the audience whistled and cheered.

Encouraged, Mitzi kicked off her shoes. Lithe, and well connected to the wild rhythms of the drum-beat, she stretched and
strained her sweaty torso. Turning away from the audience, she
unclasped the back hook of the bikini-top. Spinning around to
again face the audience she covered her bosom with the feathered band, and waved the bra above her head. In response to the
masculine demands she threw the stole into the basket. Looking
out into the black auditorium, and naked from the waist up, the
young woman betrayed no emotion.

The music stopped, and she collected her basket of clothing
before disappearing behind the side curtain. There was no ap-
plause, no acknowledgement of the performance. The strip-teaser
strutted the boards for financial reward – not for praise or
acclaim. She had no talent – although she tried her best. It was
better than the dole.

At precisely two o'clock the basement crowd piled up the stone
stairway and into the daylight. The day had grown surprisingly
warm, but the men were dressed somberly in all season grey.
Filing onto the street in an orderly fashion dictated by the narrow
exit, they blended with the old buildings surrounding the traffic-
congested junction. It was the blue sky that seemed strangely out
of place. At the doorway of the emptying Beer-Kellar, a woman,
more than sixty years and painfully thin inside a heavy overcoat
of black wool, stood looking at the wall-poster advertising the
lunchtime show. Beside her, a younger man, equally thin but
with a large haversack on his back, pointed to the picture of the
partly undressed young woman. They communicated in earnest
sign-language.

The rats in the ceiling chattered amongst themselves while
waiting for the crowds to clear. They were confused by what they
had witnessed: several hundred humans sitting in a dark, smoke-
filled room watching another human take off her clothes. They
shook their heads, and a younger rat imitated the action of the
strip-tease dancer.

Horace and Paddy decided to make their way back to their
Bold Street homes by way of the rain drain just below street

level. In contrast to normal rat policy they crossed the busy road before descending into the culvert. Standing beside the drain grid, a middle-aged man, short and round, with a heavy beard was in serious conversation with himself. On his head he wore a flat, chequered cap and occasionally pushed two fingers under the cap to scratch himself. Still talking to himself he began to dance lightly on the spot. His steps were surprisingly quick and well co-ordinated, aided by black rubber shoes. Despite the high temperature and cloudless sky, he wore a grey raincoat that reached below his knees. In itself, this combination would not attract attention: hot days were infrequent on Merseyside and its inhabitants rarely went to the expense of buying clothes for occasional use. Hot or cold, the dress code was similar. What did attract attention was the short plank of wood the man carried under his left arm. Dancing two steps forward and then one step back, his progress along the street was slow. A dancing man in Liverpool was not unusual – neither was a man in a dirty old raincoat carrying a piece of wood. It was the rusty nail protruding and bent at the end of the oil-stained tongue-and-groove that raised eyebrows. In accompaniment to his extra-ordinarily deft footwork, his right arm was raised above his head, and his extended fore-finger drew patterns in the air. With an added sprint to his gait he skipped along singing softly to himself.

On the corner of the street a delivery man unloaded tins of paint from his white van. As the round man drew level with the kerbside vehicle he began, once more, to dance on the spot.

"'e's not smokin', goin' through the motions. Full of 'oles," he said.

The delivery man, with four pens clipped to the breast-pocket of his brown dustcoat, stopped work and was about to respond to what he thought was an affront when the passer-by began singing a nursery song. "... 'ave you any wool? Yes, sir. Yes, sir, three bags full ..." The round man was happy within himself, and continued along the street.

"We're being followed." Horace said, as he looked up from the third grid. "And he's got a stick with a vicious looking nail on the end of it."

"He doesn't know we're here. He's on a different wavelength. Can only communicate with his own kind," Paddy replied, pushing his nose through the bars and sniffing the air.

"What is it, Paddy?"

"Just checking our location. We'll be on Bold Street soon."

Horace and Paddy followed the drainage system onto the street where they lived. Above ground, the man danced along the same route. Outside one of Waring and Gillow's large plate-glass windows another man, upside down with his head on the pavement and the heels of his bare feet resting against the glass, stared unblinkingly at the dancing black shoes. He wore only a pair of soiled trousers that fell abut his fleshless white legs. His jacket, shirt, shoes and socks were piled in a neat bundle beside one of the hands the man, with the small hairless head, used to maintain a balance.

"The bell's on fire. Not my fault. A bad apple. The sky's the limit. Over the hill. Don't blame me," the round man said to the upside down man. He had stopped dancing and held the piece of wood like a rifle over his shoulder.

From the ground, the skeletal man stared up at the conversationalist, his focus switching alternately between the bearded man's face and the piece of wood. He remained silent.

"It was a rear-guard action," the man continued. "All wind and farts. Pockets full of 'em. That's done the apple-cart. It was the bus conductor's fault. Where's the world going; Tobruk? Don't let 'em get away with it. You'll never get it back. They're after yer money." With a double skip the short, fat man jumped to attention and, with the piece of wood still over his left shoulder, marched away. The upside down man, out of the corners of his eyes, watched him go.

Across the street the big woman from the Sisters of Charity sat on a bench wearing her replacement plastic flip-flop shoes. Her white floral patterned dress, a size too small, was stretched tight, reaching only to her mid thighs. She sat with her blue veined legs wide apart and, as usual, strategically close to the waste-bin affixed to the adjacent lamp-post. To compensate for the heat, she had rolled her nylon stockings down to her ankles where they rested like two solid rubber rings. Middle-aged and antagonistic, she too communicated loudly with the other side of her split personality but, in conflict, her expletives were unique and profound.

"Did you catch any fish?" Betty asked when Horace arrived home.

"No. Must be too much pollution. But I've just seen the most amazing things."

Eight

As the city's single young men visit the Beer-Kellar's lunchtime sessions to view naked female flesh, the older married men go to the beer houses to get away from it. And as Raymond found entertainment in watching, from the ventilation shaft, the homeless humans arriving at the shelter with their concealed medicine bottles of alcohol, Paddy found amusement in watching and listening to the humans who frequented the upstairs public bar. In Summer he would sit quietly at the back of the empty fireplace. In Winter, when the coals burned and spluttered, he watched through a vent in the wall.

"This way, Horace," Paddy said, leading the way through a small hole into the stone-floored cellar where the beer barrels were stacked side-on over rotting bilges. Brown liquid filled the transparent plastic tubes connecting the barrels to the counter pumps on the floor above. They crossed the floor and crawled under the barrel marked 'Bitter Beer'. A second hole, concealed behind the barrel, led into a gap between the two parallel walls of brick. Fallen mortar had hardened and created a natural, but somewhat sharp, stairway. "Let me check first," Paddy said as they reached ground floor level. "Sometimes they light a fire – even on hot days '

"Why is that?" Horace asked.

"Depends on how much the landlord has had to drink. It's okay!"

Creeping behind a skirting board they emerged inside the hearth, empty of coal but with a deep recess offering maximum concealment. Side-by-side they sat under the black flue.

The public room was small and, on the opposite side from the fireplace, a wooden counter occupied a quarter of available space. Like the cellar below, the floor was stone-flagged and uncovered. At the right-hand corner of the bar a man between thirty and forty years of age, and with a disabled arm, sat on the only bar stool in the room. On the counter he had placed a packet of cigarettes, a disposable lighter and some coins. His pint pot was half full. Froth still lined the upper half of the handled glass-mug.

"It's very quiet for nine-forty at night," Horace said.

"This is when the last shift come in. Different people come and go throughout the day, but I like this lot best. They speak their minds. Just wait."

"Got me redundancy last Friday." the man with the limp arm said to Joe, the landlord, who, with shirt sleeves rolled up, was drying glasses. With a similar absence of emotion the landlord replied: "Sorry, Bill."

"They wanted to pay me by cheque. I told the wage-clerk to sod off. I told him straight to his fat face. They never paid me by cheque all the time I worked there. I said I want eighteen hundred in oncers. It's going straight on a night out and what's left is going on the horses the next day, I told him."

"What did he say?" Joe asked, holding the dried glass to the light before putting it on the shelf above the counter.

"Take it or leave it."

"So you took it?"

"What choice did I have? They've got you by the short and curlies."

"He's married with four kids, too!" Paddy whispered.

"How do you know?" Horace asked.

"Comes in every night."

"Every night?"

"Sits there on that same stool. Drinks four pints of beer and smokes seven or eight cigarettes – every night."

"He'll need to cut down now," Horace said.

"Already behind with his water-rates."

"What are those, Paddy?"

"It's what humans have to pay for water. When you've been in here a few times you learn a lot about these humans."

"I thought water came from the clouds."

Paddy nodded, pointing at a newcomer at the bar. "That's Stan, he comes in on the way home from work; goes home, then comes back again for the last half-hour. Has trouble with his nerves."

Stan ordered a pint of mild beer. He said nothing but stared at his feet.

"Thinking of buying new shoes?" Bill asked.

"Hello, Bill! Didn't see you there," Stan replied.

"Think I'm losing weight, Joe?" Bill asked the landlord.

"I do! If you want to know, you look like you've been overdoing it. Your face is full of red blotches," the landlord replied, as forthright with his opinions as usual.

"Your dead right I've been over-doing it."

"Where've you been all week? Haven't seen you," Stan said.

Horace looked at Paddy. "I thought you said he came in every night?"

"He usually does. I haven't been in myself lately. Listen . . ."

"Spent a few days with an old mate in 'ammersmith."

"That's right. I remember you saying you were going to London for two weeks," Stan said, moving his beer along the counter to stand closer to Bill.

Stan was a congenial middle-aged clerk whose few remaining teeth were complemented by ill-fitting dentures. With a penchant to smile broadly his mouth became a focal point, a greater attraction even than the wide eyes and craning of his long neck that his nervous disposition imposed into his response to any question. Of small stature, he occasionally rose onto the balls of his feet – or lifted the shoulders of his silver-grey suit. Stan complained that he had always worked under the threat of redundancy and it was that fear that had affected his nerves.

"Would have gone for a fortnight, but had to sign on today. If I'd given them me address in Smoke they'd have got me a job," Bill said with his usual straight face, and while the statement appeared factual and straight forward it was leading somewhere else.

"A job! Where?" Stan was incredulous and deadly serious. "There aren't any jobs!"

"There are in the Smoke," Bill snapped back. "More jobs in Smoke than pensioners in Southport."

"Would you work in London, Bill?" the landlord asked, leaning over the counter.

"I might. Trouble is, down there it's all bleedin' suits and typewriters."

"I wear a suit for work. This one!" Stan said, standing on the balls of his feet, his eyes and neck veins dilating.

Bill looked down at Stan's shoes, slowly lifting his head until he was looking at Stan's kaleidoscopic teeth. For a moment the two men studied each other, and then Bill said: "Waste of money doin' the pools."

"I had a win once," Stan intoned.

"How much, Stan?" the landlord asked.

"Not much. A few quid."

"I put fifty of me redundancy money on a big perm. Nowt down! Not a sausage. I've finished with 'em," Bill said, slapping the counter. "Give us another drink, Joe."

"I wish I had all the money I've put on the pools," Stan muttered to nobody in particular.

"My mate in London said to me the reason there aren't that many blackies in Liverpool is because –"

Before Bill could finish his hearsay comment Stan intervened. "There's plenty of black skinned people in the 'pool."

"Not like in 'ammersmith. It's full of 'em. You know why? Because there's plenty of work down there. They've got mo-bility."

"They're not afraid to work," Stan said. "And anyway there's work here too – if you look for it."

"Like under stones and down fairy-glens! Of course there is, for the ants and bees," Bill said out of the side of his mouth that didn't hold the cigarette.

"We've just invested in a micro-chip computer at work. It's on the secret-list," Stan announced proudly.

"Secret-list?" Bill seethed through his small, nicotine stained teeth. "Don't give me that shit. Is it on the Job Creation programme as well?"

Stan stood introspective with worry. He had mentioned a subject he had been asked not to disclose. He was sure management at work would learn of his indiscretion. If he did not have a real problem he would create one. It was the way he was. If he didn't have the fear of possible redundancy he would have imaginary illnesses.

"Stan, I hope you've noticed Bill's suit. I think he's after your job," the landlord said, pouring a measured pint.

Stan looked with alarm at the landlord. "Is that what he said?" Stan asked.

"Of course I'm not after your friggin' job. Forgot how to use a pencil years ago. It's hot in here, Joe. Have you got the fire on?" Bill said, turning to look at the hearth. Horace and Paddy moved further into the fireplace. "What's you been puttin' in the beer, Joe? I'm sure I saw the grate move."

"What's with the suit then?" Stan asked.

The suit referred to was dark grey and had the appearance of having been in a tumble-dryer. Bill blamed the creases on him being too tired to take it off when he lay on the settee watching television. Embarrassed that his attire should be the centre of attention, he removed the jacket, hanging it on the coat-stand behind where he sat. Tieless and with the sleeves of his once white shirt rolled, like the landlord's, above his elbows, he sat down. Opening the top three buttons of his shirt collar and blowing air, he said: "Is it hot or is it me?"

"Looks to me like you've had too much sun, Bill," the landlord said, looking down at the red triangle below his neck.

"Was the weather good?" Stan asked with genuine interest.

"Smashin'. Beats bagging that chemical dust. I blame that for this chest of mine," Bill coughed, patting his chest with his good hand.

"What about cigarettes?" Stan asked, moving his weight from the ball of one foot to the other.

"You offerin'?"

"No, of course not. Smoking can't be doing your chest any good," Stan said with serious concern. "They cause cancer and all kinds of things."

"It doesn't help the pocket either. Every time there's a budget who do they hit? The friggin' smoker. It's always the working man who gets ..." Bill stopped while in full flow and with his bottom six inches above the bar stool. Stan and the landlord followed the direction of Bill's stare. "The missus!" Bill whispered, sitting back on the stool.

"Get me a drink," the thirty-something woman with the large bosom demanded as she walked towards Bill.

Of greater girth than her husband, with broad shoulders and stubby hands interlinked across her stomach, she sat at an empty table a metre from where her husband sat at the bar. Bill's wife was a pleasant woman with a wit at least equal to that of her husband's – but it had a much sharper sting in the tail. She understood fully the basic supply and demand factors and would survive where others perish. Joe, the amiable landlord, poured the two beers ordered by Bill.

"Seventy-two pence to you, good sir," he said, putting the glasses on the counter in front of Bill. "And cheap at half the price."

"Seventy-two? When did that go up?"

"On his third pint and he hasn't noticed till now," the landlord said to Stan.

"It's seventy-two," Bill shouted across to his seated wife, and she fumbled in her thin brown purse.

"Come an get it if yer want it," she shouted back.

Bill eased himself off the tall stool, coughed and shuffled the four paces to where his wife was seated with outstretched hand. "And then you can sit here," she demanded, patting the empty chair to her left.

Ten minutes later Bill was back at his stool. The dry smile had returned and he lit another cigarette.

"She's gone to work. Starts tonight at the nursing home."

"You must be made up," somebody along the bar shouted.

"You gotta be jokin', son. I was goin' ter the Isle of Man this weekend for a couple of nights at me sister's boarding house. She'd got me a bed made-up. I've gotta look after the kids now." The disappointment on Bill's face was apparent. But then his face creased in a half-smile. "Mind, she's on sixty quid a week."

"Sixty quid?" Stan said. "Never."

"I'm telling youse. Sixty smackers a week. She has to put the hours in. Twelve a night and six days a week. Anyway I told her, I want the same housekeeping I used to give her. It's the sixteen pounds a week family allowance that'll cause the argument. The book's in her name. Pint of bitter, Joe."

In the presence of his wife, Bill had become subservient. On her departure he had reverted immediately to his own formidable self. "I've told her to get her name down for Sunday duty as well."

The conversation stopped and for a short contemplative interlude total silence fell on the public bar.

"Don't move a muscle," Paddy instructed Horace. "Or they'll hear."

The door to the bar-room opened, and the moment of quiet was over. Josie, the middle-aged barmaid, appeared.

"Josie! Constipated?" Bill shouted.

"Go on you cheeky so an' so," she called back. "I've been cleaning the ladies – not using it. Haven't I, Joe?"

"Have you put some paper in. Josie?" Joe asked, sharing a light with Bill from his disposable lighter.

"There's plenty already there," she replied.

It was ten minutes after ten when Stuart, the nineteen-year old son of Josie, the barmaid, arrived to join Bill and Stan at the bar. As the latest to arrive, and because of his agitated demeanour, he became the immediate centre of attention.

"Pint of beer, ma," he called. Josie scowled, and with her

tongue and upper palate made a tutting sound – but nevertheless complied with the order. "Got laid-off today," he said, turning to the older men.

"See you at the Social tomorrow, Lad," Bill said, rubbing his hands together, his protruding and mis-shapen elbow almost knocking over his pint of beer.

"There's no work," Stuart explained, suddenly serious. "It's the dockers. On strike again. They won't let us load or unload. Anyway the ships are being diverted to other ports."

"You know what you've got to do, don't you?" Bill had a smile in his eye. Reluctant to expose his small crooked teeth to the light of day he had acquired an alternative smile. "You go to the Social. Then if you've any money left you take another bus to the Supplementary Benefits office. They're making it hard, boy."

"Waste of time going to the Job Centre!"

The comment came from a short, slim man with thinning hair. With his broader wife he stood at the opposite end of the bar. Bill leaned forward, but remained on the stool. "I told the bugger it wasn't funny bein' out of work." he continued.

"Who was that?" Stan asked, sympathetically.

"The bugger at the Job Centre." Indignation was written across the face of the speaker. "Nowt doin' 'e said."

"You were a fool to walk out. You had a good job," his wife interjected.

"It were that charge-'and. 'e were the problem."

"Did your missus get her job at the nursing home, Bill?" the woman asked.

"Starts tonight."

"What about you?" the short man asked.

"I'm having six months rest. Done my bit for Queen and country."

"It's the government!" young Stuart said.

"I knew it was a bad omen that woman getting into number ten," the stocky woman shouted as she and her husband departed.

"You're right, son. That lot don't give a sod for the unemployed

112

on Merseyside. As far as they are concerned they've written us off. They've bundled us in a bag and tied a red luggage tag marked, LABOUR. KEEP WELL SEALED," Bill said, squeezing a cigarette out on the ashtray and relighting another. "If that missus, whatever her name is, walked through that door I'd string her up by her fancy hairdo."

Stan laughed, sudden and unexpectedly – like emptying a mouthful of water.

"No use laughing, Stan. Do you know another one hundred and fifty thousand school children are about to leave school. And a lot of them will be after your job," Bill continued. Stan lost his smile, excused himself and went to the lavatory. "There's over two million of us out of work, son. We're bigger than the armed forces!" Bill concluded.

Norris, the husband of Josie and father of Stuart, entered the room. As Norris was rotund, his wife was lean. The difference was not purely superficial for while they both shared a belief in family unity, and had nurtured four children through times good and bad, their temperaments were opposite: Josie had the nervous energy that denied fat a place on her bony structure. Her husband, conversely, was relaxed and ambling. And where her complexion was waxen, Norris' was rosy to the pate of his balding head – if it could be seen beneath the carefully coiffured strands of black curly hair that were allowed to grow long from the left side of the head. With painstaking care the Brylcreamed-hair was combed into the remaining hair on the right side of his head. Only from above was the bald patch apparent, but Norris always stood at the bar next to Bill. Face to face across the bar, Norris and Josie stood in their subconscious economic arrangement: a financial conduit between customer and barmaid, husband and wife. He spending his money, she recovering it in wages at the end of the week. It was a situation that suited them both for they were equally gregarious and generous of spirit. If Josie sat at home, Norris would still be in the pub. The arrangement enhanced Josie's lifestyle. They were of quiet disposition, but enjoyed gossip, and Josie, in particular, was a sympathetic

113

listener sharing her customers' joys and sorrows. She was a confidante par excellence. Only her bronchial cough or regular cigarette marred her concentration.

"You want to cut down on the ciggies," Stan said, a wide smile across his open face when he returned to the bar.

Josie looked at Stan over the rim of her spectacles, but didn't reply. The smile left his face. Stan felt perhaps his comment had been impertinent.

"I keep telling her that, Stan, but she takes no notice." Josie's husband, Norris, interjected, providing Stan with some reassurance. But Josie was at the far end of the bar, her square jaw cupped in her two thin hands as she listened, elbows on the counter, to another tale of woe. Her focus was total.

Norris, drink in hand, joined Bill, Stan and his son, Stuart, at the corner of the bar.

With less than four minutes to go before closing time, Big Jack arrived, breathless and with a heavy sports bag on the end of his arm.

"Only just made it, Jack," the landlord said, putting a pint of beer on the counter.

"Wher've you been till now?" Bill asked, looking at an imaginary wristwatch with one eye, the other eye on the clock behind the bar. "One minute to closing. That was close."

Big Jack joined the group. He was a friendly man, but insensitive to the feelings of others. He preferred confrontational conversation. Heavy in build, with bright red hair and an equally red walrus moustache, he imagined himself to be lumberjack and felt comfortable only in broad check woollen shirts and faded jeans. In argument his eyes protruded, and surprisingly, he placed his hands on his hips, standing wide legged and square-on.

"Believe you're out of work again, Bill?"

It was not the question, but the way it was said, that irritated Norris, who felt unnecessarily protective of his shorter, seated friend. Norris exhibited his feelings by staring into Big Jack's face. But Bill was intimidated by neither size nor venom.

"You have to move with the times, Jack," Bill replied. "It's become a woman's place to go to work, and a man's job to look after the house. A house-husband's work is never done!"

"This unemployment seems unstoppable," Big Jack said, adopting a more sympathetic tone.

"So does the violence," Norris said.

"Believe they've started using Stanley Knives around Myrtle Gardens on Fridays and Saturdays," Stan commented, his shoulders rising to his ears.

"And they're putting woman police on patrol because there's a police shortage," Bill said.

"There's a job for you, Bill." Big Jack laughed.

Bill looked into Big Jack's eyes, waiting for him to continue – perhaps even to withdraw the remark. With a smile, Big Jack awaited Bill's response. He knew it would be interesting.

"Five-foot-seven with a gammy arm and an army pension! Do you think I'd make it?"

"They might have an office job," Stan suggested.

"His tits are not big enough," the landlord intervened, putting stained towels over the pottery beer pumps.

"Just a minute! Just a minute! How do you know?" Bill shouted back; and only the gleam in his eye betrayed his admonishment.

"I can see down your blouse," Joe said, retreating to a corner of the bar where he suffered a coughing fit.

"Do you know, they've got manacles down at the Bridewell," Big Jack said, returning to the subject of law and order on Merseyside,

"Come off it," Stan said. He wasn't having any of that fiction. "Not in nineteen eighty."

"It's a fact!" The authoritative statement came from an off-duty policeman who had arrived behind Big Jack and who, as a comparative stranger, chose to stand at the quiet end of the counter. "We had a woman stewardess off one of the boats in the Bridewell last week. She'd just come into port that day and got herself well and truly bevvied. She went on a rampage. It took three of us to restrain her. She fought like a mad woman. Slapped her in manacles for the night. She filled her knickers during the night. Talk about embarrassed. Couldn't remember anything about the night before."

"Manacles?" Stan repeated.

The off-duty policeman indiscreetly studied his own reflection in the mirror behind the bar. He ignored Stan.

"There's a lot of stuff coming in from China these days," Norris said.

"It's not just Merseyside that's being hit. It's spreading," Stan suggested.

"It's not spreading down south. I can tell you that for sure," Bill said.

"Shotton Steel axed seven thousand jobs last year," Stan continued in a futile effort to support his theory.

"Shotton's a suburb of Merseyside," Bill said, with a wink towards Norris.

"It's in North Wales," young Stuart, who had until that point remained silent, suggested.

Big Jack stepped back from the bar and with his sports bag on the floor between his legs said: "It won't affect me. I'm doing alright. Got a house with an allotment. I'm doing well. If you work hard you get rewards like me." As he related the list of material gains he had achieved he moved on the spot like a clockwork toy, transferring his weight from one foot to the other, and although he held the handle of his beer pot, he still managed to place his hands on his hips. Leaning his body forward from the waist he placed the empty glass on the counter and then, first with his left hand, he touched the right side of his chest. He then touched his left chest with his right hand. He waited patiently for Bill's response.

Bill stood up, his feet on the struts of the stool, and looking down at Big Jack said: "I'm glad I'm not ugly like you."

As they descended between the brickwork, Horace and Paddy couldn't control their laughter.

116

Nine

Betty and Glad complained they never went anywhere. As a gesture of appeasement, Horace and Paddy agreed to accompany them to the city park the following Monday morning. Weekend was too dangerous, for it was then that the inner-city young terrorist invaded the small patch of green at the north end of Lime Street. There was no hiding place and certainly no peace for the rodent population when the back street gangs were about. And, despite their young years, they carried pen-knives and catapults. Many a Liverpool rat had lost an eye – or worse – in St Johns Gardens on a Sunday afternoon. The only visitors to the park on a Monday morning were the drunks and the insane. Those two groups posed no real threat. They were rather irritants as, when they encountered a rat, they wanted to engage the animal in conversation. As the drunks tended to slur their words and the insane talked in code it was difficult and embarrassing, and the rats did nothing to encourage communication.

The does spent two hours preparing themselves for their day out, but it was nearly eleven o'clock before the group reached the Renshaw Street underpass. The north bearing ratpass went straight past the front door of the main railway station, subterranean home to more than a thousand rats. Day and night the rat tunnel was in constant use. Sean was again on duty at the six-way junction.

"Paddy. How'se you doin'? Taking Glad out I see. Happy birthday, Glad! How was the show, Paddy?" Sean called across the busy intersection.

Glad acknowledged Sean, but turning to her husband asked: "What show was that?"

"Didn't you hear, Glad?" Betty said, but Horace nudged her into silence, and the subject was forgotten.

The sun was at its zenith when they emerged into the daylight at St George's Hall. A flag fluttered high above the Grecian-style building that reflected Liverpool's wealthy past. The four rats hurried across the cobbled forecourt where a notice declared a court was in session. The large Victorian hall separated the park from the traffic pollution on Lime Street, but the tiny park overlooked, from its opposite boundary, the entrance of the river tunnel that provided access to the Wirral Peninsula. A round-about at its mouth churned-up a constant veil of carbon monoxide.

At the south-west corner of the park, between shrubbery and low wall, the four day trippers settled down. Inaccessible to the municipal lawn-mower, the summer grass was long and comfortable. The mid-day sun was warming and the surrounding wall offered insulation from the Wirral-bound traffic. They lay side by side.

"We should come here more often, Paddy," Glad suggested, but Paddy, lying with his eyes closed, only grunted. "Do you hear me?" But Paddy responded with an artificial snore. "Bucks!" she declared. "Does Horace ignore you, Betty?"

"Sometimes," Betty replied, her eyes also closed.

"It must be ages since he last took me out," Glad continued. Paddy made another exaggerated snoring noise. "Oh shut up! I know you're not asleep. And look there's a ladybird on your stomach."

Paddy sat up. "Where?"

Betty turned to Horace. "I think I'm having a baby."

Horace sprung upright. Resting on his two front paws and with his face close to Betty's, asked: "What did you say?"

"I said I think I'm having a baby."

The four rats, all sitting up, looked in turn at each other.

"She's having a baby, Glad!" Horace stuttered.

The circumstances were so exceptional none of the four had an ear to the ground nor a snout in the air.

118

"Lend us thirty-seven pence so ah can get 'ame," the short and stocky Scotsman, with outstretched and nicotine-stained hand, said gruffly. Supported by the lush green branches of a bay willow, he swayed forwards and backwards before slowly sinking onto his knees. Continuing the downward momentum he landed on his chest. Betty and Glad stepped back, unable to tolerate the man's hot and alcoholic breath. Horace and Paddy stood their ground, inches from the man's broad and flat-to-the-face nose. The pores of that shapeless nose were open and black- and the skin of his face, knurled like a walnut, was tea-brown. Unable to maintain his head in an upright position, he rested his square, stubble-covered jaw, on the ground. "Come on, pal. Gi' us thirty-seven pence so ah can get back to Glasgi'. Ah 'aven't bin 'ame for a year. D'yer know that? An me pare old ma is dyin'. 'ave ye nay 'eart? Can't yer see am a gen ... gen, genuine bloke down on 'is luck. Look in me eyes. There's nay evil there. Am all 'eart. And me pare old ma's breathin' 'er last. Gi' us thirty-seven pence for me train fare."

"Who you talkin' ter, Jock?" a deep voice with a local accent called from beyond the bush. But the Scot closed his eyes and, without loosening his grip on the gold can of Carlsberg Special Brew, fell asleep.

Not wanting to be accused of doing something they had not done, the four friends hurried along the narrow verge between wall and hedgerow. Climbing the rear steps of the hall they entered the building and followed Paddy to an upper gallery. Betty and Glad talked excitedly. As they crept along the balcony, Paddy put one upright paw to his lips and with the other pointed down to the spacious main hall. A group of people were seated below.

Unlike the high and humid external conditions, the temperature inside the colossal building was cool. The long, high ceiling was motif covered, and an attractive frieze of white figures sculpted out of a blue background fringed the upper wall. At the top of a curving staircase a life size stone statue of one Henry

Booth stood aloft, a finger pointing admonishingly. The upper gallery was carpeted, softening the otherwise sober austerity.

"Is that the court down there?" Horace asked, in a low voice.

"Overspill!" Paddy replied, and the four rats sat down, watching through the polished wood railing the proceedings below.

Only a very small area of the ground floor was being utilised for the court hearing. To the four rats it seemed an inappropriate waste of massive space. The grand chandeliers hanging from the opulent ceiling did not lessen the tension of officialdom rising from the temporary courtroom below. A heavily built and shabbily dressed defendant stood in a waist high box. He stared down at the white-wigged and black-cloaked counsel for the prosecution.

"This man inflicted a series of brutal attacks on his wife and children," the female barrister told the judge. "On two separate occasions he broke both arms of his ten-year-old daughter. He kicked his seven-year-old daughter so hard she lost a tooth. And, your honour, he punched repeatedly the stomach of his five-year-old daughter. Furthermore, and as if that catalogue of deplorable events was not enough, he attacked, with a pick-axe handle, his wife, cutting open her head."

"Have you anything to say?" the judged asked the hunched man.

"Not guilty," the man in the dock shouted.

"Do you deny doing these things to your wife and children?"

"Well I gave 'er one in the face. She was askin' for it. Didn't 'it the kids though."

"If I may continue, your honour," the barrister requested.

"I'm sorry. Is there more?"

"Afraid so!" After he had struck his wife with the wooden handle he threw that same heavy object at his son's head."

"Have you anything to say?" the judge again asked the defendant.

"Not guilty." The man repeated the same short sentence in the same hoarse voice. "I didn't 'it 'er on the 'ead."

"Yes you did!" a woman, agitated and rising from her chair across the floor, shouted.

The defendant looked long at the woman and she sat down, turning away from his gaze.

"I'm not guilty. She's a lyin' old cow."

"You have eight children and, it is alleged, you have inflicted brutal attacks on all of them, as well as your wife. Is this how a father should behave?"

"It's 'er fault," the defendant rasped, pointing to the woman who had just said her piece. "That bastard!"

"Do you deny hitting your children?" the judge asked, putting the tip of his middle finger to his nostril and drawing the fore-finger of the same hand across his upper lip.

"It's bein' on the dole. I 'ave ter put up wi' 'er screamin' all day. Go an get from under me feet. That's all she can say. Go an' get a job. Where can I get a job in 'uyton?"

"How long have you been unemployed?" the judge asked, searching under the copious black sleeve of his gown for his watch.

"Three years."

"And how old are you?"

"Forty-three."

"Have you been to the employment bureau?" the judge asked, looking at the watch.

"Went to the Job Centre for a year, but they told me not to go again."

"Why was that?" the judge asked, shaking his sleeve to cover the watch.

"Said I was wastin' me bleedin' time."

"Who did?"

"They did."

"How can you, without a job, get drunk?"

"Don't!"

"I have heard today that you go home fighting drunk. Is there no truth in that either?"

"No truth," the man said, shaking his head and wrapping his

121

bloated hands around the brass rail at the top of the box in which he stood. He looked at the policeman to his right. "'ow can anyone get drunk on dole money?" he asked.

"Please direct your comment to the court," the clerk, seated below the judge, shouted.

"Is it true that you arrived home from the Eagle and Child on the afternoon of sixteen June and, intoxicated, you fell on top of your wife where you lay for fifteen minutes – and that you both had to be resuscitated by an ambulance man giving the kiss of life?"

"Can't remember that," the defendant answered, looking at the floor.

"This is the ambulance report, your honour," the lady barrister said, handing a document to the judge.

"It is reported here that your wife sustained cracked ribs as a result of the attack. Was it an attack?" the judge asked, turning to the barrister. "An attack?"

"I'm not sure how you would describe it," the barrister replied.

"Malicious damage?" the judge muttered to himself.

"Beg your pardon, your honour?" she asked.

"Malicious damage?"

"Assault, I would say, your honour."

"Did he actually attack his wife that day?"

"Not in so many words ... but,"

"I do think we are being side-lined by this minor issue," the judge began, but was interrupted by the defendant's irate wife. Standing, she shouted:

"You wouldn't say it was minor if 'e fell on you. Nearly killed me 'e did."

"Order in Court," the usher demanded, and the woman sat down.

"Tripped me up, she did," the man in the box said.

"Thought you said you couldn't remember anything," the judge commented.

"She's alus trippin' me up when I've 'ad a couple of bevvies.

122

Does it on purpose. Puts poison in me dinner, she does. She says she'd be better off if I was dead."

"This is the psychiatrist's report," counsel for the prosecution said, passing a wad of papers through the Clerk of the Court. The judge looked at the bundle before him, checked his wristwatch again and, deciding it was time for a cup of tea, called a ten minute recess

Huyton, where the defendant and his family lived, was a giant and compacted council estate where violence was an every day occurrence, where robbery and burglary were too common to make the local newspaper. Increasing unemployment carried in its wake increasing crime. In tandem the two concepts had developed a momentum that was stretching the forces of law and order. Discontent among the city's young and unemployed was, like an open facial sore, festering for all to see. The frustration was boiling over in the back rooms of the spit-and-sawdust beerhouses of Huyton and neighbouring Page Moss. Without the discipline and regimentation of work, the unemployed had become reluctant prisoners of their own households. Answerable only to themselves, they had become both gaoler and gaoled.

In those beerhouses referred to – and particularly on Friday and Saturday nights – the inflammation of hopelessness and cheap beer overflowed, bursting flesh and breaking bones. And the alcoholic retreats acquired new colloquial names: the bloodbath, the bloodtub, the bleeding hole, the snake pit, and the cockpit. In and out of the beerhouses, protagonist and antagonist interacted between themselves, the police, property and even with their own families. The violence had expanded until it was as repetitive as the monotony of their daily existence.

The judge returned to the make-shift courtroom and everybody – except the four rats – and on the instructions of the usher, rose to their feet.

The judge handed down to the defendant a sentence of five years in jail – but it was several hours before the slow-thinking man, one of life's born losers, grasped the enormity of what those few words really meant.

TEN

The Summer of 1980 came and went. It had been a mix of hot and cold days with rain, wind, sun and showers. It had been as confused as any Summer on Merseyside.

Betty had given birth to twins and suddenly their spacious apartment was too small. Drying nappies covered all upright fixtures and fittings, and feeding the two extra mouths became a full-time job. The additions to the family had nevertheless brought a new sense of purpose into the lives of Horace and Betty.

Back in Manchester, Betty's widowed mother, Minnie, was determined to find her missing daughter and son-in-law. While her friends and neighbours were certain the couple had met an untimely end, she was resolute in her efforts to find them. Unwilling to sit at home and grieve, she travelled regularly to the Manchester docks, their last reported sighting.

It was while listening to the rat-grapevine that she heard of two Mancunian rats who, having accidentally landed in Liverpool, had integrated so well into the Merseyside culture that honorary citizenship had been bestowed upon them. Word of this unique development had spread along the ducts, sewers and river-banks of the Manchester Ship Canal, eventually reaching Trafford Park where Minnie lived alone beneath a cereal factory. Old age and the comforts of home with a rich and regular food supply were not enough to stop her spreading dust-sheets and locking up her lair. With a small suitcase under her arm and shower hat on her head she set off along the banks of the ship canal. Without any evidence that the couple adopted by Liverpool was her own kith and kin, she nevertheless had confidence in her own intuitiveness.

For three weeks she struggled over boulders, fought her way through fern and weed and slept in empty rabbit burrows. At last, dishevelled and bloody, she reached the wide basin of Widnes where petro-chemical factories lit up the Ellesmere Port sky like Blackpool illuminations. It was only three days journey, she had been told by Runcorn water rats, from the tall chimney stacks that breathe fire in the sky to the docks of Liverpool. It was here on the sweeping bay, with its atmosphere as pungent as a thousand bag eggs and where the stranded upper waters of the Mersey glowed in the multi-coloured symmetry of chemical, oil and effluence, that she became stranded on a sand-bank. The tide had unexpectedly and suddenly swirled in and around where she walked.

Tired and weary, she had not noticed that she was walking on sand and away from the shore line until the murky waters lapped at her feet. She climbed up onto the hump of the hillock of sand, but the higher she climbed, the finer the texture of the shoal became. She began to sink in its loosely packed surface. In the embers of twilight, thousands of small, distant lights danced on the hillside chemical works, out-shining the few stars creeping into the evening sky. On an island surrounded by black sea, Minnie had sunk so far that only her head and shoulders remained free. She called for help, but in her heart realised the end was near. Nobody would be out on the polluted waters between and betwix the hours of light and dark. The years, months, weeks and days of times past flickered before her eyes like a silent movie. 'Stay in routine. It's when you're out of routine that accidents happen.' She could hear clearly the voice of her long dead father. She had always dismissed his lectures as old fashioned and fuddy-duddy. If only she had taken heed of his words of wisdom, she thought. But she dismissed his voice from her head. It was too late for such a warning. She was minutes away from a horrible death, suffocating in the turbid mix of sand and mud that would clog her every crifice until she became a permanent part of the sandbank. Forever she would be the target of seagulls, rag worms and those sea scorpions with their long sharp pincers. "Help," she screamed, so powerfully that in her deranged state she didn't recognise her own voice and thought it was somebody else calling. "Who's there?" she shouted. But there was only the sound of sea water that too was now edging up to her neck. The sea had reached the level at the top of the sandbank. It will be death by drowning, she thought. Better perhaps than swallowing rollings grains of pollution, she reasoned.

In her mind, the past became a reality and the day was warm and sunny as she swung higher and higher in the playground. Extending her short legs forward, she leaned back laughing as the swing climbed level with the upper cross-bar. With Felicity to her left, and Amanda sitting on the swing to her right, Minnie and her two friends shouted with glee as the chains supporting their three wooden seats slackened-off at the top of each forward climb, but cried in fear on the reverse climb when they looked down from a great height.

From the swings they raced across the playground and jumped onto the stationary round-about. Each with a paw to the ground, they pushed the low level merry-go-round until it was spinning freely on its axis, and the three does fell laughing to its wooden floor. Slowly it creaked to a halt and the three friends, with arms outstretched, stepped on to the worn grass and staggered in tight circles. Unable to maintain their balance they fell to the ground. And when they climbed to their feet, they went down again, exultant in disorientation. Only when their balance had returned could they take to the climbing frame – but they had to hurry – for at eight o'clock the humans arrived. How they wished they could spend all the long day in the playground and on the surrounding fields. Not only had their parents told them it was strictly forbidden, they had seen the park-keeper with his stick beating children. For rodents, the punishment – and for doing nothing naughty – was worse, much worse. The metal spike on the end of that stick was needle sharp.

Unlike the freedom their country cousins enjoyed, there were no woods or forests where they could play in the day-time. There were only the factories, but they were most definitely out of bounds on week days when factories worked around the clock on the three shift system. Some of the sprawling workshops were so big they even had yardmen who laid down poisons for the rats and mice. Other factories worked all the hours in the week and never closed. The parent rats knew all the undesirable and dangerous places and warned their children to keep away. The does usually did as they were told. It was the bucks who courted danger – sometimes with tragic results.

The muscles in their arms ached, and they dropped down from the tubular metal climbing frame exhausted. For two hours since dawn they had played and laughed until the tears ran down their faces. Rodents prefer their offsprings to sleep during the day when most human activity seemed to take place – but when the sun shone it was difficult keeping the young rats indoors.

"We'd better be off home," Felicity said. "I can smell humans."

"It's too nice to go home. Let's go to a factory," Amanda suggested.

"I don't know. What do you think? Minnie?" Felicity asked.

"It's too nice to go to bed," Minnie countered.

"I told you," Amanda said, showing her tongue to Felicity, and rubbing up to Minnie.

"But we've been told not to go near factories," Minnie continued. In search of sympathy, Amanda put her head down.

"Don't get sullen now, Amanda. Just 'cause you can't have your own way." Felicity said.

"It does sound a good idea," Minnie said, agreeing with Amanda in a gesture of appeasement.

"Let's go to the brewery," Amanda proposed. "They're not very observant there."

"Oh all right then, but I don't want to be home too late," Felicity reluctantly agreed.

Between shafts, a grey shire-horse stood in the brewery's cobbled courtyard. Harnessed to a draycart, its tail-gate against a raised loading platform, the horse's blinkered head was low in a metal bucket. A heavily built brewery worker, red faced from exertion, rolled a large barrel of ale from the platform onto the flat-backed, and equidistant-from-the-ground, cart. Pre-occupied, and not fully awake, the horse didn't notice the three furry friends hurry through the main gate. They crossed the yard and entered the open door of the yeast extraction plant where the fungus cells were combined with sugar. Having been to the brewery on other occasions, they were familiar with the layout and partial to the extract. They each took a fingerful of the viscous substance, licking the yeast as they went.

Through little windows in the side of the huge sealed troughs, hop-liquor jigged and frothed and without, it seemed, anybody touching it.

"Do you suppose there are any humans in there swimming about?" Felicity said.

"Probably," Amanda agreed.

"They'd be drowned," Minnie said.

The thought returned Minnie to reality. The water had risen to her ears, but defiantly she held her head back, pushing her throat clear of the rising tide. She tried to call out, but the filthy water filled her mouth. Twilight had gone and the night brought with it a darkness so black that the distant hillside lights and stars merged.

At eye level to the swelling flood tide, Minnie watched the reflected lights of the oil refinery frolic on the black water. On the surface, globules of oil floated freely, their tiny and perfect spheres, capturing wide but distorted segments of the festal nightscape. A universe within a universe, world without end. Her thoughts, like the unstoppable sea, were urgent and incoherent. The lights mirrored on the water were having a hypnotic effect. The minute balls of oil reminded her of the balls rolling on a dark snooker table.

Those exciting childhood days living in the cellars of the local Labour Club and in the loving embrace of protective parents. The billiard and snooker room where, after closing time, she and her brothers and sisters had free access. Of the whole social club complex, that was the room they favoured most with its six huge tables and innumerable thick supporting legs that offered concealment opportunities for their regular games of hide-and-seek. In that same room, when all the doors were locked and barred – and the steward and his wife had gone to bed, there was also much feasting on the crisps and bread-crumbs littering the floor. But there, to Minnie's everlasting despair, they had played chase-the-mice, frightening the poor little creatures to death. "Why? Why were we so cruel?" she moaned in her hypnotic state.

For a brief moment she was with her late husband on Betty's wedding day. How pretty Betty looked with the pink ribbon around her neck. Then sadness overcame her. She strained to retain those images of happy smiling faces and confetti, but while the natural release of endomorphine into her system lifted Minnie above the sense of reality, she had no control over the thoughts that crowded-in on her.

She was standing in the kitchen of her grandparents' house and granny lay on the bed beside a blazing fire. Only her hollow and yellow face was visible above the blue and white knitted counterpane, pulled tight across her chin. Small beads of sweat lay on the waxen forehead.

Minnie wavered between the despair of that tragic day and her own impending demise. Through the chinks of her anaesthetized condition she wondered whether her grandmother would be waiting to greet her, but the flashes of reflective analysis were but the sparks off a flint. Her control of thought – albeit irrational – was fleeting. In the wake of those moments there trailed, like a streaking comet, a tail of illusionary dust that carried Minnie back down the winding corridors of time. She was dancing with her husband at her own wedding. They were waltzing, and he touched her cheek.

"Hold your jaw up."

"Don't talk like that, please ..." Minnie replied, but the oily water floated into her mouth.

"And keep your mouth shut," the gravelly voice instructed.

Minnie was confused. There was no vision in her mind's eye, and she didn't recognise the voice. Something was pushing

129

against her shoulder and worse, it was moving down her lower body.

"Relax," the voice said. "Let the tension out of your body. Just let your shoulders drop. That's it. Good girl. We'll soon have you out of here."

With a whoosh like the sound of a blocked drain being released, Minnie was scooped out of the hole and rat-handled onto her back.

"Help," Minnie shouted, her mouth just above the water.

"Paddle your legs," the same reassuring voice said.

Being pulled backwards through the water, Minnie relaxed and, oblivious to the cold water lapping her stomach, watching the stars – now divisable from the artificially illuminated horizon. The hunter's moon had climbed above the Runcorn bridge, and the canopy of celestial bodies was now competing strongly on nature's behalf.

Minnie had no idea she had swallowed so much sea-water but her saviour, on dragging her up the grassy bank, had bent her double over his knee and patted her back. The oil and water gushed from her mouth.

"When did you last eat?" the stranger, silhouetted against the moon, asked authoritatively as he lowered her gently to the ground.

"This morning," Minnie answered weakly.

"Just as well. If you'd had any food in your stomach it could have got into your lungs, and that would have been the end of you."

"Thank you, sir. Thank you so much," Minnie wheezed.

"Lucky your case came floating under the bridge. I knew it was your case and you must be in trouble."

Minnie climbed to her knees, trying to see the face of her rescuer. "Are you one of the Runcorn water-rats?"

"At your service."

"Who told me the way to Liverpool?"

"The very same," the powerfully built water-rat said.

"And is that my suitcase?"

"It is, but I think the contents will need drying-out. You'd better come back with me. The missus'll sort you out; and we've got a spare bed."

"I've got to get to Liverpool. I'm a day older than I was yesterday, and I don't want to leave it too late."

"If you try to go on tonight you'll never reach the 'pool. You need a good meal and a night's sleep. We'll sort you out tomorrow."

Minnie tried to climb to her feet, but the near-death experience had stripped her of all her energy reserves. Before she hit the ground, the water-rat, in one swift movement, lifted her up and over his broad shoulder. With her small case in his other hand, and long bounding strides, he carried her across the marshy land.

"I'm Wagstaff, the chief of the local community," the water-rat said, as he scrambled down the almost vertical embankment under the railway bridge.

Mrs Wagstaff was laying the table in their riverside home when Mr Wagstaff entered the living quarters with Minnie over his shoulder. Carefully he lowered her to a seat beside the table.

"Are you all right now, love?" he asked. Minnie nodded. "You didn't lose your hat," the water-rat commented, referring to the clear plastic cap on Minnie's head. Mrs Wagstaff had stopped what she was doing and waited for an explanation.

"No, it's got tight elastic," Minnie replied meakly.

"Nearly drowned, she did," he said, at length, to his wife. Mrs Wagstaff shook her head in horror at the thought of the old doe drowning.

"There's a lot of dangerous under-currents around here," Mrs Wagstaff said. "It's bad enough for us water-rats, let alone you land-lubbers."

"She got stuck in the sinking sand," her husband explained

"Oh dear! That could have been fatal at high tide. Did you see her then, John?"

John Wagstaff shook his head. "It was her suitcase that alerted me. It came up the river as I was about to lock up the winter

131

storeroom for the night. I recognised it because ... what's your name, love?" he said, as an aside.

"Minnie," she answered apologetically.

"Minnie had passed by earlier this evening when she asked for directions to Liverpool," he continued. "She had the case under her arm, and when later it turned up without its owner I thought something was wrong."

"Liverpool?" Mrs Wagstaff said in surprise. "It's a long way! Do you live locally?"

"Trafford Park," Minnie replied, looking around the Wagstaff's living quarters. She had never been in a water-rat house. She wondered how any rat could live in a room with so many puddles of water on the floor. And the accommodation was sparsely furnished – especially for a local chief. Perhaps, Minnie thought, water-rats, with their rough, nautical lifestyle were not particular about home comforts.

"I don't know it. Is it over the bridge?" Mrs Wagstaff asked.

"Manchester," Minnie said.

"Manchester!" Mr Wagstaff exclaimed. "You've come all that way?" Minnie raised her eyebrows in confirmation and went on to explain about her missing daughter and son-in-law.

"We don't know much about Liverpool land rats," Mrs Wagstaff said, wrapping an old thin towel around Minnie's shoulders. Do we, John!"

Mr Wagstaff shook his head. "It's a sad tale all right. Like the wife said, these days we don't have much to do with the Liverpool rats, whether they're land or water. They're a breed apart and socially keep to themselves. Sometimes they come over here, but that's when we have to keep our eyes wide open and stores locked. Things have changed since I was a lad!"

"I had a doe-friend who was from Liverpool," Mrs Wagstaff said. "She was a good doe. Nothing was too much trouble for her."

"Was that Rita Lash?" Mr Wagstaff asked.

"Yes! She married that friend of yours."

132

Minnie watched the small fish swimming in a pool of water, but struggled to keep her eyes open.

"Where are they now? Haven't seen them for ages!"

"Listen to him, Minnie. Community chief and he doesn't know where his subjects live."

Minnie's jaw fell to her chest, but she shook her head forcefully to avoid falling into a deeper sleep.

"I can't keep track of everybody. Did she marry Wally?" he asked.

"Yes and they moved to Warrington. Live under the bridge by Greenalls, the drinks people."

Although the salt water had awakened Minnie's taste buds and parched her throat, her desire for sleep had overwhelmed the other two needs and she was slowly sliding off the chair. With a thud, she fell to the floor. The puddle under the table broke her fall but, dazed, she sat in the water, and the excited fish thrashed their tales against her legs.

"I am sorry," Minnie said, trying to lift herself up with the support of the chair. "I must have dozed-off."

"Come here, lass," Mr Wagstaff said, putting his large paws under her armpits and effortlessly lifting her back onto the chair. "And she was going to walk to Liverpool tonight. Can you imagine?"

Mrs Wagstaff helped Minnie to the spare room. Seaweed, luxuriant and lubricant purple, covered the floor and grey marram grass the walls. But Minnie was too tired to notice.

"I'll bring you a drink and something to eat," Mrs Wagstaff said, tucking the old doe up in bed. But by the time she returned, Minnie was sleeping soundly, and despite the generous host's efforts to awaken her, it was dawn before Minnie opened her eyes again.

ELEVEN

"I'd better be off then," Minnie said, after a breakfast of fish and larva. "That was very tasty, thank you. I feel quite full. Do you catch them locally?"

"John collects them from the farmer's pond near the motorway. But don't go yet. Wait till my husband gets back. He's going to help you on your journey."

"How can he help me?" Minnie asked, repacking the suitcase that Mrs Wagstaff had thoughtfully emptied and dried-off overnight.

"He's got an idea. Said it's too dangerous for you walking through the oil refineries that line the river. They've got security men with guard-dogs."

"Dogs? I haven't seen a single dog in the two weeks I've been following the river."

"You haven't been through any refineries yet. As well as dogs, they have electrified fencing. And they have hidden cameras. They'd see you coming a mile away. If the dogs and electric fencing didn't get you, they'd be waiting with their guns. They don't like our kind. They accuse us of committing horrible crimes like chewing cables and setting-off burglar alarms."

"They do?" Minnie said, pulling the shower cap over her head.

"They certainly do! As though we'd be stupid enough to do things like that. It's a pity they haven't got anything better to do than harass us rodents. Life's difficult enough on the Mersey with all the chemicals those humans pour into it."

"And the oil," Minnie said, recalling her close observation of the river the previous night.

"That's another thing. It leaks from pipes and ships. Have you

134

seen the river bed. No, of course you haven't. Take my word for it: it's like tar down there. Nothing could live in that. And if you're not careful, Minnie, it gets on your coat and you can't get it off. It happened to me once and I had to walk about with an oily coat for weeks before it finally washed off. You feel such a sight. Can't go anywhere. Have a sniff."

Minnie put her snout in the air and did as she was told. Not liking the smell she wrinkled her face and asked, "What is it?"

"Oil!" Mrs Wagstaff replied knowingly. "It's in the river and it's in the air. It's everywhere. Some days when it's cloudy the smell is so strong it's difficult to breathe. And then if the wind's blowing in this direction well, all you can do is go to bed and close the door."

"Have you thought about moving?" Minnie asked.

"Come and look," Mrs Wagstaff said, leading Minnie to the front door. "Look at that."

The wide silver bay shimmered as the sun cast its eastern rays over the calm waters. A continuous strip of beige sand followed the curving shoreline, and herring-gulls rolled and dived against a blue sky.

"It's a lovely day," Minnie said.

"And what about the view?" Mrs Wagstaff asked.

"It's grand! Is that a train up on the bridge?"

"The Liverpool train."

"Where's the nearest station?" Minnie asked anxiously.

"You wouldn't get on that. They're mostly passenger trains and they don't even have a guard's van. The river's your best bet. Here's John now," Mrs Wagstaff said, pointing across the sheltered still waters.

Mr Wagstaff's biceps rippled as he rowed the small, two rat canoe under the bridge. Tieing it up to the permanent iron-ring embedded deep in the bank next to the entrance to his home, he greeted Minnie: "Good morning. Did you sleep well?"

"Like a top," she answered. "And I've had a lovely breakfast of sticklebacks and tadpoles. I'm very grateful to you both."

"Throw your bag in and we'll be off," he said.

135

"Off where?" Minnie asked.

"To the 'pool. I'm going to row you there on the ebb-tide."

Shaped like a wooden clog, the little boat had been carved by Mr Wagstaff from a branch of an alder tree. For camouflage purposes the wood had been stained mud-grey. And the antique pewter soup spoon oars, that he had found on the river bed, were identical in colour, absorbing light. Only an experienced eye could see the craft when sailing mid-stream. The black bandana he wore silk-tight around his head and the gold ring in his left ear were the perfect complements to the pencil thin black moustache above his lip. For Minnie, it was plain to see why this rat of character was the local chief. Imaginative, energetic and decisive, he had all the qualities that make a good leader. And he was strong.

Soon, and with the tertiary aid of wind, tide and muscle, they were skimming through the water. Minnie sat behind Mr Wagstaff admiring his broad back, proud to be in the company of such a handsome and noble young man.

Although Mr Wagstaff considered himself to be English through and through – and a Runcornian at that – his mother had arrived one day on a sardine-carrying cargo ship from Naples, and Italian blood ran through his veins like olive oil. Although Mus Rattus by birth, she had entered into a mixed marriage arrangement with water-rat Wagstaff, a teacher of English at the rat immigration centre underneath the Cammel Laird shipyard, Birkenhead. With the decline in shipping and corresponding fall in the number of foreign rats reaching Merseyside, Peter Wagstaff moved to navigational instruction on the River Dee. After a working lifetime of teaching others, he and Silvana had retired to an embankment on the River Dee by the narrow canal passing through the old Roman city of Chester. It was a compromise that, with its Italian heritage, suited Silvana, and being based on the Dee fulfilled Peter's nautical instincts.

It was a lovely day to be sailing down the middle of a river, so wide that even the gigantic riverside structures of metal pipes, cantilevered buildings and flaming chimneys seemed insignificant. If her neighbours could see her now, Minnie thought as she trailed a paw in the water – but it was bitterly cold and a sliver of coagulated black oil wrapped itself around the second digit. Recalling Mrs Wagstaff's words about the difficulty she had encountered in removing an oil-slick attached to her fur coat, Minnie, in an effort to dislodge the viscid substance, put her paw deeper into the water, rubbing the outside of the boat.

"Are you alright back there?" Mr Wagstaff asked, lifting the spoon oars out of the water and resting them on the gunnels. He turned around, allowing the ebbing tide to carry the boat down mid-stream. Minnie had been unwise to put her paw deeper into the water for a thicker and more adhesive slick of oil had, like a coal-black eel, wrapped itself around her wrist.

"Oh dear!" Minnie cried. "I'm getting covered in oil."

"Don't worry," Mr Wagstaff said, trying to reassure the distraught and elderly doe. His concern was not just for the difficulty in which Minnie found herself. It was the way she was causing the boat to rock. "Here," he said, passing her the shell of a common sea-urchin from the deck beneath his feet. "Wipe it off with that, and please sit still."

Mr Wagstaff had achieved the status of community leader not just because of his very obvious inate attributes, but because of the able conditioning he received at the hands of his instructor father. For a water-rat, there was no greater honour than that of Water-Rat Master. Peter had invested his time and knowledge in educating his son, from the day of his very first breast-stroke to a skill level not usually attainable in a single lifetime. Only in later life did the son acknowledge his father's efforts and admit that the knowledge imparted to the infant had had maximum impact on the child's learning process. In less than a week after this first lesson, Peter had taught his son all there was to know about the International Regulations for the Prevention of Collisions at sea. He knew, for example, that at all times the skipper of a boat, no matter how big or small, must keep a constant lookout and report any other vessel sightings in a clockwise rotation system. He also knew that, although not necessarily by the book, it made sense for small vessels on a collision course to alter course substantially. He was familiar with the rules governing river navigation and that vessels must keep as close as possible to their starboard side of the channel. It had been drummed into him till his ears whistled that he must always keep well clear of larger vessels.

"Oh dear!" Minnie again sighed, looking up over Mr Wagstaff's shoulder.

"Don't worry," he said, taking her paw in his. "We'll get it off later."

"It's not that," she murmured. "It's that big ship."

"Big ship?" Mr Wagstaff said, turning to the bow.

But it was too late! The massive oil tanker was upon them, and their small craft was lifted high on the white wave that thundered up the bow and, like a matchstick over Niagara, the canoe and its occupants crashed down to the subaceous sea. Into the murky, swirling salt waters they were driven deep – where debris, according to its weight and structure, and like fossils suspended in ice, filled the silent under-river from surface to sea-bed. And then the rotating twin propellers roared over them and they were powered through the green translucency, spinning down to the coal black depths where the ancient, and barnacle covered, timbers of long dead ships rested, embedded in the tar encrusted silt. Grey, aquatic woodlice scurried in search of dead matter and greeted the two tumbling bodies with a mixture of confusion and enthusiasm.

Concussed, Mr Wagstaff and Minnie floated aimlessly, their limbs flaccid and fluid. Mr Wagstaff, head down when consciousness returned, instinctively grabbed an arm of the lifeless Minnie who drifted close by. Kicking his legs, and with a strong hold around her waist, the two rats eventually broke the surface.

The tanker that had sailed high out of the water was, like the splintered canoe, gone. With the same technique he had employed previously, he flipped Minnie onto her back and with his arms under hers, and his paws resting on each side of her face, swam towards the marshes separating the river from a parallel canal. He had swum no more than a dozen strokes when his thigh muscles began to contract. The spasms became more frequent until his legs were frozen with cramp. Only by scooping the water with his hands could he hope to stay afloat, but that would mean having to let Minnie go. It was either her life or both their lives. To allow somebody to drown was against all his teachings and principles. But the survival instinct was the most powerful impulse known to rats. The use of his legs had gone and Mr Wagstaff and Minnie, still in a lifesaving embrace, were moving naturally to a vertical position in the water. He removed his paws from her face and slowly began to withdraw his supporting arms.

"Oh dear!" Minnie exclaimed, as the water splashed her face.

Mr Wagstaff was shocked. He thought she was unconcious. Flaying the surface with one paw he wrapped his other arm around her neck. Like a paddle wheel, his solid arm cut deep into the water and gradually his body, with Minnie's head resting on his chest, resumed a horizontal position.

In the few seconds since the onset of cramp, the confused tide and undercurrents had carried the hapless couple back into the middle of the wide river. It had also carried them north towards the sea. Mr Wagstaff looked about him. He knew the river well and could see flares over the Stanlow Oil Refinery. When the waves lifted them up he could see the round, silver oil containers glinting in the sun. It is a nice autumn day, he thought, irrationally, while trying to conceive a plan that would correct a fast deteriorating situation. The refinery, he knew, had its own docks but, and more importantly, those same docks were only really suitable at high tide: that part of the river was awash with sandbanks that would, anytime, break the surface. He had to swim to a precise location north of Stanlow Point for it was there that the sand-banks stretch closest to where they floundered. As a final check before splashing out towards shore he raised his head.

"Minnie! are you awake?" he uttered, disbelief in his voice. She moved her little head on his wide chest. "I can't believe it. Your suitcase . . ."

The third turn of his paddling arm came to rest on top of the case. Manoeuvering Minnie into position, the two rats, finger tips on the case, faced each other.

"Where are we?" Minnie asked.

"See those burning chimneys over there," Mr Wagstaff said, pointing his head in the direction of the refinery. "We've got to go in that direction. Can you paddle your feet, Minnie?"

"Oh yes!" she replied, her excited voice an octave higher than its usual deferential pitch. "I went to tap-dancing lessons when I was a young doe."

At an exceedingly slow pace the small suitcase and its two passengers moved obliquely towards shore.

It was dusk by the time Mr Wagstaff, with Minnie's assistance, crawled ashore onto the narrow bank that separated the river from the wide canal.

They had landed west of the refinery, but close to the boatyard. Inexplicably they hadn't encountered a single sand-bank showing above water. It was, however, irrelevant. With remarkable good fortune they had found Minnie's suitcase. It was a connected stroke of luck that only the previous evening Mrs Wagstaff had, with her own hot breath, blown dry the contents of the case. The damp case, once refilled with warm clothing, had shrunk marginally, entrapping the air and creating a raft with incredible buoyancy.

"Are you comfortable?" Minnie asked, building a mound of earth under his head.

"I feel okay. It's just my legs. They've gone to sleep on me. It's never happened before. See that tributary over there," he said, pointing to a diversion off the canal. "That's the Shropshire Union Canal – near where my parents live. Stand back and cover your ears. I'm going to put out a distress signal."

"Oh dear!" Minnie said, stepping back five paces along the bank. "Is this far enough?"

With the back of an outstretched paw he ushered her on, and when she had gone another twenty paces he put a paw thumb up. The whistle he created through incisors and pursed lips was ultra-sonic, and so profound that the foxes on Ince Banks and all the dogs of the adjacent town of Ellesmere Port barked in unison. The bats of nearby Helsby and Frodsham filled the evening sky. Tawny owls, wood pigeons and blackbirds took to the wing. On the agricultural plane, cows mooed and horses kicked their stable doors. The people of West Cheshire had never known such hullabaloo, and, surprisingly, the sewerage works' rats, admittedly unfamiliar with naval communications, stopped feeding and returned to their nests. In North Chester the cats ran up the walls, and a security alert was sounded at the Capenhurst nuclear facility. For a seven mile radius, burglar alarms jingled, lights flashed and babies screamed. It was a cacophony of madness that even today is recalled by those who remained in the area. An unexplained phenomenon that now goes by the sobriquet of the nineteen eighty Cheshire Bedlam.

Despite the voracity of the signal, it had a precise cut-off range at seven miles and failed to reach the ear of his father by exactly point two of a mile. Mr and Mrs Wagstaff senior lived on the junction where the Shropshire Union Canal and River Dee meet. It was seven point two miles from the boat yard!

"Are you going to shout again?" Minnie asked, her paws still to her ears. Mr Wagstaff smiled and shook his head. "Can I come back now?" He nodded.

I'm going to try and have a sleep. Keep an eye out, Minnie," he said, turning on his side.

Apart from John, his own son, the older Mr Wagstaff had had another bright pupil, and he too had been taught the exceptionally difficult call. That same evening, Dewie, as the second nautical student was called, had been on the canal teaching his own son the rudiments of navigation. Recognising the call, he knew it could be made only by, other than himself, one of two rats. Turning the boat around on the canal fronting the Vauxhall Motor Works, he and his son both rowed, with all haste, towards the origin of the signal. He had registered the call by cross-referencing the vibrations on his own internal antenna and pin-pointed accurately its location.

"Somebody's coming," Minnie said, touching Mr Wagstaff ever so gently on his shoulder.

"Humans?" he asked, his snout in the air. "No," he continued, answering his own question. "It's a water-rat. Not my father, but I know the smell." He sniffed again at the air. "It's Dewie, an old and trusted friend."

Dewie jumped from the boat, leaving his son to secure it to the bank. He scrambled up the steep embankment. "John! What's happened?"

John Wagstaff explained briefly the events that had unfolded that day. "I need to get to my father's house so I can rest in safety until I get the use of my legs again."

Although the boat was of similar construction to Mr Wagstaff's former small craft, by sitting Mr Wagstaff in the bow and Minnie at the stern, the four rats could be accommodated. They left the Manchester ship canal at inter-connected and south routing Shropshire Union Canal. With extreme caution, and feathered oars, they slipped quietly passed the narrow houseboats tied-up along the coal wharf inside the yard straddling the canal. Oil lamps burned behind rows of small square windows and they watched the humans bending at the waist as they moved about inside the cramped living quarters. It was dark and the rats were lucky nobody was on the outer decks to witness their passage along the narrow stretch of water. Dewie knew the damage a boat-hook could inflict.

In normal circumstances it would have been considered a long journey for a water-rat to row: the round trip from the Ellesmere Port Boat Yard to the heart of the City of Chester being more than fourteen miles. In the event, Dewie and his family lived between the villages of Mollington and Moston at the inter-section of the Liverpool railway line and the canal. They could really be described as Chester rats.

Dewie and John Wagstaff had so much to talk about – and Minnie fell asleep – that in no time at all they were slicing through deep inner-city gullies. The moon was still full and painted strange, transient images on the upper reaches of the hewn rock-faces.

The elder Wagstaffs lived below a bank of scrubby grass to the south of the final lock linking the Shropshire Union Canal and the River Dee. It was not the ideal location for an all-water-loving rat: boat access to the higher canal was only possible by following in the shadow of a human carrying boat passing through the four deep locks on the interconnecting subsidiary canal. But then no canal could compete with the broad stretch of river that was on the Wagstaff's doorstep. And there was an added bonus: the final, and constantly leaking, lock-gate before the river was a depository for lost and discarded items floating down the canal.

At the top lock, Dewie secured his boat under the St Martin's Way bridge and, with his young athletic son, the two water-rats carried John along the tow path, over the grassy hump of a small peninsula and under low-slung bridges.

Oh dear! I can't keep up with you." Minnie said, struggling with her suitcase.

As they slid down the bank towards the river's edge they disturbed a Grey Heron. With a slow beat of the air, its wide wings lifted it off the marshland, and with its long legs extended horizontally it swooped over the dark waters and out of sight.

"Anybody at home?" Dewie called.

"Is that you, John?" Peter Wagstaff shouted sniffing the atmosphere and picking up the more familiar scent of his son.

"It's Dewie. I've got John here."

Mrs Wagstaff rushed to the door. "Whatsa the matter?"

Mrs Wagstaff was soon reassured, and her husband and Dewie helped John into the house. Minnie, unfamiliar with water-gardens, stepped on liverwort, but Dewie's son rescued her from the water before she went down for the third time.

TWELVE

Minnie was closer to Liverpool than either Betty or Horace could ever have imagined, but the football season was in its eighth week and on four alternate Saturdays, Anfield (home to Liverpool Football club) and the city centre had been awash with humanity. On the other four Saturdays it had been Everton Football Club's turn, and the district of that name had suffered from a similar, but of a different hue, invasion. However, as the two districts were adjacent, overspill was inevitable. And the city centre always took the brunt.

Both Anfield and Everton districts, as they stood in 1980, were developed at the end of the nineteenth century and beginning of the twentieth to house the employees of the Northern docks and the related industries that evolved in that north west quarter of Liverpool. In a city of deprivation there were a few patches of wealth, but they were insignificant when compared to the universal squalor that draped the four square miles like a grey shroud.

The factory closures continued, and like the lava from an erupting volcano the count of jobs lost accumulated. The whole city was sliding inexorably towards the sea and the prayers and protestations of its two Bishops were having little impact. The lava was flowing down Liverpool's streets. Those once major employers of labour were on the run: it was rumoured that Plessey, Meccano and Dunlop were looking at alternative arrangements that did not include Merseyside. From fifty thousand dock workers, only five thousand remained – and four thousand of those were on strike.

Without the pain of unemployment, that Liverpool and other

once great industrial towns and cities of the north were suffering, a malaise had swept over the whole nation. The media reported daily on the factory closures in the North and Midlands. Fearful the disease could spread to their own centrally heated shores, the people of the South stopped spending. Sales of motor vehicles fell by a third. The price of oil and petrol rose inversely, and cars were stockpiled at the Ford and Vauxhall plants. Workers were being laid-off. The shock of the Dagenham car plant lay-offs had a profound affect on southern morale.

Like an unattended municipal refuse dump, the troubles were piling up on Merseyside. It was sinking in: the shift in trade towards the east had left the port stranded on the wrong side of the country; and Liverpool was already disadvantaged with a strike reputation built on the foundations of ingrained mistrust of management and the owners of capital. They were locked repeatedly in confrontation.

The balance between union power and employer had shifted towards the unions. For a decade, wages had been forced upwards and Far Eastern entrepreneurs were rubbing their hands in glee. The variable factors of any society will interact without any apparent co-ordination. Whether it is a free or planned economy is irrelevant. If there is conflict, there will be flux. Liverpool had become the epi-centre of that conflict. Like a drowning man, it clutched at the nearest thing and embraced the militancy with its persuasive rhetoric The masses at the base of the economic pyramid had become restless. The Sunday trains south from Liverpool were packed solid, but so too were the trains north from Euston on a Friday evening. A city with a culture deep rooted and once considered durable and ever-lasting was metamorphic, slowly and reluctantly shedding its guttural English for the long vowels of the south.

It was Saturday afternoon and the Merseyside troops had returned from their labours in the south and beyond – and half were converging on Anfield to support their last bastion of tangible pride. A sea of red and white spread through the main roads and side streets; an army on the move with the capacity to outshout and intimidate the – albeit restricted by edict – most volatile visiting supporters.

A stranger to the city would not normally walk alone through the concrete undergrowth and decaying narrow streets that housed the disadvantaged. For the crowds and gangs it was a weekly ritual but, on Saturday afternoons, the hordes would not encounter any of the teeming thousands who eat, drink and sleep away their lives in the disintegrating township. Such a journey was analogous to a walk through a densely wooded forest: the uninitiated and preoccupied would not see any of the local species concealed in their habitat. But the strangers would be observed: a curtain twitches and half a face, pallid and streaked in shadow, stares, unblinking, through greasy glass. It would be another five months before the temperature rose sufficiently to tempt the indigenous adult population onto the streets. Until then, only the young, already conditioned by their environment, and the lunatics roamed the streets; the young demanding payment for not damaging parked vehicles, and the insane as unpredictable as they always are.

The inner city living conditions were microcosms of a world living on the edge of a nuclear abyss: Russia had invaded Afghanistan; the American embassy in London had been stormed by so-called Iranian students; Islamic militancy was on the increase, and the twin world powers of America and Russia still had their cold-war horns locked across the Berlin Wall. The people of the world sat back awaiting Armageddon, but the people of Merseyside, equally helpless, were more concerned with the twin problems of making ends meet and job losses.

To avoid the masses, Horace and Paddy left early for the football game, passing under the naked male statue on the stained white wall above the main entrance to Lewis's store on Ranelagh Street. Like lizards, old men in black suits and open neck white shirts lounged on street corners, absorbing the fading rays of a weak November sun.

The bleak back streets of Anfield were empty. Breathless in their proximity to each other, but gasping through the porous cardboard that covered broken windows, they pressurized the ancient sewage system housing nine thousand rats.

Out of this colourless landscape, the facade of the football stadium and its neighbouring beerhouse. The Park, appeared like a rich, but distant uncle and aunt: bright, cheerful, unreal and definitely unconnected to the surrounding slums. The twin pillars of Liverpool culture were gloss red. Even the stadium's old brick wall was painted in the same primary colour – but the sunlight shining through the broken brown beer bottles cemented into the top of the boundary wall refracted a myriad of colour, adding to the surreal juxtapositioning of wealth and poverty.

In this land of grave poverty the unemployed supporters stole, begged or borrowed a sum of money totally disproportionate to income, whether wage or benefit, in order to watch their football team kick a ball for one-and-a-half hours on a patch of flat grassland. Whether there was any psychological benefit from staring at the colour green for that period of time in an otherwise slate-grey environment was, at the local university, the subject of much heated debate. On a good day, forty thousand supporters trudged through the turnstiles at Anfield, contributing to the wealth that it displayed on its facade and annual wage book.

Those without the price of an admission ticket congregated around the gate and pay-counters searching the littered ground. The majority of those disenfranchised young children, who before the game offered, for a fee, to watch parked cars, after the final whistle baited and, like a swarm of bees, attacked the homeward bound opposition supporters. In concert they were uncontrollable: too fleet-footed and street-wise to be apprehended by the horse-mounted police who, like a conquering army, marched the visitors to the coach parks.

It was with great difficulty that Horace and Paddy navigated the underground network north to Anfield. The main underway along Scotland Road had been straight forward and without incident. It was when they began to climb up Kirkdale Road that they encountered a large gang of young rats. The reputation of these gangs was fearsome. The rat populations of Anfield and

147

Everton were long established and had suffered the same ups and downs as their unwitting benefactors above ground. When times were hard, and the humans made potato-peel soup and spread cooking fat on their bread, the rat population had gone hungry. And when those same humans used salt to clean their teeth and drank unsweetened tea, the rats knew not where to turn – except, that is, on a Saturday afternoon. For then the streets around one or the other of the two giant stadia were paved with fatty pie-crusts, greasy chipped potatoes and thickly battered chunks of cod. The discarded food covered the pavements like determined weed growing through the cracks. Whatever happened on the football pitch, the rats were always on the winning side.

After the last drunk had staggered home, the rats emerged from the grids and holes, cellars and coal-holes. From attics they slid down drainpipes and, unkempt and wet, from outdoor lavatory bowls they jumped. And fearful and partly dressed residents ran screaming indoors. Rats of all persuasions – except Chinese – scurried around the dark silent streets gobbling and hoarding. But it was the strong who benefited most, and the weak fell by the wayside.

For the humans, these districts were working class without the work. And for their rats the search was labour intensive. There was no time to develop a sophisticated culture with Temples and Palaces of Reflection. They had no time to sit and think, no time to reflect and certainly no time for building complex underground chambers. Conditions were over-crowded and many rats slept in the sewers.

Paddy knew what to expect in the drainage system below Anfield and warned Horace. The inner city rat-routes extended only as far as the Major Lester School. From there it was a case of either following the Walton Breck Road drains or deeper sewer pipes. Paddy chose the drains where there was at least intermittent light. He had, only once, travelled to a football game by the black-as-night sewer pipe, but he had been assaulted. Pragmatic, he turned the other cheek. He understood the hardships

148

and hunger the rats were suffering and was sympathetic to their territorial claims. For a population of nine thousand rats there was hardly enough food for half that number. Engrossed in the affairs of survival, and without the necessary education in ratities, the parents failed their offsprings by not imparting traditional values. However, in times of scarcity values become meaningless. Paddy knew that the gang of young rats who had attacked him were simply afraid of losing even a small share of the human waste that travelled down the pipeline. Despite their lack of learning, they understood rat nature: let one in and the rest will follow. This was really the full extent of parental indoctrination.

With nothing more serious than having their shoulders jostled by several passing local rats, they emerged eventually in the small empty kitchen behind the players' ground-floor lounge.

"We're in the wrong place," Paddy whispered, looking through the space between the partly opened door and the wall.

Horace went down on one knee, putting his head beneath Paddy's: "Somebody's sitting in there watching the television," Horace said, pointing through the crack.

"It's Cyril!"

"Who's that?"

"Plays for Liverpool. A striker or something," Paddy said, knowingly.

Creeping behind the beige-covered easy chair where the resting footballer sat watching the Saturday morning cartoon, they crossed the bare hallway and climbed the stairs.

It had been Paddy's intention to lead Horace up through the drain behind the stand backing on to Anfield Road. The access behind that standing area provided an easy ascent to the roof space where those few rats interested in football congregated. By a critical misjudgement, they were inside the hallowed building, consecrated by more than two hundred thousand football supporters. Paddy knew that if they were captured in such a place of fervent worship beheading would, at the very least, be the punishment.

"We've got to get out of here," Paddy said breathlessly, climbing the last step at the top of the staircase.

"This could be a problem. The chairman is coming up behind and I've heard he even gives people the chop!"

"Here, Paddy! An open door," Horace said, leading the way into a small room.

They had entered the V.I.P. lounge-bar.

Sheepskin, camel-haired and beaver fur-collared overcoats covered the twenty-eight men standing around the central bar.

In red and black tartan, two young and attractive women dispensed drinks in short glasses over the chrome and glass counter. Open at the front, their bolero-styled jackets allowed the white, frill-fronted blouses to spill out between brass buttons, but the ruffles were too narrow, and the cotton too thin, to hide their matching and intricately patterned white brassieres – subtle accoutrements obviously not meant for concealment.

Thick tobacco smoke filled the air, and burning cigars the nostrils. Seated at a small table by a window above an external concrete yard where the day's audience milled, two women sat in secret conversation, their bleached heads touching. Against convention they were wrapped respectively in mink and fox furs. Their hand movements were pronounced, purposefully attracting each other's attention to a diamond-ringed finger. It was in Horace and Paddy's best interest that the women had eyes only for each other and, particularly, the fittings they wore.

The two women chose not to look out of the window at the exposed bleak backyards below. The row of ruinous houses running parallel to the club's executive suite were without privacy. The black brickwalls, however, were painted man high in white paint. Messages of support for their intrusive neighbour adorned several of the house walls.

The two rats were perplexed and cowered beneath the only other table their side of the bar. It was unoccupied, but they knew it was just a matter of time before somebody sat at the table and discovered them. They couldn't go back to the staircase. Not with the infamous, rat-hating chairman standing there. Verbal communication between Horace and Paddy was impossible. It wasn't the fat men in overcoats that worried them. Their heads were elevated and noisy. It was the two women seated across the room. Should they have taken their eyes off the diamonds, they would not have ben able to miss, from their trajectory, the two uninvited guests. Like sitting targets, they sat and shivered.

Paddy, being responsible for the quandary in which they found themselves, rustled his brain. But it was a dilemma from which escape seemed impossible.

Continuing to shiver, each rat wrapped his own arms around himself. They looked at each other, for neither had ever shook so violently before from fear. In puzzlement they frowned: neither rat was easily intimidated. It was not in their nature to shake involuntarily.

"Is that better, sir?" the commissionaire asked.

"I can breathe now. Thank you, Jack. Fancy a gin and tonic?" said the tall, red faced man with gold-rimmed spectacles on his nose and a Havana cigar in his mouth.

"Thanks all the same, sir. Not allowed. I can leave the door open until they start filling the terrace," the man in the black, serge uniform concluded with four fingers to the shiny peak of his cap.

Peering beneath the tabletop, Horace and Paddy were exhilarated to see an open door leading directly from the private lounge bar to the seated terraces and fresh air. They looked towards each other, and on the whispered number, three, they made a dash for freedom.

"What was that, Jack?" the man with the cigar in his mouth shouted.

"What was what, sir?" came the reply from the commissionaire at the open door, his inflections well rehearsed.

"Could have sworn I saw something."

"Too much tonic!" his companion in a camel-hair coat suggested with a chuckle.

"That's what it is. Here, Mary, put another gin in that," the tall man said, flicking a wedge of ash to the red carpeted floor. And they all laughed heartily.

By the time Horace and Paddy reached Bold Street, they had long recovered their breath and composure. A rat's life is filled with trauma, without the capacity to dispel it a rat would soon become a nervous wreck. It is not that they forget the traumatic experiences. On the contrary every new experience is soaked up by their genes and chromosomes and mapped out for future generations. Paddy's family tree, having grown on the Irish bog, could not be blamed for that day's lack of direction.

By late afternoon the sun was already low in the sky and the shoppers were beginning to disperse. Their day was done: they had observed, furtively, strangers on the street they would never, in all probability, see again.

The heavy woman with rolled down stockings and flip-flops on her long feet was sitting on her usual bench by the litter bin. Over her regular floral dress she wore a powder-blue coat, like the dress, a size too small. On the same bench, but pressed firmly against the opposite arm, a thin woman, dressed, despite the season, also in a thin cotton dress. Coatless, she sat with her hands under the liberal white cardigan. Her dark grey hair hung limp down the sides of her face, but the three pink plastic rollers on top of her head gave some shape and length to an otherwise small and fleshless face.

Sitting motionless, except for the fingers of both hands that fidgeted uncontrollably, she stared into space. Her efforts to interlock the moving fingers had only temporary success and repeatedly they broke free from their interwoven clasp. Ten paces from the bench a street singer had returned and, in Italian, the tenor sang with such tonal quality and technique that all who passed stopped in astonishment: the man, late middle-aged and of rugged build with black, curling hair, would not, by his unkept appearance, have been out of place in the queue at the soup kitchen.

Accompanied by his own creative accordion, he swayed gently to the closing aria of La Boheme. Coins filled his upturned and

152

battered brown fedora. He had captivated his transient audience. On a signal from the singer, the thin woman in the white cardigan shuffled across from the bench. While the man packed his small accordion in its well-used case, she emptied the hat into her large, and equally well-used, black handbag.

Together, towards their favourite city hostelry, they adjourned for a long evening of relaxation.

The gift shop, on whose doorstep he had sang for their beer, was shuttered and barred. A notice proclaimed the premises closed due to a burglar, the previous evening, having removed its total stock!

THIRTEEN

Minnie had been made most welcome at the home of Peter Wagstaff and his wife Sylvana (nee Campesato). From the minute she stepped over their Parsley Fern doorstep she was treated as a long lost relative – especially by Sylvana who was of the same basic breed as Minnie and not too far away in years.

Whereas Minnie was slight of build and timid by nature – although there lurked beneath the surface of lace and lavender an unflinching determination – Sylvana was heavy of bosom and outgoing (others said boisterous). With a white streak in her black hair she remained, in essence, a doe of the Mediterranean. At every opportunity she revealed the gold-filling between her incisors and physically embraced others with enthusiasm. When she laughed she threw back her head and gargled air. She had a genuine love of rats and, if she recognised malice, kept her counsel – but also kept the malicious rats at bay.

"Are you alla righta, my luv?" Sylvana said, when she welcomed Minnie. Wet, weary and out of kilter, Minnie had stood in the doorway dripping from her last soaking.

Her husband, Peter, was of similar strong build. Heavy boned, he always said. In reality, weighting thirty percent more than the average water-rat. Born in the Albert dock on the Mersey, he had acquired knowledge that lifted him above the average river-rat.

It had not been easy, for his genetic plan had been created by ancestors who had lived for nearly two hundred years on the east bank of the Mersey. For many generations the Wagstaffs lived and bred between the Albert and Canning Docks. It had been a contented and well fed lifestyle: before the industrial revolution those two docks had been nothing more than fishing jetties

154

where the sailing smacks unloaded their catches of bass, dogfish and conger eel. The long skirted women in their box hats, and with long, white chalk pipes warming their pink faces, packed the fish in salt and twig-plaited baskets. Fish, inedible to humans, was thrown back into the sea where, beneath the wooden struts, the water-rats waited.

In those far-off days, Liverpool was but a village. By the time Peter came on the scene the hardy fishermen had been forced further along the coast, and nearly half a million humans crowded the back streets of an important cog in the industrial machine.

Peter was ambitious and studied dialects and languages until he could convert, initially, Welsh and Irish into Scouse, and Scouse into English. He became a dialectic expert and, in addition to his teaching duties, was called upon regularly to assist in disputes between the warring immigrant population.

During Peter's working lifetime, many of those docks that, as described above, were once nothing more than fishing jetties, had become nothing more than nothing. Intelligent, he foresaw the demise of the mile of docks and turned his considerable aptitude to navigation. And that, as we know, is how he came to live in the desirable and walled city of Chester.

Its wealth of long-buried Roman aqueducts and drainage systems was all that any retired rodent could wish for. Sylvana complained the streets of Chester were too clean, but that didn't bother Peter. He was content to spend the rest of his days wandering the canal and sailing the River Dee. No more energetic than the average water-rat, he had climbed above his humble beginnings by acquiring new skills. He had never been one to sit down and let life take its course. His youthful resolution had been to acquire a new skill every month. The extent of his theoretical learning was there, in his riverside home, for all to see: rows of books covered, from floor to ceiling, a complete wall. And eager-to-learn young rats were often invited to make use of his extensive library.

Minnie sat on a rocking chair in a corner of the long and

narrow living room. Crocheting a cushion, that Sylvana had thoughtfully provided, she listened while the caring couple discussed how to get her to Liverpool.

John's legs had recovered. He had borrowed his father's boat and, after dragging it up the towpath, had rowed back to Runcorn.

Peter sat at the opposite end of the room staring into space and, as he usually did in the mornings and before he was fully awake, reflecting on friends and family who no longer swam the waterways of North West England. He was a kindly man with handsome features, sympathetic eyes and black curly hair. Although Liverpudlian, and proud of it, somewhere along the line there had been Latin influence. He spent his afternoons researching his family history, but had found nothing closer to a Latin heritage than a west coast of Ireland connection. Staring into space, he rested his paws on his fat stomach and rotated his two thumbs. He was a contented water-rat.

"Gooda mornin, Minnie. Dida you sleepa well?" Sylvana said, entering the room with a basket of worms.

Minnie acknowledged that her bed was comfortable, but she thought that since she had spent two days recovering from her ordeals she should be on her way.

"Whata you think, Peter? 'ow do we get 'er 'ome?"

"Oh, I don't want to go home!" Minnie interjected.

"She wants to go to Liverpool," Peter shouted down the room.

"I knowa that. That'sa whata meant."

"I could ask Dewie if he would take her in his boat," Peter suggested.

"Oh dear!" Minnie cried. "I don't want to go in any more boats."

Sylvana looked down on Minnie, her eyelids dark and heavy. When Sylvana was happy her eyes were wide, but when she was thoughtful her appearance was sultry. With half-closed eyes, she said:

"I understanda that. You 'ad a very bad time. Your daughter 'adda no right to go off ana leave you lika that."

156

"She didn't leave me. I think they were abducted," Minnie said, leaping to her offspring's defence.

"Abducted?" Peter shouted. "Is that what you said?"

"I think so." Minnie stuttered, but raising her voice for his benefit.

"Rat-catcher, you mean?" he asked.

"Oh no! Oh no! Nothing like that," Minnie cried.

"Laboratory snatcher?" he continued – but as an expression of what he was thinking rather than a direct affront to the elderly doe.

"No! No! No! Nothing like that either." Minnie said, stamping the floor but continuing to crochet.

"Peter. Whata yer thinkin' about? Minnie saida they were ina Liverpool. Isn't thata righta, Minnie?"

Minnie nodded and said: "There's definitely a couple from Manchester in Liverpool."

"Not a many people go ter Liverpool these days. Ita musta be them!" Sylvana said. For the first time in days, Minnie smiled, but it was short-lived.

"Oh yes they do! Nuttin' wrong with Liverpool," Peter replied, defending his birthplace and slipping into the dialect as if the accent would reinforce his statement. "There's talk they're going to turn it into a museum. That'll bring 'em in."

"Make it a museum?" Sylvana said, her eyelids rising and the hint of a gargle in her voice. "The whola city?"

"Yes. What's wrong with that?" Peter snapped.

Minnie looked from Peter to Sylvana and then back again.

"Soundsa daft ter me. Where woulda they get alla da bones and armour from?"

"From under the sea, of course," Peter said knowingly.

"'ow would they knowa where to look?"

"I don't want to get into a debate. It's only what I've heard on the river. There may be no truth in it."

"Of course it'sa rumour. 'ow canna yer make a bigga city into a museum? They'd 'averta pull der 'ouses down to make a space!"

"The mistake you made, Minnie, was followed the ship canal.

157

It's brought you on the wrong bank. Then again, if you'd managed to cross the bridge to Widnes you'd have had all those factories and ... no, you'd never have made it all that way. Impossible. The best way was with our John on his boat," Peter shouted across the room.

"But it sank," Minnie replied.

"What you say?" he called.

"But it sank," Sylvana shouted. "Why don't you come and sita downa 'ere?"

"I know it sank. I'm not balmy. The idea was right. Only way!"

"What abouta the trains?"

"If it was like it was in the old days it would have been alright. You could go anywhere on those trains," Peter said, his paws still on his round stomach, but with his thumbs rotating in the reverse direction.

"We used to goa all over der place, didn't we, Peter?" Sylvana said, emptying her basket of worms into a clear jam-jar on the table.

"There's a few on the floor, Sylvana," Minnie said, pointing to the clutch of earth-worms wriggling in a collective knot.

"We wenta everywhere in those days," Sylvana continued.

"Couldn't go wrong," Peter continued. "Open wagons everywhere. I could never understand why those humans dug up all those rail-tracks.

"We used to go on the trains – when my husband was alive," Minnie concurred. Bending down, she picked up the bunch of worms and passed them to Sylvana. "In the summer we'd go on the open top wagons, and in the winter we'd travel inside the vans."

"We never wenta anywhere ina the winter, Minnie. It was too colda for me. I was brought up in Italy, you know. I knowa you'da never a know ita now – but it's a true. When I came a 'ere I speak only Napoli. You wouldn'ta believe a dat, woulda you?"

"No," Minnie replied, struggling with Sylvana's accent, but understanding the gist of what she said.

158

"Whata we gonna do? 'ow we gonna geta Minnie to Manchester?"

"I don't want to go to Manchester," Minnie shouted, throwing the cushion on the floor.

"I meana Liverpool, Liverpool. Whata we gonna do, Peter?"

"I don't know the layout of the land very well – but I've heard there's an old tunnel your grandfathers built under the Wirral," Peter shouted.

"Whata you meana, my grandfathers built? My grandfathers never seta foot 'ere."

"Figure of speech, Sylvana. Figure of speech. I'm talking about the old Roman humans who invaded these parts thousands of years ago. They were being massacred by the local population and had to build tunnels to cross from Chester to Liverpool. Brian's yer man!"

"Do yer thinka Brian the Badger knows abouta the tunnel then?"

"Probably," Peter replied.

"I'll a go anda bring 'im, Minnie. 'e only lives downa on the golfa links."

Minnie picked up the cushion from the floor. Her over-reaction had been out of character and she felt embarrassed. Surreptitiously she glanced across at Peter, but his glazed look and stationary thumbs confirmed that he had returned to a reflective trance. Minnie too was half-asleep when Sylvana returned.

"This issa Minnie, Minnie this issa Brian the Badger," Sylvana said.

"Is he asleep?" Brian asked, nodding in Peter's direction.

"Looks alike 'e's programmin' 'is genes. 'e'll bea back in a minute."

"Pleased to meet you," Minnie said, surprised at the black and white stripes on the badger's face, but trying not to show it. Although she had heard of the specie, she had never actually seen one. There were certainly no badgers where she came from. Despite his age and the wide stripes, she thought his features noble, and she saw kindness in his eyes.

159

Brian the Badger, unlike Peter and Sylvana, was born and bred locally. On the Fir Tree Farm west of Chester and on the north bank of the River Dee to be exact. He had spent his working life as a checker at the Badger Community Store, but coinciding with his retirement from the slug store the builders arrived and began putting up industrial units over his home. The timing could not have been worse. The notion of commerce on his doorstep had disturbed his peace and he resorted to chewing the leaves of foxgloves. By the winter of that year, and after the summer flowers had been consumed by the slug, the badger's primary foodstuff, and when the stalks had perished, life became too complicated. He was no longer the sane, rational controller of other badger's assets. His fuse had shortened and it ignited too easily. "Why do those dastardly humans have to move into our countryside with their little factories when their towns and cities are full of empty buildings? We can't move into their territory!" he said, repeatedly, to his wife – but the question was rhetorical, and she always shook her striped head.

And then the developers moved above his home and in their wake many more humans followed. Misfortune, much multiplied, came with his retirement, but it was fear of the unknown that compounded the situation. How would they manage in retirement and, on their new homestead, what forces for evil would they encounter, he asked himself. He worried unnecessarily, but this is a badger trait evolving from thousands of years of persecution at the hands of humans and teeth of dogs.

Reluctantly, and with Peter's assistance, they had crossed the Dee and set up home on the bend in the river across from where Peter and Sylvana lived.

By the end of the following summer, when the sun had nourished the pastures, but before September had passed, time and good neighbours had combined to heal the upheaval. There was much joy and laughter. The scars, however, remained for it had been humans of the most depraved kind who, long ago and with the aid of a terrier, had captured his school friend and tortured him repeatedly before breaking both his legs. Brian swore revenge, but conspiring for many months, as he did, he could find no remedy. He heard the hooligans were from Liverpool – and cities were no place for badgers.

Brian the badger's fears were unjustified. With its boundary fencing, railway line and roaming groundsmen, the golf-links offered security superior to that which they had experienced on the farm. For younger badgers it would have been an environment too restrictive, but for the older badgers who had done their travelling, it was perfect.

"Peter, Peter," Sylvana shouted.

"What's the matter; where's the fire," he responded, unclasping his paws and rubbing his eyes.

"It'sa Brian 'e comma ter see yer."

"What is it, Brian?" Peter asked, putting his paws back across his stomach and rolling his thumbs.

"It's abouta Minnie. 'ow do we get 'er to Liverpool?" Sylvana intervened.

"Come and sit down, Brian. Do you know about that old tunnel?" he said, continuing to talk as Brian walked the length of the long room. "The one that's supposed to go to Liverpool?"

"Of course," Brian replied in such a matter-of-fact manner that Peter was taken aback. It had been a long-shot based on, Peter seemed to recall, hearsay.

"You do?" Sylvana said, and with a whoop she threw her arms around Minnie, hugging the doe's face deep between the cleavage of her copious bosom.

"Don't you, Peter?" Brian asked. Peter shook his head. "It was built by the Romans about seventeen hundred years ago. It's in a bad state. The Victorians followed the same route when they laid down a railway track. It was uncanny. I bet the two don't vary by more than a couple of metres."

Peter, self-satisfied that his original suggestion had been so admirable, smiled at Sylvana. "Not surprising, Brian. Probably the shortest route," Peter said, falling back on his navigational training days.

"You're right! Sylvana was telling me about the terrible ordeals

161

Minnie suffered travelling from Manchester. Let me tell you, Peter, they'd be nothing compared to what's down there.''

"Whatsa downa there?'' Sylvana asked, crossing the floor and attempting to sit on Peter's lap.

"Get off,'' Peter yelped, rubbing his legs. "My knees,'' he moaned.

"'e's gotta problems these lasta two days with his knees, Brian. It wassa with carrying our John into the 'ouse.''

"Is John ill?'' Brian asked.

"No, no, he's a okay now. Wenta 'ome yesterday. Whatsa downa there?''

"I don't know for sure. Never done the tunnel. Only what I've heard. I've got a map that my Great Uncle Boris gave me just before he died. Parts of the tunnel are inhabited by strange things.''

"Humans?'' Peter asked.

"Half-and-half.''

"'alfa-and-'alfa?''

"Uncle Boris and his mates, when they were young, of course, did a survey. He marked on the map where the different underworld creatures lived, but he could never bring himself to talk about them.''

"Did he see them, Brian?'' Peter asked, leaning forward in his chair.

"The one thing he did say before he died was . . .''

"Go on, whata 'e say?'' Sylvana asked excitedly, her ear close to Brian's head.

"Give the badger time to get his thoughts together, will you,'' Peter reproved.

Minnie, head bowed, continued to crochet, but listened intently.

"He said some of them are like shadows.''

"Like a shadows? 'ow you mean?'' Sylvana asked.

Peter, himself anxious to hear the answer, did not admonish his wife for her intrusive questioning.

"Said they had no bodies, as such. Just shadows. I've heard of

162

other badgers who strayed into the tunnel only never to be seen again."

"'ow you know they wenta into the tunnel if they were a never seen again?" Sylvana asked perceptively.

Ignoring the question, Brian continued: "There are not just shadows down there. Different creatures live in different parts. For example under Birkenhead there's a tribe who attack strangers with their eyes."

"How?" Peter asked, his mouth open.

"They can stab with their eyes. Like knives!"

"Are they human?" Peter asked.

"It's a debatable point. Some of them do look human, but others are half-animal."

"Poora animals," Sylvana sighed.

"It's too dangerous for an old doe to travel to Liverpool by the tunnel," Brian concluded.

Minnie put the cushion on her lap. She stared long and hard at Brian. "I'm not old!" she said.

"I didn't mean that. I meant ... well, you know what I meant," Brian stammered.

"No I don't," Minnie shouted back. "I'm not afraid of any old shadows. Where's the entrance?'

Brian looked at Peter, and Peter lifted his shoulders. Sylvana crossed the room and returned with the jar of worms. Without speaking, she held the jar in front of Brian.

"Thank you," he said, slowly lowering the wriggling worm length-wise into his mouth.

"Minnie?" Sylvana asked, holding the jar at arm's length.

Minnie shook her head. "I've got to get to Liverpool. How long will it take in the tunnel?" she said.

Brian looked towards Peter again, but Peter averted his eyes towards the ceiling and pretended to whistle.

"The tunnel under the River Mersey collapsed hundreds of years ago. The Roman tunnel finishes under Hamilton Square station. From there, the only way you would get under the river is by the railway tunnel. But that's as dangerous as the old Roman tunnel. It's electrified," Brian explained.

"How long?" Minnie demanded.

"From here to Birkenhead?" Brian asked.

"From here to Liverpool," Minnie replied, pausing between each stressed word.

"What would you say, Peter?" Brian said, looking for support.

"If the tunnel is straight . . . is it?"

"More or less. Give or take a few twists and bends."

"Two to three days," Peter said.

"If you show me where the entrance is, I'll be going," Minnie said, rolling the cushion around the needle. "I won't be able to finish this. I'm sorry."

"You can't go on your own. You 'earda whata Brian says."

"Why don't you go with your friend?" Brian asked Peter.

"With 'issa knees? You musta be jokin'. And 'e 'as the 'aemorrhoidas."

"What about you, Brian?" Peter said, reversing the rotation of his thumbs.

Brian shook his head. "Wouldn't go down there if you paid me. Anyway, I've got a few complaints to make this week. Another badger family has arrived on the links and their kids are running all over the place. They'll spoil it for everybody."

"There's no a control of the kidsa today, Brian. They runna wild."

"That's the trouble. Different when we were young! My father used his paw to knock sense into me. Can't do it today."

"I'll take you, Minnie," Peter said, rising to his feet, but having to lower himself slowly back into the chair. "I'll be alright in a minute."

"You'lla never get anywhere witha those a knees."

"I'll take a stick."

"I'll get you the map, Peter. You know what they call the tunnel?" Brian said, but without waiting for an acknowledgement, continued. "The abode of the shadows of the dead."

164

FOURTEEN

That same evening, Brian the Badger returned with his late Uncle Boris's old map. In the neat hand of a surveyor, and with the same attention to detail afforded to an ordnance survey, the map had been drawn in the dye of a blackberry on the pale green leaf of a Bog Pondweed and sealed in aspic. Apart from the folds, where the aspic had been nibbled and the leaf unthreaded, the map was as good as new. Brian had returned to the Wagstaff's home wearing a little woollen hat with a colour co-ordinated dark green rucksack on his back.

"Where are you a goin', Brian?" Sylvana asked, as inquisitive as ever.

"Can't let Peter go on his own, can I?" Brian said. "Got me complaint off me chest and I'm ready to go."

"I'm a goin' too, you know. Isn't thata right, Minnie?"

"It is Sylvana and I'm very grateful to you," Minnie said, repacking the contents of her case on the table. "And I'm grateful to you, Mister Badger."

"Brian, please." he insisted.

"It's very good of you all. I don't know what to say," Minnie said, putting a garment of underwear to her cheek to check its dryness.

"Good evening, Brian," Peter said, entering the room with his rucksack over just one shoulder. "Where you off, then?"

"With you."

"I thought you had some complaining to do?"

"Done it. Told them straight. If they don't keep their kids under control there'll be trouble."

"And what did they say?" he asked.

165

"Told me to mind my own business. I wasn't standing for that. I said I'd report them."

"To whom?" Peter asked.

"I don't know. Didn't go into detail. They seemed to get the message."

"Whata you got in the baga, Brian?"

"Hey, woman! That's personal," her husband interjected. "What if Brian was to ask you what you had in your handbag. Wouldn't like it, would you?"

"I justa wondered if 'e 'ad any weapons an' things in case a trouble."

"I've got my stick," Brian said, swinging the willow-cane over the table. Minnie ducked but it caught the empty jam-jar, knocking it on its side. "And I've got a torch and two spare batteries, a whistle, a thermal blanket and a box of matches. Be prepared for the worst. That's my motto."

"Is it waterproof?" Peter asked.

"What?"

"Your torch?"

"How do I know."

"Mine is."

"Well it would be. You're a water-rat. Where'd you find it?"

"Had it ages. Found it on the towpath. Went for a walk one morning and there it was."

"That was a stroke of luck."

"For me," Peter said, pushing his arm through the second shoulder strap of his back pack, "but a disappointment for somebody else."

Sylvana knotted the gold tasselled, black headscarf under her chin and Minnie pulled her clear plastic shower cap down to her ears. With Sylvana clutching her red plastic handbag, and Minnie her small suitcase, the two does followed Peter and Brian onto the canal bank.

"I'd better locka-up. Don't want the mice makin' a mess whila we're out," Sylvana said, sliding a staple into the door clasp.

166

"Which way, Brian?" Peter asked, his baseball cap at an acute angle, and hobbling with two sticks for support.

"It'sa not so warma, Minnie," Sylvana said, putting her arm into Minnie's. "Give us a warma."

The pressure was high, but there was a frost on the air that formed a halo around the misty, reclining on its back, half-moon. Holding the map to its weak light, Brian, with the first digit of his black paw, followed the heavy, wavy line north-west from Chester's cathedral, the starting point of the secret tunnel.

"That's where it starts, under the cathedral. We'll need to do a bit of burrowing to find it, I suppose," Brian said, struggling to find the original folds of the leaf.

Clambering up the overgrown riverbank, they followed an easterly course, crawling under the low bridge across which vehicles raced in a continuous procession of dazzling headlights and exhaust smoke. From the, inaccessible-to-humans, canal tow-path, they emerged on the strip of land separating the auxiliary waterway to the River Dee from the main canal channel. Short-cutting over the knoll, they joined the primary waterway with its substantial tow-path. By the time they had climbed the path to the highest of the four northgate lock-gates, Minnie had to sit on one of the short black and white bollards at the water's edge. Her nerves had just been tested again: as they approached the lock-gates a train had roared over the overhead bridge, frightening the life out of the distraught old doe.

The canal had originally been blasted out of sheer rock, but the deep, fern-lined gully was illuminated, much to Brian's disgust, by electric lights attached either directly to the rough rock face or on the top of long, thin black posts. High above their heads, the narrow 'Bridge of Sighs' ended against a flat brick-built wall, missing a huge and adjacent square hole in the wall by several metres. Two swans dozed in the shadows.

"This way," Brian said, taking up the lead and leaving the tow-path by a sweeping and snaking path. At the top of the pathway, they climbed the solid wooden steps to the city's east wall. It too was illuminated, and in a line they hurried along the elevated and paved footway. Squeezing through the iron railings, they dropped into the rear garden of the cathedral and landed on a grassy bank that shelved gently to a wider expanse of grass. The cathedral stood tall and sombre in the moonlight.

Too cold for humans, and marginally off the beaten track, the cathedral precincts were as quiet as its ancient, flat-stone grave-yard: conditions ideal for rodents of North European origin – less so for rats, like Sylvana, from warmer climes. Brian complained about the wide open space between their position and the cathedral. They stood under a leafless oak tree to reconsider the map.

"Does it show the exact starting point?" Peter asked, rubbing his knees.

Brian shook his head. "I wish I could talk to whoever it was who drew this map. I'd complain, I would. You'd think they'd show exactly where it begins. It could take me a week burrowing under this lot."

"Well-" Peter began, but before he could say another word, and like a white sheet falling from the naked branches of the tree, a Barn Owl swooped low. Only its blood-curdling shriek denied it the status of a flying ghost. The four rodents dived to the ground.

"You stupid owl," Brian shouted; but unconcerned by the opinions of others, the mass of white feather slowly swept the air and disappeared over the old Roman wall.

"What are you looking for?" a strange, high-pitched voice with a strong Welsh accent asked.

The travellers spun around; they could see nothing but a pair of eyes peering out of a thick laurel bush.

"Who goes there?" Peter asked, raising and pointing one of his two sticks towards the shining eyes.

"More like, who you goes where?" the voice behind the eyes replied.

"Don't talk stupid," Brian complained. "Why are you hiding?"

"If you don't mind! I was sleeping before you lot came in to disturb me."

"We'rea very sorry," Sylvana said.

"No, we're not," Brian shouted.

"Keep your voice down, boyo, or you'll have the caretaker out. I accept your apologies, missus, but I don't care for your friend's tone. It's not very animal to talk like that. After all, life is too short for such a demonstration of anti-social conversation," the voice continued.

"Don't talk crap," Brian snapped.

"He's a righta. Brian. We shoulda be more polite," Sylvana said in support of the hidden stranger's philosophy. "Life issa too shorta!"

"I'm sorry," Brian muttered reluctantly.

"Who are you?" Peter asked.

"I know who you are," the voice said. "You're Captain Wagstaff who sailed the Dee. Used to see you around a lot in those days."

"What's your name?" Peter asked, unsettled by the inequality of the situation.

"'e's notta really a capitan!" Sylvana said.

Peter looked towards his wife, expressing facially his disappointment at her interjection.

"I'm Ollie, the Water Shrew. Remember me?" the Shrew said, stepping out from behind the bushes.

Peter craned his neck. In the improving moonlight conditions, he studied the dark furred creature with the white chest. "Is it Ollie Jones from Flint?"

The shrew walked towards the group with an extended flipper and Ollie and Peter, both with the water connections, shook their organs of prehension.

"Good to see you again, Peter. How's retirement?" Ollie asked.

"I miss my old mates on the water; and it gets a bit boring sitting around the house in winter."

"I haven't seen you out on your boat for a while."

"The blood's too thin now for winter sailing."

"And issa knees are a no gooda now," Sylvana said, as usual having her say. "'e's a full a aches and painas."

"Is that right, boyo?" Ollie asked.

169

"Where's the entrance to the tunnel?" Minnie moaned.

"It's my weight, Ollie; putting too much pressure on the old kneecaps."

"Sorry, Were you talking to me?" Ollie asked Minnie.

"Where's the tunnel entrance," she requested.

"What tunnel?" Ollie asked.

"The tunnel to Liverpool," she affirmed.

"Ollie won't know, Minnie. He lives on the canal," Peter explained, sympathetic to her over-riding concern to be reunited with her daughter. "And besides, he's Welsh!"

"Are you talking about the Roman tunnel, madam?" Ollie asked.

"I've got to get to Liverpool before Christmas," Minnie said, nodding her shower-capped head.

"Do you know the tunnel?" Brian asked, trusting that enough time had elapsed for his initial verbal insult on the Welsh water shrew to be forgotten.

"I've heard about it often. I hear its got something of a bad reputation as far as the Mole population, for example, is concerned. I don't live here. I've been calling on a common shrew lady-friend and I was on my way home when I thought I'd have a nap in the bushes. I had such a busy day today, you know. It was one of those days, Peter. You know, when nothing goes right. It started this morning with –."

"What have you heard?" Brian demanded, his irritation returning.

"About the tunnel?"

"Of course, shrew. What do you think I mean?"

Never one to stretch himself to make up for small stature nor, for that matter, imbued with an aggressive streak to compensate for the same comparative inadequacy, Ollie accepted his limitations, but had adopted a polite manner that could usually disarm even the most aggressive verbaliser. "I do beg your pardon, sir, please forgive my stupidity," he replied, with an undulating lilt as soft and melodious as the angel's harp that serenades the buried dead in the middle of the night. "The tunnel to which you refer has an entrance in the graveyard over there, but exactly where I don't know – and I do not really want to know."

"Why is that, Ollie?" Peter asked.

"You know it was built by the Roman legionnaires using Welsh slave-labour, don't you?"

"Get on with it, shrew," Brian insisted.

"Ollie," the shrew corrected.

"Okay ... Ollie! Get on with it. We haven't got all night."

"Hundreds of those Welsh men died, but the victims never forgave them."

"Forgave who?" Sylvana asked.

"The Romans with their fancy little skirts and tinny breast plates. When a slave died in the tunnel those Romans buried the body where it fell. Later, when they'd conquered most of these parts, they stopped using the tunnel, but it served another purpose: they created catacombs for dead Roman legionnaires."

"Catacombs? Like inna Italy?" Sylvana said. "Issa that a righta, Ollie?"

"I haven't been to Italy, ma'am, but I suppose they must have them there too."

"What are catacombs?" Minnie asked.

"Where they stored the dead. On shelves like they do in the shops," Ollie said.

"Do they store a the dead inna shops?" Sylvana cried.

"Of course they do. They even freeze them" Peter sighed.

"'umans?" Sylvana asked.

"Oh no! They're too clever for that. They don't store their own kind on the supermarket shelves. Just our kind," Peter said, rolling his eyes.

"They eata rats?" Sylvana asked.

"Probably," Peter said, more as an aside.

"I've never been inside a shop so I can't comment, but I'd be surprised if they'd eat rodents after what they say about the rat population," Brian said thoughtfully.

"How do they know what they're eating, the way they cut the

poor creature and wrap it in cellophane. There'd be a war if we did that to humans," Peter said.

"You lot eat slugs and earthworms. What's the difference?" Ollie asked.

"They've no brains. They're parasites. Anyway, who are you to talk, Ollie? You eat water invertebrate yourself." Peter replied.

"I don't go and killed them and wrap them up in, what do you call it?"

"Cellophana," Sylvana answered.

"Will you lot please keep your voices down."

It was another strange voice calling from out of a darkness that draped itself around the distant bushes like a black mist.

"Why?" Brian shouted.

"Because you're making a noise," the voice barked back.

It sounded too tough to argue with, and Brian apologised.

The shrew, badger and three rats each put a paw above their eyes peering into the darkness.

"'ow canna those deada Welsh never forgive – if they are a dead?" Sylvana asked reflectively. However, before Ollie could reply, the newcomer shouted across the field:

"Because their shadows live on."

'Shadows?' Brian thought. "What shadows do you know about?" he shouted back.

In silence, the group waited for an answer, but it seemed the newcomer was no more. Just as they had about given up on the stranger, it called out" "Come over here. To the berberis bush."

Apprehensively they crossed to the north corner of the oddly shaped building.

"Well?" Brian asked. "Are you coming out?"

"I'm here!" the voice said, now behind them on the open lawn.

They turned and caught their collective breath. It was a fox – and a dog at that, Sylvana noted.

"A foxa!" Sylvana said, at length recovering her breath.

"Don't worry. I'm a friendly urban fox. My name is Freddie. Afraid my parents were not very imaginative. Couldn't help hearing what you said back there. What do you want the tunnel for?"

Minnie explained her problem again, but at first the fox couldn't believe that anyone would want to go to Liverpool – let alone a whole family. It was the tears welling in her eyes that convinced him it was not a leg-pull.

"Do you know where the entrance is?" Peter asked politely.

"Yes I do. First there are things I need to tell you. You know this place was once a Roman town, fortified and with its own port on the River Dee? At one time there were more than six thousand soldiers."

"I'm a from Napoli, Freddy?" Sylvana said, putting a paw in the air, and showing the gold filling between her incisors.

Freddie nodded his acknowledgement, but continued: "Although the Romans were under attack from all sides, their main fight was with the Welsh. They wanted the metals in the Welsh mountains."

"I'm Welsh," Ollie said, with a smile.

Again Freddie acknowledged the comment. "It was a vicious war. They captured many of the mad Welshmen," he continued – but he was again interrupted.

"Mad Welsh? Aye, boyo! Where'd you get the mad from?" Ollie asked.

"I'm talking about men who lived in mountain caves two thousand years ago. Things have improved a bit since then. Well anyway, the Romans captured so many Welshmen they had them build a tunnel where they could be kept. Some bright spark thought it would be a good idea to build tunnels instead of roads. They could use the cavemen, who were good at that sort of thing, and they could then travel without being ambushed. So they built the first tunnel to Birkenhead, and then continued under the River Mersey to what is now called Liverpool. The problem was, when they emerged from beneath the river, it was bereft of civilisation. a bit like today!"

"Just a minute, just a minute," Peter interjected. "It's one of the finest cities in England."

173

"Some a times you say it's a good, and then its a bad. Make up a yer mind," Sylvana said, readjusting her headscarf.

Freddie the fox studied Peter's expression, but as he could trace no suggestion of a smile, perplexed he continued. "Many Welshmen died in the tunnel. Accident, malnutrition, disease. Hundreds were buried in the tunnels. There they would have lain had the Romans not decided to bury their own dead in the same tunnels. Not covered by earth but exposed to the atmosphere! That's when the trouble started. It was too much of an insult – even for the dead. The Welsh spirits called on Thor and the Roman dead retaliated by calling on Mars. It was fairly equal until the Welsh brought in Odin, the god of thunder. Their spirits have been fighting ever since. Once the dead are disturbed there is no stopping the rot. It's a chain reaction. It was then made all the worse when somebody built a church above the tunnel in AD907. Then it became an Abbey, but the real damage came in 1540. With the king's dissolution of the monasteries, the Abbey became what it is today."

"Whatta difference did thata makea?" Sylvana asked.

"There were other things like civil wars, but it was really the confusion caused by the dissolution. It was too sudden and Odin, Thor and Mars, who still to this day have their subalterns down in the tunnel, were incensed; it even reached the god Hades. That was it. When he arrived he dragged in the dead spirits of warring factions from all over the world. They will forever be locked in mortal combat and although their bones will be crushed by conflict into dust, they will be reconstituted. And the conflict will continue until the end of the world."

"Let'sa go backa 'ome, Peter," Sylvana pleaded.

"No! No! No!" Minnie said, loudly.

"You'll be okay if you ignore what is going on and don't, for goodness sake, get involved," the fox concluded. "Do you want to go down?"

"Yes, yes," Minnie cried, and Peter, Sylvana and Brian reluctantly agreed.

"Follow me. The stone is two-by-two and twenty-two, from

those who died together above the son of Owen." The fox said, leading the group around to the graveyard.

"This is the entrance," Freddie said, putting a paw on a square flat stone.

"How long to Birkenhead, Freddie?" Peter asked.

"Three days." Freddie said.

"Peter asked Ollie, the water shrew, to get a message to his son in Runcorn for him to meet them at Monk's Ferry, Birkenhead, in three days time.

"No problem, boyo. It's as good as done," Ollie said. "And don't you go working too hard when you get home now. You hear me?"Ollie said, waving his flipper before heading for the canal.

With the aid of Peter's two walking sticks and Brian's willow cane, they forced the stone flag out of the earth where it had lain for 155 years. Black and ragged cobwebs covered the entrance to the hole in the ground.

"Where'sa yer torcha?" Sylvana asked, nudging Peter's arm.

With his stick, Brian cleared away the matted web, but it clung to the willow cane like glue. Peter shone his torch into the void. The tunnel was four sided and two metres deep.

"How will we get down there? It's too deep. The fool who made this hole made it too deep," Brian moaned.

"There's stepsa goin' downa the side," Sylvana said. "Shina yer torch over 'ere, Peter."

The ladder of rusted metal was attached to one of the brick-lined walls, but some of the bricks had become, over time, detached and lay in a mound at the base, partly blocking the entrance to the shaft running horizontally north.

"Who's gonna goa first?" Sylvana asked.

"Me," Minnie shouted.

"Brian and I will go first. We'll need to make a clearance at the bottom," Peter said, allowing his two sticks to slide down the gap between ladder and wall. Going down onto his knees, he slowly lowered himself backwards over the hole.

"Be a very careful," Sylvana instructed.

Painfully he descended into the darkness. Brian followed and with the light from a torch they cleared the broken bricks to allow a passage into the tunnel.

Minnie was the last to descend the ladder. Freddie the fox dropped her suitcase down to Peter's waiting arms.

"I'll put the stone back in place," Freddie shouted down – but the intrepid four didn't hear him: they had entered the tunnel where rows of shelving displayed hundreds of dusty skulls and collective bones in small, neat piles. They didn't hear the flagstone drop into place but felt the draught.

"Oh dear!" Minnie said, following the light beam from Peter's torch as it fell on the yellow skulls where spiders crawled in and out of the black eye and nose sockets.

"They're only bones, Minnie," Peter said, reassuringly. "Can't do you any harm."

"What do the spiders feed on? Can't be any flies down here, Peter. Don't eat rats, do they?" Minnie asked, a tremble in her voice.

"They're cave spiders, Minnie. Feed on insects."

"How canna you tell?" Sylvana asked, not entirely convinced.

"Look," Peter said, closing in on a shelf of bone. The four travellers put their heads close to a group of black bodied spiders resting on the lower rim of an eye socket. "See the bands of red around its legs. That tells me its a cave spider. It's the only spider in these parts that lives in the dark."

"Canna we eata them?" Sylvana asked,

"Hungry?" Peter answered her question with a question. Sylvana shook her head and the gold tassels on the headscarf reflected the torch light. A spider, attracted by the swinging tassels, leapt from the skull where it had rested and landed on Sylvana's nose. It scrambled up towards the tassels hanging over her forehead and vanished under the scarf.

"Get it off," she screamed. "Get it off!"

"Take your scarf off and shake your head," Peter instructed; but before she could unknot the connected corners a terrifying scream filled the tunnel. Sylvana threw her arms around her

176

husband, and Minnie jumped into the arms of Brian the badger. The two bucks stood fixed to the ground.

"What a was a that?" Sylvana said, torn between two dilemmas as her paw searched anxiously through the space between hair and scarf. With a shiver she threw the spider to the ground.

"I don't know, but I don't like it," Peter whispered. "What do you think, Brian?"

"I think we should go back. What do you think, Minnie?"

Minnie nodded her agreement but before they could move, the shadow of a man dressed in a skirt and breastplate ran screaming past the horrified group. In close pursuit, he was followed by the shadow of a second, but woolly shaped and axe wielding, figure.

The first shadow ran up the wall and disappeared into one of the skulls. The second shadow, oblivious to the visitors, shouted 'moc' and, head down, returned deeper into the tunnel from where it had first appeared.

"Let's go back " Minnie cried, disentangling herself, picking up her fallen suitcase and pulling on Brian's arm.

Peter, with his torch, led the way back to the entrance. He climbed the ladder but could not move the heavy stone. Freddie had allowed the slab of stone to fall on its own weight: it had landed with such force that it had recreated a concrete seal. Unknown to any of the four, Freddie had placed moss-laden rocks on top of the stone in an effort to maintain the secrecy of the tunnel.

"You have a go, Brian," Peter said, climbing down to the rubble covered base where standing was difficult.

Brian huffed, puffed and complained about shoddy workmanship. He also cursed, but apologised quickly to the does.

"Issa there another dooraway?" Sylvana asked.

Removing his backpack, Brian withdrew the folded leaf and, unfolding it at the right section, asked for torch-light. "What do you think, Peter?" he asked, pointing to a small cross cutting the north west line on the map at a place identified as Dunkirk.

"Dunkirk? Have you got the right map there, Brian?" Peter asked, urgency in his voice.

177

Unfolding the whole leaf, Brian flattened it against the wall. "Shine your torch on the top," he asked. "See that."

"What's that, Brian?"

"Read the title."

"Can't make it out. It's too high."

"Okay, follow the line. See Dunkirk?" Peter nodded. "What's the next name?"

"Is it Eastham?"

"Yes, and after that?"

"Rock Ferry?"

"Correct. It is the right map! Must say I didn't know there was a Dunkirk around here."

Sylvana and Minnie, in each others arms, stood in the corner of the shaft furthermost from the black hole leading into the tunnel with its resident shadows and screams.

"We've got to go on, there's no other way," Brian said, putting away the map and pulling the bag back over his shoulders.

"It could have been a trick of the light that caused the shadows," Peter suggested.

"What abouta the scream anna the voice? Wassa that a tricka?" Sylvana asked, her black eyes flashing.

"I can't explain it – but there's an explanation for everything. Should we go on?" Peter said.

"It's the only way," Brian agreed.

With Brian holding the torch, and waving his cane before him, he led the way past the silent skeletons. Minnie and Sylvana, arm-in-arm, followed with Peter, on two sticks, taking up the rear. Nobody dared speak, fearful of waking the dead.

"It musta bin a tricka the light?" Sylvana said, an uneventful hour into the tunnel after leaving behind the ancient bones of the long dead.

Walking in the dismal light from a single torch, they encountered nothing more sinister than rockfalls that littered the ground, but caused no obstruction. The occasional long-eared Natterer's Bat that fell unexpectedly from the roof to interweave the group caused no alarm. The few active bats were the light

178

sleepers – or perhaps sleep-flyers – for it was hibernation time and the majority of the hundreds of other bats hanging upside-down from the upper stratum were in a deep sleep. It was the odd vipera berus that frightened the life out of the assemblage – particularly the all-black variety for, even with their zig-zag marked back, they were difficult to see in the shadows. Suddenly such a snake would slide from under a rock, its head raised, forked tongue flicking and its vertical evil eyes fixed on its target. They knew that a single bite from the adder, as it was commonly known to humans, could kill a rodent on the spot.

Like a pig in a python, the tunnel widened, and the deafening roar of thunder followed the fork lightning that struck the ground of an anti-chamber. Like an irregularly shaped tube of light, the electrical discharge, partly embedded in the ground, remained upright. Backs again to the wall, they stared in disbelief at the brightly illuminated tableau where human skeletons dressed in shabby clothing fought each other. 'Long live the Catholics,' the group to the left shouted, and the group to the right responded: 'Long live the Union.' The opposing civil armies clashed. The Catholics attacked with pitch-forks and American baseball bats, and the Protestants responded with spades and flag-poles. Wide-eyed, the four rodents watched in horror as skulls complete with flat caps were knocked to the ground – only to be replaced immediately.

"Turn your torch off," Peter whispered. "They might see us."

"You're right. If they see us we're done for," Brian said, switching off the torch and holding his cane stick before him. "How many do you count?"

"Hundreds," Peter replied. "Are you alright, does?"

Minnie and Sylvana, holding each other, shook their heads.

Accompanying a long roll of thunder, a dark-coloured voice bellowed: 'We want power. Kill! Kill! Kill!.'

'They want union with Eire,' another, but unseen, lighter and trembling voice called from the right. 'Don't be deceived. They've been to Africa for tuition.'

'Lock 'em up and throw away the key,' a contralto and strident voice shouted from the roof of the side cave.

Suddenly the fighting stopped, but the skeletons stood in frozen animation and the fork of lightning, like a black burnt-out match-stick, collapsed and died. The silence, after the crunching of bone, was just as unnerving.

"Let's go," Brian whispered, switching his torch back on.

They had taken only two steps when a roar of thunder, rumbling at first but increasing in volume, travelled along the tunnel towards the terrified foursome. In a huddle, they crouched close to the ground, but the thunder dissipated and a second fork of lightning, like a bullet in a barrel, spun around the tunnel, following the thunder that it usually preceded. The water-rat, badger and two does fell to the ground. When they lifted their heads to see if they were still alive, they were confronted by a re-enactment in the wide side chamber. The glowing tree of light, more vibrant that its predecessor, had impaled itself in the exact place where the previous fork of lightening had landed. The tableau-vivant burst into life and the two opposing armies of skeletons went once more to war. Broken finger bones flew through the air and skulls were fragmented to dust. It was only after the last two battling skeletons had ground each other to nothing that the light went out and silence and blackout were reinstated.

Stumbling into each other, but using the side wall on the opposite side of the tableau as a guide, they hurried on towards their destination. Confident that they were clear of the warring dead, Brian switched on his torch.

"I thought it a wassa the end," Sylvana said, a paw to her heart.

"What did you make of that, Brian?" Peter asked.

"An illusion! Somebody – probably that fox – is having us on. That's what I think," Brian said, turning to look back anxiously over his shoulder.

"It was too real!" Peter continued, shaking his head.

"'ow canna the skeletons be real? It don't make a sense."

180

"I agree, Sylvana, but who could make bones do all those things?" Brian asked.

"Lights! They do it with lights," Peter said emphatically.

Minnie said nothing and the four travellers kept walking into the pregnant tunnel.

For five hours they walked along the tunnel and at hourly intervals the thunder and lightening brought with it different sideshows. Repetitive in all things except clothing, the group became blasè, curious only to what uniform the armed skeletons wore. They didn't even bother to stop, but continued at Minnie's best pace until Brian called a halt. He had noticed a recess in the tunnel wall with a low platform.

"This looks like a good place to sleep," he said, swinging the bag off his back and throwing it on the ledge.

"Oh dear! My feet are very sore," Minnie said. "I could do with putting them in a bowl of mustard and hot water."

With their silver thermal blankets up to their noses, and heads resting on their bags – except Minnie who had taken a woollen twin-set from her suitcase and rolled it into a comfortable ball – they were just about to collectively ooze off when Sylvana said:

"Did a you notice, it was always a 'umans killina 'umans. It's a crazy. Why do they do that?"

"Go to sleep, please! We've got a long way to go tomorrow," Brian instructed.

"They were skeletons," Minnie whined.

"'uman skeletons," Sylvana corrected.

"Trickery, that's what it is," Brian said, reaffirming his theory, but Peter was unsure.

"How do they reconstitute themselves?"

"What does a thata mean, Peter?"

"Putting themselves back together again," he explained.

"There you are a, Brian; 'owa could a they do that?"

"Lights! Now let's all get some shut-eye," Brian said, pulling the lightweight blanket over his head.

With the hostilities they had that night witnessed invading and dominating their dreams, they all thought the sound of marching feet was imaginary. But the studded boots and singing army was soon upon them. From their recessed ledge they looked into the tunnel as the four-abreast troops passed within centimetres of their sleeping place. Wide-eyed above their blankets, they watched the never-ending column of men. In khaki coats and tin helmets they walked backwards, but even with their heads facing the wrong way they marched in time and with confidence. Stiff-legged and with their arms by their sides they sang repeatedly:

> The kindest thing to all mankind
> Is the front's the front and the backs behind
> But we are British and don't give a damn
> For we survive on bread and spam.

The boots of the marching army kicked the ground into a dust-storm that settled on the four exhausted itinerants, covering them like a large electric blanket. Warm and comfortable, they slept for four hours, an hour longer than the itinerary suggested by Freddie Fox allowed.

After a shared bag of peanuts for breakfast, they set off for Birkenhead – but nobody mentioned the army nor could they explain the blanket of soft brown dust that covered them during the night. The border-line between truth and illusion is a flexible concept at the best of times. For our journeying bucks and does the fragile border had been consumed by illusionism.

For two and a half days they walked, talked, and watched nearly two thousand years of human wars, but each re-enactment always ended in death and destruction. After only their first three shows the travelling rodents anticipated how each subsequent tableau would finish, and eventually failed to notice the pandemonium at their feet.

"Why they don't a learn? Why they keep a fightin'?" Sylvana sighed.

"Do they like dying?" Minnie asked politely.

"They like killing. They don't care who. Like what they nearly did to my school-mate," Brian said.

"What a was a that?" Sylvana asked.

Brian explained, and the two does put their paws to their respective cheeks. Minnie allowed a little moan to pass her lips.

"And those hooligans were from Liverpool, Minnie. Don't know why you want to go there," Brian said, his temper rising.

"Can't blame all the humans of Liverpool for a cruel act by a few," Peter philosophised.

"Human's don't care who they hurt," Brian seethed.

"What about what a the farmers do; eh? eh? Settin' a traps, put in uppa barbed a wire and, and layin' poison by the fox 'oles."

"Don't get yourself worked up, Sylvana," Peter remonstrated. "You'll have your blood-pressure up again."

"I don't a know how the poor foxes getta through the spring the way the sheepa farmers put out the dogs at lambing. I wouldn't likea to be a fox," Sylvana continued. "And the poora cubs. Don'ta stand a chance, they don't."

"The farmer says it's his livelihood he's protecting," Brian said.

"It's a the greed," Sylvana interjected.

"What would those scoundrels from Liverpool say they hurt my school-mate for? They wouldn't have an answer. Thugs they are," Brian concluded, hitting the ground with his stick.

FIFTEEN

It wasn't until they entered the last lap of their journey to Birkenhead, and had passed under Rock Ferry, that they encountered direct aggression. Two donkeys with shaven heads and rings through all four of their stiff ears blocked their way.

"Hello!" Peter said. "Is this Hamilton Square Station?"

The two donkeys looked down at the questioner, but seemed to have trouble keeping their eyelids up.

"What's it ter yer?" the donkey with the black eye drawled in a fake American accent.

"We're looking for Hamilton Square Station?" Brian said, standing on his toes.

"So what?" the second, and scarfaced, donkey snarled out of the side of his large mouth.

The donkey with the black eye pulled back its upper lip – where a few hairs grew – and guffawed through its long yellow teeth. The second donkey did likewise.

"Can you please let us pass," Sylvana pleaded. "Minnie 'ere 'assa to go to Liverpool."

"A friggin' foreigner, Rocky," the donkey with the red scar down its cheek said. "What's in yer bag?"

Peter sprang to his wife's defence. "Never you mind," he said, leaning heavily on his two walking-sticks.

"'ere,keep that out or I'll nut yer," scarface hissed, with an ear indicating its own nose.

"My son is the Chief of the Runcorn Water Rats. I'm warning you," Peter shouted.

The donkey with the black eye put out its tattooed front right leg. Placing its hoof against Peter's chest, it pushed him to the

184

ground. The two donkeys looked at each other and guffawed again.

For Brian, that act of aggression was inflammatory and it ignited his fuse. Before the donkey had time to put its hoof back to the ground he attacked: with a broad sweep of his willow-cane, he brought it down on the donkey's hind quarter. A second stroke wasn't necessary for the two donkeys raced away down the tunnel and out of sight.

"Oh dear! That was awful. I thought they were going to rob us," Minnie cried.

"Thanks, Brian," Peter said, struggling, with Sylvana's assistance, to his feet.

The ground began to shake, but for the four adventurers it was nothing new: for three days the tunnel had reverberated to the beat of war-drums and thunder, the ground had trembled beneath the battling warriors, and trains roared overhead. But this was different. The disturbance was more of a swell than a storm, and the train passing overhead was moving slowly. It stopped, and then there were human voices and the staccato rhythm of high-heeled shoes. Tired and dusty, they looked at each other, curiosity written across their furrowed brows.

"Minnie, I think we've arrived," Brian said, a grin spreading slowly across his striped face.

"In Liverpool?" she asked, somewhat bewildered.

"Birkenhead," Peter said. "Sounds like the railway station."

The clashing of the elevator's metal gate and drone of an overloaded lift confirmed Brian's assumption. Artificial light from the station's corridor drew symmetrical black patterns on the accumulated oily waste at the base of the lift shaft into which the four war-weary hikers had climbed. As the elevator ascended for the second time, Brian, by paw tips, lifted himself up to look through the grill.

Unobserved, an old rat sat sleeping in a dark corner of the lift-well. Oil-stained and covered in fluff, like the thick carpet of waste overlaying the floor, he was, to all intents an purposes, invisible. It was his spluttering as he gasped after a missed breath that gave him away.

Peter smiled down at the brown rat with oil-splashed whiskers. "He's well away," he said to Minnie.

"Oh dear, we mustn't wake him," she replied.

Wedged in a corner between two walls, the old rat stirred and in a slumbering state tried to reposition himself into a more comfortable position. He opened one eye, watching the newcomers, but didn't speak.

Lowering himself down from the ledge of the outer lift cage, Brian rubbed his paws together to remove the dirt. "It's definitely a railway station – but there's a lot of boots and shoes moving about."

"What does that a mean?" Sylvana asked.

"It means we're bang on target."

"Like a shootin'?"

"If you like," Brian said, too irritated to offer clarification.

"It means we're on the right route for getting Minnie back to Liverpool," Peter intervened.

The old rat's large eye followed the conversationalist's lip movements:

"Watch yer 'ead," the old rat remarked casually, as the base of the elevator descended. "Sit down," he demanded, and the four fell onto their backsides. Slowly the prototype elevator descended, creaking under the weight of thirty-two passengers.

"We didn't need to sit down," Brian complained, as the elevator stopped well clear of their heads.

"What?" the old rat asked, a paw cupped behind his ear.

"We didn't need to sit down," Brian said.

"Luke at me when yer talk," the oil-stained rat said. "I'm a bit Mutton and Geoff."

"Why did you tell us to sit down?" Brian demanded for the third time.

"Me neck was achin'."

"What do you mean your neck was aching?" Brian continued.

"Yer wha?"

186

"Oh, never mind," Brian said, throwing his arms up in frustration.

Sitting waist high in forty years of soft, polluted refuse, Minnie commented on how comfortable it was and how pleased she was to have the opportunity to sit down. Sylvana agreed it was a cosy location but said she didn't care for the smell of lubrication. Although Peter said nothing, he was extremely relieved to take the weight off his knees. In a semi-circle they sat facing the one-eyed and partly deaf Birkenhead rat. After the traumas of the previous days, the respite was welcome. All four knew they were back in the land of gluttony and waste.

"Do you live here?" Peter asked.

The old rat shook his head, but then confusingly nodded. He didn't answer immediately, but his one eye was watchful. "Sort of," he answered, his eye fixed on Brian's striped face.

"Is this Birkenhead?" Brian asked. The old rat nodded. "What station is this?"

"'amilton! Anything else while yer keepin' me awake?" the old rat said, closing his eye.

"Can you tell me the way to Liverpool, sir," Minnie asked, respectfully.

Opening his eye, the rat scratched himself, pursed his lips and spread them wide. Placing the back of his head against the wall, he took a deep breath. Exhaling, he said: "Down two flights of stairs, end of the corridor turn left. Yer on the platform. Turn left an' keep goin'."

"Where are the stairs?" Brian asked.

"Through that gate," the old rat said, pointing to the metal grill, once again visible as the elevator ascended.

"We're so close?" Peter said.

"It's a long walk, mind. Over a mile through the tunnel. Better to go after midnight when everybody's gone 'ome."

"Does the station shut down then?" Brian asked.

"Turn yer 'ead ter me when yer talk. I can't see yer lips."

With sighs of exasperation, Brian turned his head towards the local rat. "Does this place close at midnight?"

187

That's what I said. Re-opens at 'alf-five in the mornin'. At midnight they turn the electrics off. That means there's no tunnel lights, but also no leccy in the rails. Lost a few mates that way. Which part of Liverpool do you want?"

The old rat followed Brian and Peter's head direction. Sylvana snored quietly and Minnie, conscious that she was the centre of attention, became coy.

"Where? I don't know. Anywhere I suppose," Minnie sighed.

Peter related Minnie's sorry tale, and the old rat asked: "You've no idea where they're livin'?" Minnie lifted her shoulders. "Luking at me you'd think I knew nuttin'. The truth is I meet a lot of Liverpool rats down 'ere. 'eck they come from Moorfields, Lime Street an' all over the place. I've 'eard about two Manks livin' in the posh part of town."

Minnie grew excited and threw her arms in the air. "Where? Where?" she shouted.

"Luke at the oil on me. I'll bet you think all Birkenhead rats are like this. First impression an' all that."

"Oh no. I hadn't noticed," Minnie lied. "Where's the posh part of town?"

"Bold Street. Very 'andy for Central Station. Right next door."

For three days Sylvana had been a pillar of strength. Pragmatic and giddy in equal parts, she had restrained emotions where insanity threatened, and provided humour in the face of adversity. While the contradictory personalities seemed natural and simplistic, in reality Sylvana had to work at them and the morbid conditions those three days had imposed required super-rat effort. Exhausted, she lay buried in the rubbish with only her head showing. The soft gargling sound deep in her throat and the eyeballs rolling around behind her closed eyelids betrayed her internal turmoil. Peter lay next to her and in no time at all the elderly couple, with heads touching, were snoring, and Sylvana's eye movements had stopped.

"Is there any way we can find out the names of the Mancunians living on Bold Street?" Brian asked.

"I'm not sure," the old rat replied.

"Is there?" Minnie whined.

"What's the matter with your face?" the rat asked, his one eye fixed on Brian's face.

"Nothing. Why do you ask? Is it dirty or something?"

"Did yer paint yer face yerself?"

"Don't talk rot. Of course I didn't. It's natural," Brian snapped back. He could feel the white of his face turning red.

"Quite smart," the old rat remarked in his usual laid-back manner.

"You think so?" Brian asked, feeling altogether more amicable.

The old rat nodded his head, but he was still having trouble keeping his eyelid up. Brian had no intention of letting him go back to sleep. He had too many questions that needed answers: "How will Minnie know when she gets to Central Station?" he asked.

"It says so on the wall. Keep ter right."

"And how do we get to Monk's Ferry?"

"Easy!"

"How?"

"Dead easy!"

"How?" Brian shouted.

"Am not that deaf. Downstairs at the end of the platform you'll come to six stone steps leadin' into the tunnel. Luke above yer 'ead; yer'll see the cables. Just squeeze into the ducting and it'll take you down to Woodside Ferry. Follow the shoreline south. It's not far. Now if yer don't mind I'm goin' ter 'ave me winks."

"How do we know when to make a move?" Brian asked.

"You'l soon find out," the old, oil-stained and fluff covered rat said, sliding down the wall and disappearing beneath the dust depository.

"He said when the lights go out," Minnie said, picking up on the old rat's earlier comment.

Brian was the last to fall asleep, but first to awaken. The darkness was total. By touch he woke his colleagues, and Sylvana, from Peter's shoulders, climbed through the elevator's lattice-work gate. Minnie did likewise but from Brian's shoulders.

189

Brian then crouched down and Peter stood on his shoulders, but there they remained. Peter was simply too heavy for Brian to straighten his legs. Sylvana took one arm and Minnie the other but, pull as they did, they couldn't budge the overweight water-rat with bad knees. Sylvana's pragmatism deserted her as she contemplated the horrible thought of her and her husband having to journey back along the tunnel of death and destruction. And then she broke into a cold sweat as she recalled the Chester entrance had resealed itself. With added vigour, she pulled at Peter's arm until, in pain, he cried out.

"You're pulling me arm out of its socket."

"Luke out," the old rat said, forcing his way out of the waste. "Get on my shoulders," he instructed. Effortlessly he lifted Peter up to the gate, and Brian watched in disbelief. "Your turn," he told Brian.

As he rose up on the old rats back, Brian asked: "Where'd you get the strength?"

"Don't think 'cause am old, am useless. We're 'ard nuts us Birkenhead rats!"

Turning sharp right they crept, unnecessarily, down two flights of stairs and in the darkness tip-toed along the narrow corridor and, as instructed, turned left. There it was before them: the railway tunnel to Liverpool.

"Which a way we goa?" Sylvana asked, rubbing her eyes; still not fully recovered from the short, but deep sleep.

"Right?" Peter suggested.

"No! No! No!" Minnie exclaimed. "He said left. I remember distinctly."

"That he did. Let's go," Brian said.

As we know, rats and badgers, have reasonably good eyesight in the dark. Although it has limitations and can be compared to the human eye looking through frosted glass, Brian, Peter, Sylvana and Minnie had other attributes that should not be overlooked: a penetrating sense of smell and perceptive whiskers. Blindfolded they could have found their way to the six steps

190

without falling off the platform or bumping into the wooden benching lining the curving walls.

"This is where we part company," Peter said, a distinct croak in his voice, and Sylvana threw her arms around Minnie. Brian stood aside wiping the tears from his eyes. Breathless in Sylvana's bosom, Minnie fought for air. She was anxious to complete the last leg of her journey to Liverpool.

After much hugging and paw-shaking, Minnie walked down the steps into the wide bending tunnel with its rough, rounded roof.

With the assistance of a cable hanging loose, Brian, Peter and Sylvana climbed into the roof ducting as advised by the old rat. With Peter's navigational skills, and empirical knowledge of Birkenhead, the group of three soon arrived at Monk's Ferry where John was waiting in his father's boat. It would be the following morning before they reached home.

Minnie, however, was closer to her destination, and as she walked along the dark cinder-track between the damp wall and cold steel rail her heart began to accelerate. 'What if it's not Betty and Horace,' she thought. 'What will I do? How will I get home? Oh dear'. The thoughts brought with them a drop of temperature every bit as cold as the River Mersey. And then, from somewhere near her beating heart, a spark ignited a warm glow that spread through her whole body as she recalled somebody's comment that nobody from Manchester ever goes to live in Liverpool. It can only be them she thought – but then a cold wind blew over her as she recalled those other words: 'Nobody in their right mind goes to Liverpool!'

"Oh dear," she said aloud as she stumbled along. "Both Betty and Horace are in their right minds. It can't be them."

The first half of the railway tunnel deep below the River Mersey was downhill and comparatively easy. As Minnie approached the middle sector, where the incline levels off before climbing up to the opposite side of the river, she saw a flickering light on the tunnel wall. Slowing down, and moving her suitcase to her right hand lest it should catch on the wall and make a noise, she hesitatingly came to a halt. She could hear human voices. At that point, where the ground is flat and in a recess off the tunnel, four men in black boiler-suits knelt in a small circle around a spluttering butane gas-lamp. One of the four men was dealing playing-cards.

"Wha' kinda 'and is this, man?" one of the four said, as Minnie crawled by – but the same man, seeing Minnie out of the corner of his eye, threw a brown apple-core at her. "Is you shakin' up dese cards?" he complained, not allowing himself to be distracted from the gambling session. The apple missed Minnie, but fearful of a follow-up attack she ran uphill until, breathless and with a chest she was sure would explode all over the railway lines, she found a suitable cleft in the wet wall where she could hide and rest. Putting down her case she picked up the scent of other rats. Inside the crevice, four white eyes stared out of the black hole.

"I'm sorry to be intruding. I was running away from those humans?" she explained to nobody in particular.

"The cleaners?" a buck voice said.

"I don't know," she replied.

"Kneeling down?" a doe voice asked.

"Yes, yes. They didn't chase me though. Threw an apple."

"Where is it?" the deeper voice asked.

"What?"

"The apple."

"Oh dear. I don't know where it landed. It didn't hit me. Must be on the railway line.

"Go and get it, Rosy," the buck instructed.

With an excuse-me, a thin doe squeezed past Minnie and ran down the side of the track, returning with the core. With another apology the doe squeezed back into the fissure.

"Where are you going?" the buck asked, a mouthful of apple affecting articulation.

Minnie told them about her missing daughter and son-in-law.

"Is she called Betty?" the voice asked.

"Yes! How did you know?"

"And Horace?"

192

Minnie was ecstatic and clapped her paws. "How, how do you know their names? Did I just tell you? Oh dear..."

"They live under the pub on Bold Street. Doing all right for themselves," he continued.

"Are you sure? How do you know? Can I believe you? Oh dear, I'm so confused."

"Don't worry, missus. We can take you. We've done our courting for tonight. We live just across the road from them in the main sewer," the slim doe said, again moving out of the inner darkness and reassuringly touching Minnie's arm.

It was just before dawn that the trio scrambled up the two long and stationary escalators, ran across the Central Station concourse and navigated the passageway onto Bold Street. The young buck led the way at a pace that Minnie and the young doe carrying, on her beau's instruction, Minnie's case, found challenging.

Drained mentally and physically, Minnie stood outside the door where the buck had left her. With her shower cap pulled tight over her ears, she called meekly: "Betty?" Three times she called out her name before mother and daughter stood, speech-less, facing each other. For a whole two minutes they stared into each others water-filled eyes, both confident they were dream-ing. And then they fell into each other's arms and the tears flowed freely.

"How did you get here, mother? Mother! Mother! Mother!" Betty cried, smothering the elderly doe with kisses. "How? How? I can't believe it. Let me look at you. Am I dreaming? Don't say, yes." And once more they fell into a warm embrace. "How did you get here?"

"It was nothing. I got a lift," Minnie said, with all the under-statement mothers impart on their offsprings when talking about their own troubles. Betty would never know – but Minnie would be a stronger and wiser rat than she was before leaving home on her epic journey from Manchester to Liverpool.

SIXTEEN

By Christmas Eve, Minnie had been installed in her own small apartment along the corridor from her daughter and son-in-law.

For the first week after Minnie's arrival, Horace had been well pleased with the uplift in Betty's disposition. The earlier arrival of the babies had brought the smiles back to Betty's face, but they were superficial. Behind the facade was an emptiness. The unexpected arrival of her mother immediately filled the void, and they all rejoiced.

The fact that Minnie slept on the settee did not, at first, mar the reunion. It was the constant flow of advice in all things infant that Betty found irritating. The baby and the accoutrements of the nursery had imposed their own limitations on available space. As far as Horace was concerned, Minnie exasperated an existing and adverse situation. She had commandeered the best chair in the house and whichever way he looked she was there: straight-backed and shower-capped. Without the pressures of fatherhood perhaps his tolerance would have been more elastic.

"Paddy, you've got to help me," Horace pleaded.

Paddy provided the space and the two friends converted the unused storeroom. Horace arranged Minnie's transfer that same day. Horace and Betty had thought Minnie content to share their facilities and sleep on the settee. However, her own underlying discontent grew in equal measure to that of her son-in-law. Alone at least in her own little lodgings, she punched the air and let out a yelp.

"Do you fancy going up to the pub tonight, Horace," Paddy asked, as they swept away the sawdust of their labours. "It's a real eye-opener on Christmas Eve. No use going too early. Things don't liven up until about ten."

By ten o'clock they were installed in the wall cavity looking down onto the proceedings through a ceramic ventilation grill at ceiling level. Flames licked out of the fireplace, their summer-time stand-point. The bar-room was filled with humans, some in fancy costume, the likes of which Horace had never before seen, and the atmosphere was heavy with tobacco smoke that wafted through the air like a sculpted cloud. It rolled over the nicotine-stained ceiling before encircling the light cables and disappearing into the landlord's living-quarters above.

The recession, by the Christmas of nineteen eighty, had begun to bite sharply affecting the sales of even the long established industries north of Watford. Neither were the traditional reces-sion-proof businesses, such as brewing of beer, ring-fenced from adversity as they had been for hundreds of years. A major brewery reported a thirteen percent drop-off in sales, and at brewery board-meetings up and down the country hasty plans to stop the rot were put into place. Under-pinning the short term and panic proposals were plans of a more serious consequential nature: the targeting of the youth market and alternative pro-ducts.

The decline in alcohol sales were inverse to the increase in violence. That analytical sector of society looking on from afar and professing, with government funding, to see clearly the correlation between drunkenness and violence had to return to their drawing boards.

In Liverpool there were underlying tensions as there were in all mixed communities: the white populations of the deprived areas distrusted the blacks and the middle-class white; the elderly black distrusted black youths – and the Chinese distrusted everyone, including themselves. The city had no inherent wealth, but a workforce with a reputation for spontaneous strike action. The factories were falling down like a row of closely positioned dominoes. Unemployment was high and rising. Many of the young and old had no money. Aimlessly they loitered on street corners.

The rise in Scouse unemployment had not happened overnight. It had been persistent: twenty thousand out of work in 1966. Forty thousand by 1971 and rising.

The disparate private shipyard owners had, in the twentieth century, become less fragmented, eventually coming under a single body: the Mersey Docks and Harbour Board. In 1966, Liverpool had been the UK's major export outlet and yet the docks still lost £2,000,000.00. The cause of the loss was attributed partly to investment in creating an infrastructure for the growing – and less labour intensive – container business. And to repeated, unofficial strike action by the dockers. It was reported that in 1971 there were approximately a hundred such strikes, culminating in a national strike and the demise of the Harbour Board as it was then constituted.

The strike mentality was like coal dust: it got under the skin of anyone down wind and was difficult to remove. It was still blowing in 1980.

And crime was rife: parts of the city had become no-go areas. The 'Piggeries', a three-sided rectangle of four storied housing units, with external walkways built around a depressing communal yard of dark grey concrete, was out of bounds for traders and police alike. It was the majority, the law-abiding and non-car owning citizens, who suffered. In those rancid and clustered environments there was no room for the apportionment of blame.

As the dissolution of the monasteries was attributed to Henry VIII so to did the dissolution of industry have its scape-goat. The people of Liverpool pointed their collective finger at Mrs Thatcher, the prime minister of the day.

In the Liverpool of 1980 there was no place for pride or prejudice, and sophistication was not in the Scouser's dictionary.

Entangled in the web of unemployment, their repartee, surprisingly, remained intact.

"There's Joe, the landlord," Paddy whispered.

"Where?"

"There, in the white shorts."

"Well, well . . ." was all Horace could say.

Joe, the amiable and chain-smoking landlord, had entered the room wearing a rugby shirt (quartered in black and red), his forty-year old school cap and white baggy shorts. On his feet, he wore black wellington boots, and around his neck, from a piece of string, hung a policeman's whistle. A cigarette dangled from his mouth. Removing the cigarette he shouted: "Order!" There was no response and he blew a blast on the whistle.

"Watch me friggin' ear," Bill said, covering it, as best he could, with his invalid arm. "You'll make me deaf!"

"Sorry, Bill. Didn't know it was your good ear. Order! Order!"

The landlord's words were lost in the bedlam, and he again put the whistle to his mouth. The third whistle brought a moment of calm.

"Get on with it," a voice from the crowd shouted.

Self-conscious and sober, Charlie Chaplin sat next to Count Dracula. At the bar a ship's captain called for a pint of bitter and a gin and tonic.

"The brewery says I'm not selling enough of the golden nectar so I'm going to keep an eye on youse lot. To help you though, and through the generosity of me heart, I'm going to give youse lot a half-pint voucher every time you order a pint or short."

A deafening cheer filled the small, stone-floor room where standing customers stood shoulder to shoulder, back to back and face to face. The older clientelle sat along three walls. A young woman, pig-tailed and dressed in a short black gym-slip, carried a large plate of biscuits and cheese cubes. An older woman in black cloak and conical hat sold raffle tickets. On the bar top, with the beer slops and over-flowing ashtrays, paper plates supported small sausages pierced by sticks. Peanuts spilled over into the beer dregs.

"Makes yor mouth water!" Paddy whispered.

"Why are they wearing those strange clothes?" Horace asked.

"They're an odd lot those humans. They always want to be somebody else."

"You mean like trying to escape from themselves?"

"Exactly. They spend so much time looking into mirrors that eventually they've seen enough. I think they realise sooner or later that the reflection in the mirror is never going to be anybody of note. The sad thing is, there isn't anything they can do about it. And as they grow older, the unhappier they become with what they see in the mirror."

"By the sound of it they've got themselves into a right mess. Is that Stan coming in the door?"

"There's an example of what I was saying. He's turned himself into a nervous wreck."

"Evenin', Bill," Stan said, choosing to stand next to his seated bar friend. "Where were you yesterday?"

Bill tapped the end of a cigarette on the counter top, put the cigarette in his mouth. With the long flame of his cigarette lighter poised he hesitated, and from the corner of his mouth said: "Didn't you get me sick-note? Christmas post again!"

Not really expecting an explanation, Stan had asked the question simply as an opening gambit. "What have you come as, Bill?" he continued, the apprehension in his wide-eyed stare contradicting the broad grin that exposed his unco-ordinated teeth.

"A businessman. Obvious in't it?" Bill replied curtly, dusting dandruff off a shoulder of his dark blue blazer. Beneath the jacket he wore an off-white shirt unbuttoned to his white, hairless and flaccid chest.

"Where's your tie then?" Stan asked.

"Oh dear, I've forgot to put me medallion on. Bet the ruddy wife's gone out in it again."

"Pint, Josie," Big Jack called as he approached the bar. "Where've you been, Bill? Not like you." He put his red, curly head close to Bill's face.

"Want a puff?" Bill replied, blowing smoke in Big Jack's face.

Big Jack withdrew. "Seein' as youse lot would put Punch to shame I'll tell you. I've 'ad a two day 'angover."

"Two days! Come off it, Bill," Stan said, rolling onto the balls of his feet. "They don't last that long."

"Mine do," Bill confirmed, inhaling deeply on the cigarette.

"Mine don't." Stan said, shaking his narrow shoulders.

After a moment of uncharacteristic silence, concluding with four smoke rings rising from his pouting lips, Bill explained: "It was a two dayer, okay? Went down to Yates' on Lime street. Did the pubs around the Cavern, then a club or three. Finished up in a gamblin' den."

"Ladbrokes?" Big Jack asked.

"'aven't got a clue. We was mob-'anded and must 'ave 'ad ten pints before ten."

"That's like poetry," Stan said with a toothy smile. Bill was unhappy at being interrupted in mid-flow and his expression alone was enough to wipe the smile from Stan's face.

"When we got on the roulette table I was up ter 'ere." Bill continued, a finger on his prominent adam's apple.

"Stupid gambling after you've been drinking," Stan said, regaining some of his limited composure.

"Don't remind me. I've been broke since. 'ad to borrow off the wife to come out tonight."

"That the end of your redundancy money then?" Big Jack asked.

"You must be jokin', son. That went ages ago. It was me dole that I lost. All of it."

"What did the wife say, Bill?" Stan asked, with genuine interest and strong visual images of the verbal fury he himself would face in such circumstances.

"Not talking to me," Bill replied, pain etched across his face – but quickly bursting into laughter, said: "It's bloody marvellous!"

By eleven o'clock, half-an-hour after the usual time for last orders, the young woman in gym-slip had been well handled, and young men staggered bent and fuzzed. Bonhomie and tension

199

were imparted freely and logical conversation, a commodity rare at the soberest of times in the bar-room, had long departed.

Joe blew his whistle. Josie, her naked arm swinging like a pendulum on a clock, rang the ship's bell above the counter, and a youth, wearing his grandfather's black trilby and mother's winged sunglasses, asked for another drink.

Red face and with his old school cap on the back of his head, Joe, once again behind the bar, leaned forward, spread his hands on the counter top and replied quietly: "'aven't you got a 'ome to go to?"

The youth shook his head and Joe stretched himself to his full height and shouted: "Ladies and gentlemen, Merry Christmas to youse all and goodnight." In the face of anticipated abuse he smiled contentedly, his prominent eyes rolling in delight at the bulging cash register.

The two rodent friends returned to ground level. It had been an entertaining show, but they felt dizzy from all the secondary smoke they had inhaled.

"I don't know about you, Horace, but I think I'll take a walk on the street to clear my lungs."

"Will it be safe? Usually a lot of people out on Christmas Eve," Horace said.

"They'll all be sozzled," Paddy replied, putting a paw to his mouth and coughing.

Brightly coloured lights criss-crossed Bold Street, and the open pub door painted a cream swathe across the pavement where men lay dazed, sleeping or comatose. To avoid stepping into the roadway, Horace and Paddy reluctantly walked over the prostrate assemblage of Liverpool's mankind. Polystyrene cartons of half eaten potato chips lay scattered beside the inebriated figures, and in the shadows, hard-backed earwigs nibbled, their tail pincers vibrating in appreciation.

The next morning there was considerable activity in all rat households as the does prepared meals from exceptional ingredients, and presents were exchanged and unwrapped.

For weeks preceding the alleged anniversary of the birth of the human son of God, the dedicated, and not so dedicated, followers of the competing Christian religions of Catholicism (we are true believers), Protestantism (ours must be the true religion: we have the greater number) and all those other religions allied to the fragile concept of Christianity forgot their differences. For many, the nouns of the faith were useful expletives. For all, it was a time when memories were either manufactured or recalled – only to be subdued quickly under the soporific influence of intoxication. It was also a time when money, no matter how scarce, materialised and was exchanged for unusual foods, inappropriate gifts and wrapping paper.

In the early hours of Christmas Day, the Adventist to Unitarian churches had opened their doors to respectability dressed in collars and ties, hats and veils, and with full wallets and purses. And the congregations thanked the Lord they had jobs, and for all the assets that righteousness and obedience to the church or synagogue had bestowed upon them. They knelt and prayed for more, while on the unclean city streets the homeless were joined by the drunkards who knew not what they had celebrated. And from the pulpits, the virtues of mercy and sympathy were extolled, but the combined writings of Matthew, Mark, Luke and John did nothing to encourage the flock to go out into the streets and search out the poor and needy. And provide shelter? Well that was beyond all contemplation.

The food that found its way into Betty's kitchen was not a supply that Horace would want to encourage. It was a question of acquiring those stocks that filled the shops and larders in the run up to Christmas. The chicken meat was too dry, the sprouts too hard, the potatoes too soft inside their roasted jackets, and the speckled stuffing and green and red jellies were fit only for human consumption. Minnie, who was helping her daughter prepare the midday meal, remarked that once, back in Manchester, they had found a turkey, but that it seemed to last forever. Horace had spent the morning attending to the demands of the babies and was uplifted when Paddy called enroute to see his cousin, Douglas, at his home beneath the old, inner city church.

SEVENTEEN

The streets were deserted and traffic-free, and the pair were able to breathe the comparatively fresh air instead of having to pass through underground pockets of carbon monoxide. So quiet were the streets, they could hear their own breathing. As they slid down the grid outside the empty church a white robed Sister of Charity emerged from the house opposite. Sockless in open sandals, she hurried towards the River Mersey.

"Douglas!" Paddy shouted down a flexible tube that his cousin had installed between the drain and the church basement.

"Go away," came the reply.

"It's Paddy."

"Don't give a sod if its the Pope himself. I'm having a lie-in."

"It's nearly mid-day," Paddy insisted.

"I don't care if it's nearly midnight. I'm not getting out of bed."

"We're coming in."

"Who's we?"

"My friend and good neighbour, Horace."

"Oh him! Come in if you want. Close the pipe after you. I don't want any more flood water in here."

It was difficult walking through the bending extraction tube suspended over a large hole where soil erosion had occurred. The square mile between Berry Street and Hanover Street had fallen into severe neglect until, beyond repair, the local authority had turned its back on the squalor, and the problems of decay – especially below ground – intensified.

Years before, Douglas, in his more active years, had cut a small hole in the church's basement wall and the tube was a perfect fit.

Sealed with a rubber distributor cap from an old Ford Cortina, the entrance was water-tight.

Douglas lay on his back in bed, the brown blanket pulled up over his head. Curious, Horace studied the small room with, at one end, a white lavatory pan, and at the other, Douglas and his bed. The pan did not appear to be connected to any drainage system and neither did it enjoy the facility of a flush. Douglas had converted it into a food storage unit. The middle of the closet was occupied by a table, one chair and two biscuit tins. On the table, a quarter candle sat at the apex of a pile of curled grease. Its long, blackened wick hung dejectedly. Horace sat on a biscuit tin, and Paddy on the other. They watched the bed for signs of life.

"Is he asleep?" Horace asked, eventually.

"Are you asleep, Douglas?" Paddy asked.

"Leave me alone."

"It's Christmas Day," Paddy reminded his cousin.

"So what?"

"Food'll be plentiful tonight, to be sure."

"Around here? You must be joking."

"Are you ill?" Horace asked, but the rat under the blanket didn't reply.

"More like lazy in his old age," Paddy said.

"Lazy? You'd be in bed if you lived here. I'm telling youse."

"Why is that. Douglas?" Paddy asked.

"Because," Douglas shouted, springing up so fast the Horace almost fell off his biscuit tin chair, "they've turned this place into a mad-house."

"Who?" Paddy asked.

Sitting up in bed he pulled the blanket up to his nose so that, between his black woolly hat and the dark brown blanket, only his eyes were exposed to the chill air.

Talking through the blanket, Douglas explained: "They've turned it into a social club or something."

"Who have?" Horace asked.

Douglas turned his head towards Horace, but didn't reply immediately. He was pre-occupied with the previous evening's events. At length, he said: "Foreigners or something. Kept me awake all night with their singing and foot-stamping."

"I thought the church was empty," Paddy said.

"It was once. Not anymore. I'll have to find somewhere else to live. But I don't want to leave. Why should I be forced out by Johnny-come-latelies?"

"Is there nothing you can do?" Horace asked.

"Who can a rat turn to in time of trouble, I ask yus?" Douglas said, letting the blanket fall about his shoulders.

"Nobody wants to listen to us Merseyside rats. You're right there, Douglas," Paddy agreed. "They even call us vermin."

"We could bring in a few hundred mates and they may think there's a plague and clear out," Horace suggested.

"I thought of that. That would be suicide. They'd bring in the rat-catcher and that would be the end of me. I only hope they don't find out there's a cellar beneath the church. That would be just as bad."

"They're bound to find it eventually, Douglas," Paddy said.

"Do you think so?" Douglas asked, looking into Paddy's eyes for the truth of his theory. "I don't want to move. I'm too old and set in my ways."

"I could probably find you a room in the complex," Paddy suggested.

Douglas continued to stare unblinkingly at Paddy. "You know I like to be alone," he said.

"You used to go out and about at one time. Gregarious Douglas they called him, Horace."

"That was then. I'd get spivved up and chase the young does. These days I'd rather tend my store of oats and seeds," Douglas said, throwing back the blanket to reveal a red and white broad-striped nightshirt reaching down beyond his feet. He threw his legs over the side of the bed, summoning up the energy to put his feet on the floor and stand up. "Everything gets that bit more difficult the older you get, Horace. I used to swim in the Mersey –"

"Before it was polluted," Paddy said, offering clarification to his younger Mancunian friend.

"Before it was filled with all that chemical stuff. By the time they've finished, those so-called humans will destroy the earth."

"There'll probably only be us rodents left, ' Horace said.

"You could be right?" Paddy said, nodding his head in agreement.

"What do you want, our Paddy?" Douglas asked.

"Nothin'. I've come with me kind friend, Horace, and we've come to wish you a Merry Christmas an all that?"

"Merry Christmas?" Douglas scowled.

"You know what I mean. It's what they call it up there."

"Why have youse come in the morning when you know I don't like visitors at that time of day."

"It's after twelve, be Jasus. It isn't morning any more. Is that right, Horace?"

"It is, Paddy. Another morning we'll never see again."

With a deep breath, Douglas stood on his feet, shuffled inside his nightshirt across the room and sat at the table. Striking a match on the leg of the table he lit his candle. From a pocket inside his shirt he withdrew a pair of grey, woollen, but fingerless, gloves and pulled them over his paws. He wrapped his paws around the flame.

"Is it cold today, or is it me?" he asked.

"You're feeling the cold 'cause you've just got out of bed," Horace suggested thoughtfully.

"And you've got a lot on your mind," Paddy said.

"And you didn't sleep very well," Horace continued.

Alternately Douglas's visitors offered explanation that he would rather not have heard.

"It is December."

"You're not getting any younger!"

"Do you think you're starting with a cold?"

"You're too near the surface."

"When did you last eat?"

"You need a wife to keep you warm in bed."

"Shut up! Both of youse. There's nothing wrong with me that a bit of peace and quiet wouldn't cure."

"Oh yes there is," Paddy argued. "You're becoming an old nark. You're getting to be like a crusty, old hermit crab. Why don't you get yourself a doe."

"I don't want a doe. I've got enough problems as it is."

"What problems?" Paddy asked.

Douglas pointed his paw at the ceiling. "That lot up there, for a start. Come to think of it, that's me only problem. I was very happy when I could get a full night's sleep."

"It won't be like that every night," Horace hinted. "They were probably celebrating."

"Every Friday and Saturday they celebrate. I feel like going up and taking a bite out of somebody's leg."

"Don't do that. Don't ever, ever think of biting a foreigner. They'd call in their army with all kinds of chemical weapons. We'd all perish," Paddy cried.

"I know. I'm not stupid. There's no harm in thinking."

"Fantasy can sometimes become reality. You might get so angry you carry out the actions of your thoughts," Horace informed the older buck.

"I said I'm not stupid. Have youse two come here to torment me?"

"Of course not, Douglas. We're sorry to hear of your troubles, but I always say, don't kill yourself, for things can only get better," Paddy asserted.

"What are you talking about? Rats do not kill themselves. Only humans do that," Douglas said, despairing that he was being drawn reluctantly into a debate.

From the same pocket of his nightshirt that had held his gloves, he pulled out a crumpled cigarette. In amazement, Paddy and Horace watched Douglas put the cigarette in his mouth, lean over the flame of the candle and start blowing smoke.

"What you doing, Douglas, me only cousin from across the sea? Have you gone mad? Those things kill," Paddy shouted.

"I've never before seen a rat smoke a cigarette," Horace exclaimed.

"For me nerves. I've watched those humans all me life and they say it keeps them calm. I'm so desperate, I'll try anything."

Three weeks of lost sleep had affected Douglas's appetite as well as his nerves and, in the four week since Paddy had last visited, his cousin had lost weight.

"Don't stoop to human failings, Douglas. You'll only bring disrespect to the whole rodent population of Merseyside and beyond. We're above such mediocrity. Don't let human depravity taint your lungs. You must rise above your adversity. Together we will conquer your problem."

"You're right, Paddy," Douglas said, squashing out the cigarette on the table top. "I'll use my will-power."

That afternoon the three rats went around the back streets of China Town collecting empty rice bags and fruit boxes, dragging them back to the cellar beneath the old church until Douglas's room was filled wall to wall and floor to ceiling. With Paddy's building skills, they soon created a false ceiling, sound proofing it with sacking.

It was late evening before, from a building site on nearby Slater Street, they had acquired all building materials necessary to seal permanently from the world the internal doorway to the basement closet.

"Even if they find the cellar, they'll never know this room existed," Paddy said, proud that his former building skills had not deserted him.

In a day, by the dual powers of conversation and cooperation, they had overcome what one lonely rat had considered insurmountable. Douglas was humbled and resolved to move back into rat society, passing on his experiences to younger rats, and help those rats weaker than himself. Lest he should forget, he painted large above his bed the words that Paddy had left him with as he departed: 'No Rat is an Island'.

EIGHTEEN

4 July 1981

The early part of the year drifted by the way they do, and the people of Liverpool went about their daily lives. Like the majority of volcano-side villagers, there was no alternative: the population was born and bred there and lived a life of self-denial.

In reality, Liverpool was a city in dire neglect – not that those lucky enough to have jobs noticed: they were too busy passing through life to care. And they had been blinkered by familiarity and local media that did not do enough to advocate positive action. By painting portraits they overlooked the landscape. The city workers arrived in the morning and departed in the evenings for sedate Southport in the north, and pastoral Wirral in the south. But those commuters living in the few tree-lined suburbs of Liverpool itself – and who considered themselves a social strata above the inner-city dwellers – were beginning to feel uncomfortable. A local newspaper, although a medium of population appeasement, made full use of the statistics supplied by pressure groups.

With a headline banner, it reported: 'Merseyside has entered the eighties on a tidal wave of rising crime with violent offences up by over a third.' The headline was supported by police statistics: incidents of wounding up by 34.8%. Robberies up by 10.2%. The incident of burglary – up. Thefts from motor vehicles, people and arson – all increasing. In a five month period 47,757 crimes were recorded. This figure did not include non-reported crime, but a conservative estimate suggested it was at least equal with reported crime.

For the previous year, the total number of crimes reported to the Liverpool police stood at 120,000. By a strange coincidence the number of Liverpool men without employment was also 120,000 – give or take the variable inaccuracies in any survey.

The unemployed on Merseyside in 1966 was 20,000. Five years later the number had increased to 40,000. The unemployed figure then gained a relentless momentum of its own, spiralling out of control. Those inner-city dwellers, who remained after the workers had departed for their centrally-heated homes, did not need to read statistics. The evidence was all around them.

'In the early hours of Saturday morning,' a local radio reported, 'a teenage girl was slashed with a Stanley knife as she left a back street nightclub.' The knife-blade, curved and razor sharp, had, with a single stroke, sliced through three layers of clothing to expose flesh and muscle. As the girl lay bloody on the pavement she was encircled by a mob of drunken youths. They pushed, shoved and argued for a better view of the dying girl. When the ambulance arrived, they refused to be moved and a struggle ensued An ambulance man was knocked to the ground and two youths climbed inside the open ambulance and lay on the beds. A lone policewoman, helpless in the face of such a mass demonstration of drunken disorder, was hassled. In a pool of dark blood, the teenager lay with her kidneys exposed to the night air. Only the arrival of a police patrol car caused the crowd to disperse.

As the ambulance sped away, the police car received a message that the Stanley knife wielding assailant had struck again: a young man had been found lying in the vicinity of the Birkenhead tunnel entrance. The maniac with the knife had travelled a mile from the scene of his first crime and attacked, from behind and in similar fashion, the helpless victim walking home after a night in one of the many decrepit, back street beer-clubs of the Duke Street area of the city.

In the evening the same radio station reported that a young Australian female lecturer had been attacked on the steps of the Anglican Cathedral. Her attacker had struck from behind, knocking the woman unconscious before stealing her cash, traveller's cheques and passport. She was a tourist returning for a brief visit to her family roots. The previous week it had been a Canadian tourist who fell victim in the same location. He had been attacked by three black youths who had taken all the possessions he carried.

The acts of violence were both mindless and motivated. The only common denominator was that the crimes were committed by small groups or individuals. The previous evening, events had taken a different direction and acts of vandalism and aggression had spread wide over the run-down district of Toxteth.

Horace and Paddy had gone out for an evening stroll, calling on Paddy's friend on point duty at the rat underpass outside Lime Street Station.

Although the sky was flat grey, the evening was warm and humid. It had been a hot Summer's day and the heat had lingered into the evening. From the underpass the two friends decided to take some air and, climbing up onto the curved roof of the railway station, watched the never-ending traffic below.

"What will they do when the oil runs out, Paddy?" Horace asked.

"They'll find some other way to pollute the atmosphere. Look at her down there."

It was that time of the day when it is neither light nor dark; a time when people can be defined, but neon lighting is already effective. The strings of lights added a garish mantel to the old black buildings. Against a wall, beside the lighted window of the cafeteria at the station approach, a woman leant confidently. In early middle-age, she wore matching skirt and blouse of black taffeta. The frilled neck of the blouse was open to the third button, and the hem of her skirt, its thread hanging loose, was seven centimetres above her boney and black fishnet covered knees. Thin and pallid, her white face and bleached hair would have appeared as one had she not allowed the natural dark roots to grow through. Above where she had shaved away her eyebrows, two thin, arching pencil lines had been drawn. The carmine red lipstick, like the unnatural eyebrows, did not follow the true shape of her once regular features. The years

210

and labours of her profession had taken their toll, but thick face-powder covered the cracks. A dirty, white plastic handbag hung from a lean, bare arm. Both elbows were angled away from her slim body and her ringed hands rested on narrow hips. Two elevated and nicotine stained fingers held a smoking cigarette. Her black, high-heeled clad feet crossed so that it was the sole of just her right foot that carried her weight. The toe-cap of her crossed-over left shoe touched the ground for balance. Her relaxed posture disguised a vigilant eye.

The young raced aimlessly between beerhouses, and the old made raucous laughter behind the patterned windows of Yates' wine bar.

Confident, in the growing shadows and debris that filled the street, the two rats strolled along Renshaw Street, looking in the do-it-yourself shop windows as they went. They had decided to visit Chinatown and perhaps sample some of their cuisine that seemed to be growing in popularity.

On the steep, stone steps of St Luke's shell of a church, Paddy recognised most of the dozen men drinking from large brown bottles. He had seen them at the soup kitchen. The young man in the holed Fair Isle jumper was a newcomer. Each man sat alone. The analogy of the bomb-site and the homeless men was not lost on Paddy.

By the time they reached St George Square, the epi-centre of Liverpool's Chinatown, the natural light was failing, but the square of Chinese restaurants shimmered with paper lanterns.

"They start again!" a thin Chinese man in a black suit shouted to an equally thin man across the street.

"Who?" the Englishman asked.

"They! Mad kids with sticks. They run around streets hitting people on head." the Chinese man said, hurrying towards the local Chinatown pub.

"Where?" the Englishman shouted.

"Toketh."

"Where's Toketh?" Horace asked.

"I'm sure he means Toxteth. Let's go and see what those humans are up to again."

"Sounds dangerous?" Horace said.

"They won't see us in the dark," Paddy replied confidently. "Might be a good show."

From the square of gaily lit lanterns, they padded back along Great George Street, turning east up Upper Duke Street before threading through the narrow back streets to Faulkner Street. Horace was familiar with the area, for it was here that he, and Betty, had watched the confrontation between shopkeeper and council employee. As they crossed the junction with Grove Street, low key chanting filled the evening air.

"Don't look now, Horace, but we're being followed."

Horace turned. Twenty metres behind, dozens of children and youths, some armed with sticks, stones and bottles, marched aggressively, filling the street like a dust cloud. The way ahead appeared clear, but the zulu-like chanting had grown more urgent, and the rhythms of war vibrated around street corners.

Horace and Paddy hurried towards Upper Parliament Street – but this proved to be a major tactical error: suddenly they were surrounded on all four sides. Like swarms of angry bees, the rampaging juveniles floated through the streets. only ragged curtains hanging through jagged windows ventured out of doors.

"It's gang warfare," Paddy said; but the gangs were not fighting each other. They had united with a common goal. "This way," Paddy shouted, taking Horace by the arm and leading him through a paint-chipped iron-gate into a narrow garden fronting one of Upper Parliament Street's terraced houses. Through the railings, they watched and listened to the mob shouting and swearing at an unseen enemy.

The properties that lined the street had, when Liverpool prospered, been elegant: their owners privileged and pampered. Seven pitted stone steps separated shoe-scrape and pavement from the tall, heavy and pillared doors. Like Liverpool itself, the houses had fallen into disrepair and the multi-roomed accommodation, with a history of individual prosperity, was segmented into lonely and damp bed-sits, mainly for the old and unemployed.

"Kill the pigs," the crowds shouted in unison as police vehicles rolled slowly up the street. The main gangs retreated east while smaller groups dispersed into the streets north and south of Upper Parliament Street, their chosen battle-ground; but then, unexpectedly, the swarms returned armed with milk bottles. In the rear, very young children carried rocks and provided additional ammunition. Milk bottles with burning fuses twisted through the air, exploding on impact and spreading fire along the ground. The smell of petrol overpowered the stench of poverty and decay.

Curtains moved and the frightened occupants bolted doors. The streets screamed and burnt. Windows were shattered and the police, in the face of a massive bombardment of burning petrol and broken glass, retreated. Ambulances arrived, and police bodies were repaired by the roadside.

With reinforcements, the police, unarmed and unprepared for mass confrontation, were still confused. Their intelligence had been flawed and they were not trained to counter a riot on the scale of what faced them. The police continued where they had left off, but in the meantime, and like a trained army, the rioters had reorganised themselves in preparation for a pincer attack under maximum diversion. Charging the police from three different directions, the force of Law and Order was out-manoeuvred and out-numbered. The key junction of Upper Parliament Street and Princes Road fell under the control of the primary gang.

Princes Road, another area with faded memories of wealth and gentility, retained its wide road and central tree-canopy, but its classically built houses in 1981 accommodated hirelings and the poor. It also housed those respectable inner-city dwellers with and without jobs who lived there, not by choice, but circumstance. Toxteth was an area where respectability and the disreputable lived side-by-side.

A saloon car drove down Upper Parliament and like the parting of the Red Sea the crowd allowed it to pass. It stopped and four youths climbed out. The crowd closed in around the vehicle, turning it on its side. In quick succession a second and third vehicle arrived and, carbonized, they burnt like beacons, lighting up the street and throwing long shadows across the road. Smaller fires were lit at intervals and black, putrid smoke spiralled from incinerated rubber.

"I can't breathe," Paddy complained.

"It's getting to my eyes," Horace said, wiping the tears from his cheeks.

Young children formed circles and danced wildly around the fires while the denim clad army of older children ran shouting up and down the street.

Lined behind clear shields, the police charged the burning barricades but were repelled. They regrouped and charged again – but for every two steps forward they retreated one step. Battered, bruised and bloody the police pressed uphill until at last their persistence was rewarded. The swarms of youths disappeared into the shadows of the terraced back streets and council estates.

"That show is going to take some beating," Paddy said, as they hurried home. Fragments of stone, metal and glass covered the streets and the pair had to proceed with extreme caution. It was impossible to use the underground rat passageways as petrol had seeped through the ground and it would be a day before the danger decreased. Shocked by the scale and ferocity of what they had just witnessed, Horace and Paddy walked in silence, their eyes fixed firmly on the ground.

The police had followed the fragmented gang and, like the aftermath of a war-torn battlefield, a strange silence remained where the injured were being treated in the light of flickering flames. At the back of the giant Anglican Cathedral, police and ambulance vehicles lined the kerbside. Policemen sat on the pavement, backs to the cathedral railings and receiving medical attention. Others sipped tea, steaming in the cooling night air.

On Berry Street, the glass of shop windows littered both sides of the window frames. Shopkeepers, called from their beds, stood perplexed outside their ransacked premises. Of a row of shops, only one plate-glass window remained intact – but fractured in an intricate spider-web design that spread from a central hole to all four corners. It had held firm to its puttied frame despite the battering from a fluted metal dustbin that evidentially lay on the ground. Its former content trailed along the footpath.

The next day, and concerned that such wide and indiscriminate use of petrol-bombs could destroy whole areas of ratland, Paddy with Horace's help, held meetings with all the rat community leaders of central Liverpool. Already one of the main ratways, that leading from the defunct south docks to Wavertree in the west, had been put out of action. Of primary concern to the Chinese rat population was their close proximity to where the riots had taken place – and the potential for disaster. With their reliance on coloured paper-lanterns to dress their pagoda they were more vulnerable than, say, the Bold Street rat complex with its stone structures. The leaders of all the rat communities, including the Chinese and Black rats, agreed that contingency plans had to be put in place that very day. Paddy had reported that the police had suffered many wounds, and because of the police record for taking leave for injury, he doubted that the force would be able to mount a concerted rebuff to any other disturbances that weekend.

All day, messenger rats scurried between the different communities. Paddy's warning had been timely for spasmodic rampaging had continued throughout the day. Paddy had estimated that about five hundred children and youths had swarmed the streets, and prophesised that that was only a fraction of the disenfranchised youth. Add to that, he had said, the children who are allowed to run wild in search of excitement and adventure and you are well into the thousands.

"All da 'omes we rent could be destroyed," the black, baritone rat leader said, and the indigenous rat communities were relieved that their immigrant brothers would unite in the common cause. As we have noted earlier, survival is the strongest drive known to rats. This instinct has been mentioned again because of the widespread nature of the danger that the humans suddenly and unexpectedly, posed to the rat population.

For decades the people of Liverpool had treated all rodents with respect, housing them, feeding them and providing all the necessary furnishings for their accommodation. The people of Liverpool had nurtured rats and mice, and the local council had done nothing to discourage the practice – except by inadvertently reducing the size of the human population. Then the rats had adopted safeguards.

Although the youth of south Liverpool similarly meant no harm to the Merseyside rat population, consequential ignorance is no excuse in the eyes of rat-law. Threatened, they must retaliate.

Toxteth, that square mile of decay where narrow streets of houses, as soot black as the slaves that their docker forebears shackled in those cold, damp warehouses down the road, had a restless day. Decomposing vegetable waste filled the intersecting and regular alleyways with the stench of a gangrenous sore.

Allied historically to the heart of Toxteth, but now alarmingly stranded like a bad tooth in the dentist's chair, young gentlemen played squash at the Racquet Club.

A few doors away, the brightly painted cinema at the junction of Upper Parliament Street and Princes Road prepared for the first show of the evening. Across the road, and an anathema to the local population, the Anglican Cathedral towered out of an unexpected valley. Megalithic, brown, sharp-edged and over-powering. Close in geographical proximity to the inhabitants of Toxteth, but in reality light years away, it had the appearance of a Medieval religious structure built to intimidate. No longer fearful of divine intervention – nor the tied arm of the law – the sons of a dispirited and broken Toxteth were on the loose.

For all its symbolism, the cathedral was wasted on its neighbours that it had been built to serve. Of course, the status of those neighbours had, over the previous seventy odd years that it had taken to build, changed.

An Act of Parliament in 1885 authorised the construction of an

Anglican Cathedral in the diocese of Liverpool. The diocese had been created five years earlier when the industrial expansion in Lancashire (when the county had been all embracing) forced independence from Chester.

Work on the construction began at the beginning of the twentieth century, and King Edward VII laid the foundation stone in 1904. The building was completed in 1978.

While Sunday prayers were being said inside its vast and stone-cold nave more disturbances outside continued, and shops at both ends of Upper Parliament Street were looted. Retailers fought off the raiding youths who had arrived with domestic tools of destruction. Bus shelters lay flattened and street lamps destroyed.

That evening, as the mature population moved into the dark, back street beerhouses, the children and penniless youths moved onto the streets.

By dusk, the young from Edge Hill Wavertree and Princes Park had arrived to support their allies of Liverpool 7 and 8. Armed, as had been the earlier rioters, with rocks, petrol bombs and kitchen utensils, the mobs roamed the streets, looting and hijacking cars for their petrol and subsequent combustibility.

Once more the police and crazed youth faced each other. Under a constant bombardment of exploding petrol bombs, aimed from behind burning barricades, the police were taken by surprise at the veracious and co-ordinated attacks. Milk vans in the locked dairy compounds were loaded with crates of empty milk bottles and driven to the battle front. Those children under nine years, and without the required strength to throw stones, filled the bottles with petrol, sealing the bottle necks with paper and cloth. Their class-mates ran to the frontline with the glass bombs.

The police were losing the battle. Without the right kind of fire-proof clothing and counter-offensive weapons their role was passive and aimed at containment. A policeman, ablaze from head to foot, ran into the arms of a waiting fire officer who extinguished the flames and passed the casualty on to the adjacent ambulance. The wounded officers and men lay along

217

the street, and the ambulances ferried the injured to the surrounding hospitals that had been put on emergency status. The hospitals overflowed and Toxteth began to burn: the Racquet Club was soon ablaze and, like the cinema up the road, red and white flames danced out of the roof, their windows exploding. The foam padded cinema seats melted and the black, noxious smoke poured out of every hole. In an alcohol or adrenalin induced frenzy, the rampant mobs shouted and cheered at their work. They screamed at the police and the other authority employees. Mass hysteria had taken over and the children and youths were bereft of sanity.

"They're losing the battle and part of China Rat Town has been damaged," Paddy reported from the rat command headquarters in the valley behind the cathedral. "We can't wait any longer. We go in ten minutes from now."

Rat couriers raced along ducts, drains and sewers. In relays they reached every rat community in the city. The lean rats from Pierhead community skipped and jumped over the sleeping homeless; fat wharf-rats hurried as best they could; business sector rats slid down lift shafts and bannister rails; black rats hurtled along the main Toxteth sewer pipe and the China Town Rats arrived armed with axe and cleavers. Filling every inch of the hidden church-yard, the rats lined up in orderly fashion, their local commanders knowing exactly which entry or back street they would use to launch an attack on the crazed school children and youth of south Liverpool. All day they had plotted and planned their strategy. It would be a multi-pronged attack such as the allies used to mount their final approach to Germany in 1945. During the afternoon of that Sunday, Paddy and Horace had visited the library to study the history books in the military section. They would not attack from the ground where they would be seen in the light of the burning vehicles and buildings. They had another plan.

Rat commanders, Paddy, Horace, Douglas, Raymond, Porky, Lofty and Ginger stood on the raised ground facing the thousands of regimented rats. Paddy stepped forward.

"The fight may be long. It will be hard and some of youse may not return. But we will fight on the streets; we will fight in the alleys and we will fight in the school playgrounds. And if the fight goes on, we will fight in Sefton Park. Good luck, rats, and may Pluto be with you," Paddy shouted, clicking his heels and saluting.

The army of rats cheered and the warring humans stopped what they were doing and looked at the sky. Shaking their heads the antagonists resumed hostilities.

Climbing the grassy banks, a quarter of the army of rats led by Paddy and Horace filed silently through the iron railings on to Upper Duke Street and fanned out into the alleys and streets north of Upper Parliament Street. Half of the remaining troops emerged at the front of the cathedral and headed south, circumventing the battle-streets before turning east and splitting into divisions. The remaining rats climbed down into the main sewer pipe and in orderly fashion marched east beneath where the fighting raged. From the sewers, they entered the houses lining Upper Parliament Street and secured themselves behind front doors.

On the appropriate tick of their inbuilt clocks those rats rushed like water out of the doors. The rats occupying the areas to the north, south and east poured over roof tops and down walls. Other rats leapt out of street grids. The attack was so well timed that simultaneously the rats bit into every available calf, spitting out denim, cotton and blood. Screaming, the terrified children and young men ran home where they cried for antiseptic and plasters.

With incredible misfortune, the chief of Merseyside police, with approval from London (and not being able to see what had happened behind the burning barricades) gave the order for twenty-five gas canisters to be fired into the mob. It was the first time, allegedly, the gas had been used in mainland Britain.

Those rats near to where the canisters fell suffered the most damage and other rats had to provide mouth-to-mouth resuscitation. Paddy was badly affected and, after reviving his heart,

Horace carried him down to the sewer. The sewers were crowded with wounded and eye-damaged rats. Those with lung damage were carried on makeshift stretchers and the blind rats shuffled home, an outstretched arm on the shoulder of the rat before it. By the time the police moved forward, the industrious rats had recovered all of their injured colleagues from the street. The streets were empty.

Small, spasmodic disturbances continued through the week, but the perpetrators were those who had not suffered rat bites and were few in number. The police called in reinforcements from all parts of mainland Britain until the Merseyside Police Force was swelled by an additional two thousand personnel. But the war was over and the enthusiasm of the unruly mobs was tempered by a determined army of rats as well as, of course, overwhelming police superiority.

NINETEEN

After the last throb of violence had passed, cause and attribution were debated in every beerhouse in the land. Questions were asked in the House of Lords. The Liverpool riots of 1981 had become the centre of world attention. Government ministers, with trepidation, journeyed to Liverpool, a city not previously on their agenda, and interlocked with council leaders and the Police Chief. The city's church leaders debated with the Community Relations Council.

"I have great trust in the vast majority of the people of Merseyside and I hope they'll put this behind them," a Government Minister declared, and a member of the public shouted:

"Yer Tory policies are ter blame Mass unemployed is to blame."

"We should give them hope for the future and that is the best way of putting this behind them," the minister, with detached and superior intonations, continued. His verbal elegance matched by a back-tilted head and jutting chin. Down his nose, he looked at the nameless faces in the hall. He most definitely was not the people of Liverpool's favourite politician – if they had one at all! And he knew it.

While the analysis of the riots continued in council chamber and Houses of Parliament, thieves, under cover of darkness, smashed shop windows on Liverpool's main streets. Fleet-footed, they raced through the labyrinth of back streets embracing video recorders and black bin-bags full of smaller electrical goods. The daring, with bent knees, struggled with television sets. With the expertise of professional removal men, groups manoeuvred dishwashers, washing machines and tumble dryers. Men and women, with fingers through coat-hanger hooks, ran through the side streets, their swag swinging over their shoulders.

And the cross-party recrimination continued. Liverpool's Young Socialist Party blamed the police and called for a one day strike. The Community Relation's Council blamed unemployment and police harassment. The Relations Liaison Committee called for equal opportunity for the black and Asian community in the work place. Again the C.R.C. intervened:

"The community faces excessive deprivation in housing, educational opportunities and certainly in terms of jobs. And on top of that comes the fact that we live in a racist society. We have no evidence to suggest that the troubles were anything but spontaneous."

Another spokesman argued that the disturbances could not be racial as there was an equal number of white youths involved in the riot. He expressed concern that there was no machinery available for mediation.

"I have no sympathy for the police and their sus laws," a young Toxteth housewife told a local newspaper reporter. A councillor, with one languid eye on the ballot box, said the responsibility lay with the insensitive Authority.

The Home Secretary visited the two hundred police officers incarcerated in the Royal Liverpool Hospital.

"It's the government's fault," another councillor declared.

"No, it's the police," said a Mrs Jenkins.

"It's the police authority and that council chairperson!" a brave policeman said from his hospital bed. "She's taken away our power."

"A whole series of inter-related causes have got together in a dangerous chemistry," a Liverpool member of Parliament announced, a deep frown spreading across his forehead.

The Toxteth Member of Parliament thought it was unemployment and over-policing. He called on the police to walk the streets and befriend the inhabitants of his constituency. Images of sun-splashed days, men with jobs and docile children passed through his mind. He wanted to turn the calendar back to those less volatile days.

The Liverpool branch of the National Union of Teachers said they saw it coming.

Merseyside's Senior Community Relation's officer said: "It was a spontaneous reaction of anger and resentment." He couldn't explain why the gangs had arrived in hijacked cars armed with hammers, knives and baseball bats. Or how, so spontaneously, the eight-year-old children had learned to make petrol bombs.

"From the tele," an old scouse sage shouted, removing his flat cap and scratching his bald head. "All we see every night is Northern Ireland."

"'e's right," the fat woman, turbanned and wrapped in a faded yellow pinafore, agreed. "All we get is violence."

"We have lost our way. We are losing religion the same way we have lost our morality. On the Costa Brava the young and old women of Britain have a reputation for promiscuity. Their sexuality has been liberated by science and Hollywood. They think it is a game. The youth are rebelling against the lost values of motherhood," a vicar shouted from the pulpit.

"They smashed up my Jag!" a local printer seethed. "The next time I won't stop. I'll run the buggers down."

Another community relations officer agreed that those innocent motorists travelling to and from work through Toxteth, and whose car windows were still being shattered around them while they cowered beneath the dashboards, were the victims of violence. But continued: "I do not see how you can say the stealing of milk-floats and the syphoning of petrol from stolen cars could be anything but spontaneous."

"These riots were incited by political extremists," the Liberal leader of the city council announced to the Liverpool Echo, but then continued: "the deep rooted cause was unemployment coupled with the removal of a physical police presence from that area. You can't say the cause was bad housing because a lot of the area has been re-developed to a high standard. It really is hooliganism on the grand scale, and it all stems from the anger and resentment that's growing in urban communities at the waste of human resources in terms of lack of employment. The cause that must concern central government is the bewilderment that some ten thousand jobs a year can disappear from the city."

By the Tuesday, following the weekend of riots, most of the shop windows on the south side of the city had been boarded in reparation and, in those adjacent districts as yet untouched by the violence, for protection. Smoke continued to drift into the air from the smouldering shells on Upper Parliament Street and low atmospheric pressure ensured the smell of burnt rubber did not rise above nose level.

A sense of calm returned to Toxteth on Wednesday, but white businessmen in the nearby city centre complained of being jostled by passing black men.

In that uneasy truce, the Home Secretary, in the security of Liverpool's Chief Constable, Ken Oxford's, blue, bullet-proof Jaguar toured the area. The Home Secretary, Mr William Whitelaw, did not step onto the streets, but stayed closeted in leather upholstery.

Later that day, inside the oak panelled committee room of the Town Hall, Mr Whitelaw concluded: "I was very sad to see the damage done in Toxteth. To see what happened to one of the great centres of our country . . . their violence was destroying the hope for jobs."

In the House of Commons, Mrs Thatcher insisted that unemployment was not the principle factor in the Liverpool riots. "At the appropriate time I will visit the area," she said haughtily.

"The area is deprived and neglected, not least by you," a North West M.P. responded. "You have consistently refused to visit the city, and also refused to meet the People's Marchers for Jobs." She was urged to visit the city of Liverpool to witness the effects of her stringent policies.

"The failure of this Government's economic policy is obvious," Denis Healey, an opposition Member of Parliament declared. "We have the highest interest rates in history and yet money supply has increased by nearly fifty percent.

There are nearly three million people registered as unemployed, and manufacturing output is twenty percent lower than in 1979 when Mrs Thatcher came to power! Inflation doubled in the government's first year."

The Prime Minister was unmoved.

"If you want a job get on your bike." her trusted lieutenant, Norman Tebbit, told the unemployed. He smiled, and the Prime Minister, touching her dyed and coiffured hair, nodded regally.

Down the road from Toxteth, the Odeon Cinema was open for business as usual and the film 'Chariots of Fire' was playing to full houses.

The rats were given no credit for the part they had played in restoring law and order to the troubled streets – but then only the rioting mobs knew, and they were not likely to admit to humiliation by so small an adversary. And, of course, in Liverpool the rats had always been taken for granted.

TWENTY

As promised, Ginger, Lofty and Porky delivered a parcel of dresses for the young girls who lived and played in the cold shadows of the three Ugly Sisters tower blocks.

"Look who is 'ere," one of the girls shouted, as the three rats entered the concrete compound. Her four friends appeared from behind the brick walls at the bottom of the thirteen broad, grey steps leading from the upper level where the three high-rise blocks stood. "'ave yer brought us some clothes from the tip?"

The girl asking the question had dark brown hair and a waist level nylon tunic of similar colour. It was unfastened to reveal a crumpled, off-white shirt. Her faded denim trousers were torn and hung baggily from the knees, their creases aggravated by being tucked into ankle high suede boots. She looked taller than when the rats last saw her, but it could have been an illusion caused by the high heels of the scuffed boots she wore. Leaning against the central iron handrail of the steps she smiled and her dark eyes narrowed above high cheekbones. She scratched the hollow of her neck where her shirt was unbuttoned.

"Here you are, luv," Porky said, handing her the parcel.

Excitedly she tore away the newspaper wrapping, handing a frock to each of her friends. The five young girls held up their gifts and another girl said: "They're too small!"

"They would have fitted you the last time we saw you," Lofty said, dejection in his voice and face.

"We've grown since then," a third girl cried,

"We get bigger everyday till we're eighteen, me mam said," the girl with the pony-tail explained. She wore boots identical to the dark haired girl but with a wide, black corduroy skirt. The lapels

226

of her tight fitting and stained jacket curled outward. Both the skirt and jacket were of a style discontinued many years before. The top button of her plaid collarless shirt was also undone, overstating the length of her neck. Her sand coloured hair was swept back off her broad forehead. Her slim body, confident posture and long pony-tail gave her the appearance of a young filly.

The three rats sat in a line on the bottom step, angry with themselves for not remembering that children, even in deprived areas, continue to grow.

"Don't worry," the third girl said. "We know you meant well."

"They'll do for our little brothers and sisters," the second girl said reassuringly.

"It'll make a nice duster for me mam," the girl with the pony-tail exclaimed.

Coming to the front of the group, the girl with the round, white face bent forward and put her right hand on her knee. She threw her head back and laughed loudly: "Me mam could make a pair of knickers," she said, holding the small flowered frock to the waist of her silver-coloured satinet dress.

"Don't be stupid," the girl with the pony-tail chastised. "All knickers are black."

"Me mams are white, see," another girl said, sticking out her tongue. Like the clothes her friends wore, her short-sleeved cream shirt and matching shorts seemed too big for the wearer and of another era. Originally cream in colour, her concertinaed boots would, when new, have reached her knees. Her face shone and her dark hair clung behind her ears as though she had just washed.

"My mam 'as 'oles in 'ers," the girl in satinet said, laughing and turning on the spot.

"There's a man coming. Sit still and don't say anything you three," the formidable young girl with the pony-tail instructed the rats.

"Pretend you're dead," the girl with the round face suggested. And the three rats lay on their sides.

227

"Hello girls," the man with a camera around his neck and note-book and pen in his hand called as he approached.

"What do you want?" Miss Pony-Tail asked.

"I'm from the papers. What do you think about the riots we've just had?" he asked, flicking over the pages of his shorthand note-book and chewing the end of his pencil.

The five girls looked at each other and the girl in the denim trousers put a finger to her temple.

"Don't know what yer talkin' about," the satinet girl said, pushing back her light brown hair, pouting her lips and sticking out an ample chin. "Take me picture."

"In a minute. Come on girls; what comment have you got to make about the trouble in Toxteth?"

"Where's Toxteth?" the denim girl asked.

"Down the road over Islington. Come on girls, you're having me on," he said, leaving his arm suspended in a southerly direction, "it's been in all the papers."

"We don't read the papers," the girl in the billowing corduroy skirt replied.

"It's been on the tele every night this week. Don't you watch the news?"

Four of the five girls shook their heads and the same four jostled in anticipation of having their photograph taken. The fifth and silent girl remained in the background, forever observant but saying nothing.

Her dark curly hair spread attractively over the shoulders of her beige woollen jumper, but her sad face betrayed no other emotion.

"Yer from the news?" the girl in the cream shirt asked.

"Yes," the young reporter confirmed.

"Me dad used ter buy a paper till yer put yer prices up," she continued.

"Come on, take our pic," pony-tail demanded.

The four girls continued to jostle, none wanting to be on the end of the line.

228

"Stand on the step. Watch you don't stand on that lot," the reported proposed.

The four girls climbed over the prostrate rats and stood on the second step. The silent girl climbed higher, leaning against the central metal handrail.

"Come down and get in the pic," the girl in satinet called over her shoulder, and reluctantly the quiet girl moved down to the step above her friends. "I'm a model for Vogue," Miss Satinet continued. Putting a flat hand to the back of her head and looking to the grey sky, she fluttered her eyelids.

"'er a model?" pony-tail replied. "She's nowt but the Gretham Street slag."

"'ey, mop 'ead. Let's 'ave less of that," the satinet girl replied without altering her pose. "Come on, I'm getting a stiff neck."

In friendship they jostled and vied, but the girl with sad eyes stood apart with a half hint of a smile.

The girl in denim trousers put the thumb of her left hand in her mouth and two fingers of the same hand up around her nose. Her right hand was deep in her trouser pocket.

The girl in the cream shirt smiled and ran a hand through her limp hair. "It's me they wanna see."

"No it's me," another replied, while the satinet girl cried:

"What's the fee?"

"D'yer want a comment about this disgustin' place," Miss Pony-Tail asked.

The reporter shook his head. "No, that's not news," he said, putting the camera to his eye. "It's the riots they want to read about. Get a bit closer. That's good. You at the back. What's your name? Can't you do better than that. No, that's no good. Look, can you pick up a few stones and throw them. We need a bit of action."

The quiet girl on the third step moved down to face the newsman. Lifting her eyes to his, she asked: "Would you like to live here?"

"Go on, get off," the girl in the corduroy skirt shouted as the man hurried away. "I'll bring me dad. 'e used ter be a docker."

"Yer want to take some pictures of this disgustin' place and the dead rats," the girl in satinet shouted, waving a small fist in the air. But the reporter didn't hear her words. He didn't want any trouble with ex-dockers.

"That wasn't very nice, girls," Ginger said, sitting up on the step again.

"I've got bad back lying on that," Lofty said, standing up and stretching his long legs.

"You're too tall, that's your trouble," Porky said.

"I didn't mean to insult you. I don't know what made me say it," the girl apologised.

"That's all right," Porky said, shrugging his shoulders and looking at the ground. "We know you're all our friends."

"That's right!" the pony-tailed girl agreed. "You're like family."

"Well, we've got to be on our way. We're going to a big rat ceremony down town," Ginger said. "One of our mates is being honoured today."

"I wish we could all live in nice houses with gardens like those you see on the tele," the girl with sad eyes said. "Can't you help us, Ginger?"

Ginger looked at his two mates and the three rats smiled. "Of course we will. I'll organise a rat infestation next week. You'll be rehoused in no time."

TWENTY-ONE

Paddy slowly recovered the use of his lungs but would never walk again. Glad said she would care for him forever, and Horace and Betty pledged their support.

With the agreement of the Council Members of the Bold Street Rat Community, Horace was to be appointed in Paddy's placed as leader, an honour never before or since bestowed on a Mancunian rat. The investiture was to be held in the Isenergic Temple.

Minnie, on the front row and in her shower cap, smiled proudly, and Betty wiped away a tear as Horace strode onto the stage.

From his mobile bed at the back of the hall, Paddy held up a thumb, and Horace nodded. Paddy's friends – and now Horace's too – stood to attention: Raymond raised an eyebrow, Douglas clasped his paws above his head and Ginger, Lofty and Porky waved. Glad, holding Paddy's free paw, blew a kiss.

On a side balcony beside the stage, John Wagstaff and his wife sat with Peter the Water-rat and Sylvana. Brian the Badger and his wife sat behind. Respectful of the importance and solemnity of the occasion, they all sat quietly – except Sylvana who leaned over the parapet. Dressed in her black dress and gold tasselled black head-scarf, she called in a hushed voice:

"Minnie!" Minnie looked up and Sylvana grinned widely, her gold filling catching the light. Sylvana pointed to herself and then to her companions. "Do you wanna ccme for a sail on oura new boata this afternoon?" she whispered.

Minnie half raised her right arm and moved her paw. Smiling, she shook her head, reflecting on life's little twists and turns.

EPILOGUE

Like the giant factories and massive warehouses that once lined the well-oiled northern landscape, the twentieth century came and went.

And surprisingly, Liverpool was still there, smaller and with many of its former features converted to museums, souvenir shopping centres and exclusive water-front apartments, but remaining in bold typeface on the Atlas of Great Britain.

However, a glance at that map is all that is needed to see the problems it will face in the twenty-first century. And, as if to confirm its geographical misplacement, the proper noun is printed over the sea.

The end of the twentieth century brought with it a marked reduction in the human population of Liverpool. Conversely, a rat-catcher reported, the rat population continued to increase.

All the humans who appeared in this book really were part of the twentieth century and, although they would not agree, they all, in their own small way, made their contribution to history. They all played an important role, bringing warmth and humour to their friends and love to their families. They were real people, some who often struggled to make ends meet; who argued when times were bad and laughed when times were not so bad. They suffered pain – often in silence – and tolerated fools. A spade was a spade, and, for many, a pint beer a luxury. And the local politicians tried their best.

The twentieth century would not have been complete without the characters who appear in the pages of this book for every man, woman and child who ever lived has brought some happiness to others. Even those rioters brought about change for the better, attracting Central Government and European investment to the city. In the longer term that investment may be gone, but all will not be lost.

One day, in the distant future, when oil runs out – and the Far East is disadvantaged by distance – the tall ships will, once more, bring prosperity – and the casual labour system – back to Liverpool.

But what you must not do now is close this book thinking you have just read a fairy story. Please do not forget the people living on the back streets of Liverpool and all the other former industrialised cities of the world. Neither must you consider that the author has, by implication, tried to mislead you: we all know that rats and badgers have lives that run a shorter distance than humans.

Because of this inequality we had to leave friends behind in the last century. However, if you are ever on the rivers Dee or Mersey, watch out for unexplained movements on the waters' surface. And the next time you are in Liverpool keep your eyes on the drains.

Finally, if by nature you are sceptical and find it difficult to accept what you have read, you might check out the data. But proceed with care: I wouldn't want you to finish up in that old Roman tunnel!